AWAY FROM KEYBOARD COLLECTION

CALL SIGN: REDEMPTION

PATRICIA D. EDDY

If you love sexy romantic suspense, I'd love to send you a short story set in Dublin, Ireland. Castles & Kings isn't available anywhere except for readers who sign up for my mailing list! Sign up for my newsletter on my website and tell me where to send your free book!
http://patriciadeddy.com.

PROLOGUE

Five Years Ago

Trevor

THE ABANDONED OFFICE building on the outskirts of downtown Caracas is missing half of its windows. A hint of the sea carried on the winds tempers the stench of piss and death. One day, I'd like to be sent on a mission to a nice resort. Or a golf course. Hell, even a college locker room would smell better than this place.

Moving silently through the fifteenth floor, I scan for hostiles. Half a dozen desks are turned on their sides, but most of the building has been trashed. My targets are two floors below me, and by the heat signatures, I'm looking at two guerrillas and three hostages. Any other time, I'd call those good odds. Especially since one of the hostages is Air Force Lieutenant Commander Austin Pritchard. The man's a legend. He has more combat medals than anyone I know, which is saying something. But he's been held for almost a week now, and I have no idea what they've done to him.

This mission has been fucked from the start. By rights, I shouldn't be here. My handler tried to keep me out of this, but I told him I didn't give a fuck what he—or anyone else up the chain—wanted. I was doing this. Sanctioned or not.

I'm the only one who can. And after this job, I'm out. For good.

As I reach the edge of the building, the wind picks up. Fuck. If there's anyone hiding on this floor, even the slight sound of my pants whipping around my legs could get me killed. They're made for stealth and flexibility—like the rest of my clothing—but that means they're not skin-tight. Dropping to my knees, I pull out my rappelling gear.

Two floors. Eight meters. A little under twenty-seven feet.

One last check on the thermals. Same three hostages. Kneeling, by the looks of it. Hands probably bound.

Two hostiles. One leaning against the wall three meters from the hostages, another circling them. I don't give a fuck about the one moving. He'll be dead before my feet touch the ground.

The other one...he's the reason I'm here.

The rope knots around one of the window supports, and I check that it's secure enough for my weight. One breath. Two. Three.

Bring him in. This is what you were trained to do.

If there weren't two men with very lethal guns waiting to kill me as soon as I breach the thirteenth floor, I'd laugh. No one's trained for this. Not when one of the hostiles is your best fucking friend. Or was.

Gripping the rappelling release in one hand and my gun in the other, I balance my arches on the edge of the window.

Do it.

I push off and let myself fall, squeezing the control handle so I slide down the rope until physics takes over, and I swing back towards the window.

My first bullet shatters the window, and I burst through in a shower of broken glass, releasing the rope, tucking, and rolling forward until I come to my feet again. The second shot takes out the guerrilla circling the hostages, and then it's just them, me...and Gil. The man I'm supposed to *retrieve*.

"I should have known they'd send you," Gil says as he springs for Pritchard. Hauling his hostage up by his bound arms, Gil presses a knife to Austin's throat. One of the man's eyes is swollen shut, blood trickles from his split lip, and he groans as his feet scramble for purchase on the dusty floor.

"They didn't. I demanded to be the one to bring you in." I don't take my eyes off of Gil as I sidestep one of the other hostages, a man a good fifty pounds overweight who's breathing heavily. One of Venezuela's richest bankers, and one of the most vocal opposers of *El Presidente,* Marcos Farías.

"Not happening. Walk away, Trev." He presses the serrated blade harder against Pritchard's throat, and a trickle of blood wells on the dark steel. "Walk away and I might even let big brother here live."

"Gil," Pritchard rasps, "think of Dani."

At the mention of his sister, Gil's brown eyes turn cold. "Dani turned away from me the day she started calling your parents mom and dad."

"We...welcomed you...into our family," Austin manages as the knife digs deeper.

"Gil, you're going to kill him. There's no coming back from that." I take a single step closer, my gun steady. "Let him go, or I end you."

"And fail your mission? That's not the man I know. The one who follows orders blindly. Without question. Without giving a single *shit* who you destroy along the way." Gil shifts his hold on the knife. "Last warning, Trev. Drop the gun."

Blood flows freely down Austin's neck. The blade is less than a centimeter from his carotid artery, and if I don't stop the bastard now, he'll kill the man who saved me from myself after I broke Dani's heart all those years ago. Meeting Austin's gaze, I wait for understanding to dawn in his hazel eyes.

"Okay. Okay." I raise my hands, taking my finger off the trigger. The moment of shock registers on Gil's face for a split second before Pritchard draws in a breath and slams his head back against Gil's nose.

Blood spurts, and I fire a single shot, hitting Gil in the right arm. The knife clatters to the ground, and I tackle him as Austin collapses.

My first punch slams Gil's head to one side, but he wraps his legs around my waist and flips me over. I register the scrape of the blade on the dirty floor a second too late, and Gil drives the knife deep into my shoulder.

The pain steals my breath, but I still manage to bring the gun up and wedge it under his chin. "Give...it up," I manage. "You're...coming back...with me."

"Never." He twists the blade, and the sound that comes out of my mouth is something between a groan and a whimper. It feels like someone's shooting me full of electricity while simultaneously setting me on fire.

Pritchard, who's managed to free himself from the zip ties, hauls Gil off of me and throws him five feet into a half-rotten desk before he staggers and falls to his knees. "How could you do this to Dani? To me. You're my fucking brother." His voice is hoarse and weak, but there's an edge that tells me he's not in danger of dying. Not yet.

Gil springs up, a pistol he pulls from an ankle holster in his hand. "I'm not. Your parents only wanted her. I found my home. My father's people welcomed me with open arms. With the Loma Collectivo, I'm who I was always meant to be."

I wrench the blade from my shoulder and struggle to my feet, blood running down my arm and soaking my black shirt.

The wound isn't fatal, but it hurts like a son of a bitch and I'm getting light headed.

"Gil, last warning." I lean against a pillar, using the exposed metal beams to steady myself. "You know I'm faster. Better. We have to take you in."

"To a black site where they'll torture me until I don't know my own name?" Gil laughs as he sights Pritchard, who's grabbed the dead guerilla's gun and is now drawing down on Gil with me. "Never." He aims at Pritchard's heart. Fuck. Austin's not wearing body armor, but I am.

I see it in Gil's eyes a split second before he squeezes the trigger. Desperation. The boy I met in my very first foster home, the one who taught me so much about how to survive in the system, the man I trained with for five years, the one who had my back and saved my life a dozen times...he's begging me. And I can't let him down.

I jump in front of Austin, and as Gil fires, so do I.

"Trevor? Breathe, man. *Breathe!*" Austin's voice echoes like I'm underwater.

Forcing my eyes open, I groan and rub my chest. The bullet hit just right of my heart, and I try to do as ordered, but fuck. I think it cracked a rib. "Shit."

Austin's face says it all. I did what I was trained to do. Fire a kill shot under the worst of conditions. Only this time, I didn't just kill an enemy combatant. I killed my best friend. And Austin's brother.

"Got an exfil plan?" Austin asks. Grief flashes across his features, but a moment later, he schools his face into a mask. "Ruiz can't walk. Gil broke his leg when they captured us. And I don't have long before I'm going to need medical."

With a grunt, I push up to sitting. "Roof. Give me a minute. I can help carry him."

"No. Fogerty and I can handle him." With a nod at the other hostage, a thin, wiry man wearing a shell-shocked look on his face, Pritchard grabs a roll of duct tape from a duffel bag next to Gil's body, pointedly *not* looking at the man his family adopted as a teenager, then proceeds to bind my shoulder.

"Thanks." I test my arm, finding it better than I expect, and stare at the man I just executed. His eyes are open and fixed on the ceiling. The bullet wound to his forehead is neat and clean, just a drop of blood around one edge and some burned and blackened skin. He looks...almost at peace. "We can't leave his body here. You and Fogerty get Ruiz. I'll take Gil."

Meeting Austin's gaze, I wait for him to say something. Anything. I just killed his fucking brother. But then...I don't know what the hell Gil did to Pritchard the week he held him prisoner.

Finally, Austin claps a hand on my uninjured shoulder and squeezes. "I'm glad it was you, Trev. Anyone else..."

"I know." Anyone else would have done their job. Taken Gil in, let him disappear into the CIA's worst-kept secret. Hell, that's what I should have done too. Because now, anything Gil knew about the Loma Collectivo is gone. They're a scourge on the Venezuelan people, kidnapping, terrorizing, and more. And we just lost our only link to their leader—Gil's birth father, Jorge Sosa.

"He didn't want redemption." Austin stumbles as he heads for Ruiz and Fogerty, but braces himself on one of the overturned desks, takes a shuddering breath, and then, with some effort, straightens. "You took his pain away."

God, I hope I did. That I didn't just make the biggest mistake of my life. I fired the shot for Gil. For Austin. For Dani. But most of all, I did it for me. Because I don't think I could have lived with myself if I hadn't.

Hauling Gil's body in a fireman's carry, I'm hyper-aware of the distinct lack of a heartbeat. And that I'm the one who killed him. I jerk my head towards the stairs. "Time to get the fuck out of here."

In more ways than one. As soon as we land back on United States soil, I'm turning in my resignation. I can't take another life on order. Not after tonight. It would end me.

Four Days Later

STANDING in front of my handler, Oliver, I adopt the standard at ease position, hands crossed behind my back, prepared for my dressing down.

"You realize we'll never get intel on the Loma Collectivo if we can't detain one of their members, right?"

"I'm aware, Ollie. Do *you* realize it was kill or be killed?"

"You had a vest."

I roll my eyes. "And how often have we seen Kevlar fail? He could have tried to shoot me in the head. I made a decision. You weren't there."

He sits back, steepling his fingers in front of him. "No, I wasn't. But the two hostages you *didn't* know gave me a pretty detailed account of how things went down. Pritchard backed you. Of course."

Shit.

"Who are you going to trust? A banker and a contractor who were so scared they'd pissed themselves? Or me and Pritchard?" I reach into my jacket pocket for the envelope that's weighed heavily there since I got dressed this morning. "You know what? It doesn't matter." Dropping the envelope in front of him, I swallow hard. "I'm out."

"What?"

"I quit." I turn to leave, not knowing what else to say.

"Sit your ass down," he snaps. When I do, he levels me with a hard stare, his dark brown eyes almost black. "You're going to let this op be the end of your career? For fuck's sake, Trevor. You're the best damn SSO we have. You think on your feet like no one else I've trained in fifteen years, and you're throwing it all away?"

"I'm not 'throwing it all away,'" I say, unable to keep the harsh edge from my voice. "I'm taking a path that doesn't force me to choose between my best fucking friend and my country."

"This is a mistake." Oliver shakes his head. "I won't sign off on this."

"Then I'll take it to Smythe. Because I can't kill another person on *orders*. There's too much blood in my ledger already, and Gil...shit. I *know* it was the right thing to do. But that doesn't mean I'll be able to sleep easy again. Ever."

Ollie stares at me like he doesn't know who I am anymore, and he's probably right. After all, *I* don't know who I am.

"Take a week to think this over, Trev. Please."

"Answer's going to be the same. I wrote that letter before I left for Venezuela." With a small shrug, I run a hand through my hair and wince as my stitches pull taut. "I'm done. Don't try to delay the inevitable."

Picking up his desk phone, the man I've worked under for five years punches a four-digit number. "This is Senior SSO Oliver Benton. I need an SSO processed out. Trevor Moana. Do it today. He'll be in your office within ten minutes."

The tension I've carried since leaving for Venezuela rushes out of me so completely, I'm surprised Ollie doesn't hear the *whoosh*. "Thank you," I say quietly as I push to my feet and offer Ollie my hand. "If there'd been any other way..."

"There was," he replies as his fingers tighten on mine. "I should have stopped you from going to Venezuela. I'm sorry, Trev."

"That wouldn't have kept me here." As I turn for the door, I blow out a deep breath. "You'd have needed to stop Gil from turning in the first place. Everyone dropped the ball on that one. But no one more than me."

THE BAR on the outskirts of Langley is quiet for a reason. Special soundproofing makes each booth practically a cocoon. Austin's waiting for me when I arrive, a pint of beer cupped in his large hands.

"You do it?" he asks after I give the bartender my order and slide in across from him.

"Yep."

The man looks like he's about to punch something. Or crumble into pieces. "I told Dani," he says. "Some of it."

"Did you tell her why?" The bartender brings over a pint of pilsner, and I nod my thanks.

"No. She doesn't have a lot of memories of him. She should keep the good ones. Not the ones we..." Austin trails off, then rubs his fist against his heart. "All she knows is that you and I were injured in the same op that killed Gil. And that he died quickly. Mom and Dad...they don't know either. We're having a family memorial at the house next week. Nothing formal. If you can come..."

"No."

"Trev—"

I can't be there. Can't pretend I'm not the reason the whole family's grieving. "I should have seen the signs. Done something sooner. He almost killed you."

Austin stares at his hands folded on the table as I look him up and down. He hid his pain from me until we got on the transpo out of Caracas. Gil broke two of his ribs, then tortured him with hundreds of shallow cuts to his torso the day before I flew in. No wonder his voice was so strained. I don't know how he managed to stay upright.

"We both should have. You're..." Pain tightens small lines around his lips, and emotion churns in his eyes. "You're practically family, Trevor. Shit. How many nights did you eat dinner at our house when we were in high school? You spent spring break with us every single year."

"And I'm the one who put a bullet in his brain."

Austin opens and shuts his mouth, then shakes his head. "Fine."

We sip our beers in silence until I can muster the courage to ask the one question I can't get out of my head. "How'd Dani take it?"

Austin huffs out a breath, then winces and wraps his arm around his ribs. "She didn't cry. She never cries. After I told her...she hugged me, then shut me out. Like always. Said she was fine."

"Dani's...always fine." The spirited girl I met in high school never let anyone in. Except me. Once. For one beautiful, perfect week. The first year Gil failed to contact her on her birthday. I found her crying behind the Pritchards' barn, and she let me comfort her. A few days later, we shared a kiss I've never forgotten.

But then I broke her heart. All because of Gil. And Dani never opened up to me again.

"Don't ask me how," Austin says. "Or what she hides behind that smile of hers."

Anything that can hurt her.

She's a product of the system. Just like me. The first thing you learn? How to survive without letting anyone else see your pain.

"Austin, if you need to talk..." I say. The beer sours my stomach, and I slide it to the center of the table.

"Nothing really to say. You saved my life. The rest...I just want to put it all behind us." He doesn't look at me, and I don't push. If he wants to keep his emotions locked away, that's his business.

I drop a twenty between us. "I'm leaving Langley tomorrow. Heading up to Boston. I know a guy up there who runs a security and investigation firm. Second Sight. He's been trying to get me to interview with him for a year. I figured I'd finally take him up on it. Anything to get out of this life."

Austin nods. "You know how to reach me." As I stand, he adds, "Take care of yourself, Trev. I mean it."

Dani

After the five hour drive from New Haven to my apartment outside of Washington DC, all I want is to crawl into bed and hide away from the world. We didn't have a funeral for Gil. Just a little gathering at home. He hadn't truly been part of our family for years, and though we were close until the Pritchards adopted us, after that...it was like he wanted to forget I even existed.

Despite my exhaustion, I pause on the way in to check my mailbox.

The package slip makes my heart skip a beat. It's from *Gil*. He must have sent this just before the mission that took his life.

My eyes burn, but I don't cry. I never do. The package locker contains a fat United Express mailer, and I tuck it into my bag as I climb the stairs to my apartment.

It feels so empty. Not that Gil ever visited. I've lived here three years, and he never once even came to dinner. Austin drives up from Fort Bragg once a month.

Inside, I set my electric kettle and fill a mug with licorice root tea—something Betsy Pritchard—the only mother I've ever known—introduced me to when I was in high school. The sweet scent calms me and gives me an emotional and physical boost at the end of a long day. There's nothing that will make me feel even close to normal tonight, but my nightly tea ritual brings me a semblance of normalcy.

With a steaming cup in my hands, I sink down onto my couch and run my fingers over the envelope.

Daniella Rosa Martinez.

I haven't been Dani Martinez since the Pritchards adopted us. And Gil's the only one who ever called me Daniella. To everyone else I meet, I'm Dani.

I don't understand why he sent me something now. Before his death, I hadn't talked to him in five years. Why?

My hands shake as I tear open the envelope. Inside, there's a letter dated three weeks ago, a flash drive, and a small stack of photos.

Daniella, mi hermana. I'm sorry I stayed away for so long. My next mission will be dangerous, and there's a chance you won't want to speak to me if I return. So I left this with someone I trust and asked him to mail it for me if the worst happened. Not long after I joined the CIA, I traveled to Venezuela and found my father. I have never felt such a connection to another person.

I glance at the top photo. It's Gil, standing next to an older man who looks just like him. Plus thirty years or so. The next picture is that same man, many years ago, holding a baby. The photo's a little grainy—age and perhaps emotion have wrinkled it—but I can see Gil's birthmark on his left arm. The crescent shape stands out bright red against his skin.

There are four pictures of Gil as a child. In the last, he looks to be close to six. It must be one of the final photos taken at his father's home.

Setting the pictures aside, I return to the letter.

Papa said after Mama took me from him, he searched for us, and eight months later, we appeared in El Paso, Texas. You had just been born. By the time he flew to the United States to bring us home, Mama had died, and we'd been lost to the system.

If you're reading this, I'm either gone, or you've finally decided to cut me out of your life forever. I need you to know that I'm sorry I wasn't the greatest brother. I wanted to be, but you were so happy with the Pritchards, and I couldn't be. Not when I knew I had another father out there somewhere. I never belonged. You did. You do.

I used the CIA's resources to perform a full DNA workup on you last year. I'm giving you the opportunity to have the same connection I did. That sense of belonging. Daniella, I tracked down your father. He's Venezuelan, and all of his information is on the flash drive.

I'm sorry I could not give this to you in person. I love you, mi hermana.

Gil

I close my fingers around the drive, and the tears I've held back for years spill down my cheeks. I never wanted to know who my birth father was. Not really. Only in that vague "everyone wants to know where they come from" sort of way. I'm a Pritchard. When I took the job with the Washington Post, I changed my last name so no one would know Austin and I were related. He was already a big deal in the intelligence community, and I didn't want anyone to think I was treading on his connections.

But Monroe? It's Betsy's—my mother's—maiden name. They're my family. My mom, my dad, and my older brother.

I don't need what's on this drive to feel a connection. I don't want it. I want Gil back. The Gil who protected me in every foster home. The Gil who taught me how to ride a bike and throw a punch and lock my emotions deep inside where they'd never hurt me.

But I'll never have that again. Gil's dead, and even with my family around me, I always feel alone.

CHAPTER ONE

Present Day

Trevor

"GIL, last warning. You know I'm faster. Better. We have to take you in."

"Never."

The sound of gunfire wakes me from sleep with a shout, and I sit up and rub my chest where Gil's bullet fractured a rib. Even five years later, I can still feel the bone cracking. Still smell the blood all around me.

Gil was only one of forty-seven kills I made for the CIA. But his ghost haunts me more than any other. The rest...faceless, nameless men—and two women—I never thought twice about. I was following orders. Doing my job. Until I had to kill my best friend.

Staggering out to the kitchen, I turn the tap on full blast and fill a glass with cold water. I'm tempted to go for the vodka, but that never ends well. Last year on the anniversary of Gil's death, I went on a bender and didn't show up to work at Second Sight for three days. Dax threatened to fire me.

My phone buzzes on the counter with a new text message.

Austin: *I don't know why I wake up at the exact time he died every fucking year. How does my brain even know?*

Shit. I woke up at 3:14 a.m. It's an hour later in Caracas. I fired the kill shot at 4:14 a.m. local time.

My fingers are clumsy with my emotions running so high, so I activate voice to text. "Just got back from the west coast yesterday. You should have seen it, man. Dax and Evianna, Ryker and Wren, Ripper and Cara. A triple wedding. When I was there, for a day or two, I almost forgot. Almost."

The phone rings, and I put it on speaker so I can open my kitchen window. The frigid air helps ground me. Reminds me I'm in Boston, not Caracas. That I'm safe. That I have friends. A group of people I can count on.

"Dani called me," Austin says. "Otherwise, I might have forgotten too. And what does that say about me?"

"That you're human." The kitchen window isn't enough, so I head out onto my balcony. I'm only wearing a pair of pajama pants, and my feet are bare. The icy concrete makes my soles tingle, and the wind sends snowflakes pelting my chest.

"She wanted to talk about him. Wanted *me* to talk about him."

Rubbing my chest where the bullet hit, I sink into the snow-covered patio chair. I don't care that I'm quite literally freezing my ass off. The physical pain is a hell of a lot better than the mental anguish. "She didn't really know him. He never let her in. Not after your parents adopted them."

"If I could change one thing," Austin says, his voice rough, "it would be that. He never should have cut her out of his life."

Dani's heart-shaped face flashes through my memories. Her laugh. Her smile. She was always so *real*. Like she saw everything about a person with just one glance. "If it weren't for Dani, her mother never would have escaped Venezuela. And if Gil hadn't cut her out, who knows? His bastard of a father might have gone after her too. You know that."

"I know." The defeat in his tone matches my own emotions. This is the one day a year I let myself feel...much of anything. "She's the best of all of us, you know."

I choke out a laugh. "Yeah. She is. She still working for the Post?" I'm not sure why I'm asking. I read every article she writes. But Austin doesn't know that.

"Yep. International affairs and human rights."

Whistling, I reach my tolerance for the cold and snow and push to my feet. "Want to pour one out for Gil sometime next week?"

"I wish I could. The President's sending me on this bullshit publicity tour. I'm supposed to convince a dozen foreign governments that we don't torture people anymore."

My snort escapes before I can stop it, and over the line, Austin snaps a warning, "Trev."

"I know, I know. Officially, we don't condone any acts of torture. But you and I both know we still have plenty of black sites all over the world. I'm not having this debate with you." Shutting my patio door, I head back to my darkened bedroom.

"And you don't need to. Fucking hell, Trev. What Gil did to me... What he told me he did to dozens of others. What happened to Richards. McCabe. Holloway. Do you really think I condone that shit?"

"No! I never did." Frustration and a hint of shame start to warm my chilled skin, and I sink back onto the mattress and rest my elbows on my knees. "How long's the trip?"

"Three weeks. I leave day after tomorrow. I'll call you when I'm back." And with that, the call disconnects.

Fuck. I don't have a lot of friends, outside of the men and

women at Second Sight, the security and investigations firm I work for. And I just insulted one of the few people I know I can always count on. Tossing the phone on the nightstand, I sink back against the pillows and try for the sleep I know won't come.

WALKING into Second Sight knowing Dax isn't here is odd. He and his new wife, Evianna, are spending a week in Canada with Ripper, Cara, Ryker, and Wren. Watching the three couples get married just a couple of days ago made me feel almost...normal.

After rescuing Ford's fiancée, Joey, from Afghanistan, discovering Ripper'd been held there for six years and tortured so brutally he didn't even remember who he was, then pulling off an extraction the likes of which belongs in a fucking movie, I feel like I've found where I belong. Even if I don't really know how to act around any of them. Not really. Not after being bounced from foster home to foster home. When my dad died, I was only eight, and the system swallowed me up and never let me go. Too many times, I thought maybe I'd found my family, only to have the system yank me back again.

I nod at Ford as I head to the coffee machine. I couldn't get back to sleep after talking to Austin last night and I'm intent on two things this morning. Caffeine, and silence.

Until I see a flash of gold on his hand. I stop mid-pour, the coffee teasing me with its rich scent, but this is more important. "Uh, Ford?"

He arches a brow, but the hint of a smile tells me he knows exactly what I'm going to ask. "Morning, Trev."

"Want to tell me about that?" I nod towards the hand he has braced on his hip.

"Private little ceremony on the beach in San Diego." He grins, using his thumb to twist the ring around his finger. "Felt so wrong to take this off in Snoqualmie, but after what the three of them went through…"

"It was their day." I top off my cup, then offer to fill Ford's as well. "So, tell me about it."

He leans against the counter, his hands shoved into his pockets. "Joey didn't want anything fancy. Just her mom, her sister Geri, and Geri's husband." Ford's eyes take on a warmth I hadn't seen until he found Joey again, and he shakes his head. "Should have happened twenty years ago. Now, everything feels…right."

Sliding the coffee pot back under the machine, I meet his gaze. "Everything was right the moment the two of you saw one another again. Congratulations, Ford." I clap him on the shoulder, the closest I ever get to a hug, and smile. "And make sure Joey knows if you ever fuck up, she can call me to kick your ass."

He laughs, and I muster just enough energy to join in before heading for my office with my coffee cupped protectively in my hands. As happy as I am for Second Sight's co-owner and his new bride, I've reached the limit of my ability to handle small talk.

Dammit. It's been five years. I should be…better. I should at least be able to sleep through the fucking night. But somehow, seeing my friends find their forevers has made the nights since ten times worse.

Dax, Ryker, and Ripper are brothers in every sense of the word. When they're together, it's so obvious, it's painful. I had that once. Now, my best friend's dead—by my hand—and Austin? Last night broke something between us. Or at least damaged it. The bond we shared was forged through shared pain. I didn't think anything was strong enough to sever it.

Turns out, I'm an idiot.

So I'll hide out in my office and catch up on all of the emails waiting for me after a few days spent across the country. Maybe after that, chasing a lonely dinner with three or four shots of vodka won't sound like such a bad idea.

CHAPTER TWO

Dani

I SHOULD HAVE KNOWN BETTER than to try to work today. I spent half the night staring at the ceiling and the other half pacing with occasional breaks to pull out the flash drive Gil sent me right before he died.

And then at 5:00 a.m., I finally opened it.

Luis Rojas.

Born: March 4, 1961 in Calabozo, Venezuela

Current Location: Unknown

The drive is still sitting on my nightstand, but the information is burned into my brain. Now that I know his name, I can't stop thinking about who this man might be.

The Pritchards are the only family I've ever known—besides Gil. They adopted us when I was nine and pulled us out of a group home where we were regularly punished for speaking Spanish to one another.

Though Gil and I had vowed not to trust another adult for as long as we lived, after six months of constant love, acceptance, and support from Betsy, Steve, and their son, Austin, I gave in and started calling them Mom and Dad.

They're my family. My parents. The only ones I've ever needed.

The one photo next to my computer is the very first picture we took together. It was our second day with them, and they insisted a photo of all five of us belonged on their wall.

So why can't I stop thinking about Luis Rojas?

After I boot up my computer, I pull out my thinking putty—so very like the childhood toy that I used to stretch over the comics in the newspaper so it would pick up their images—and start squeezing it and rolling it around in my hands. It's silly—needing something to help me focus—but it works. Plus, my hands are crazy strong now.

This one is purple and sparkles, and I let my eyes unfocus as the putty stretches and compresses between my fingers. I have an article on the latest trade agreement between Mexico and the United States due by 5:00 p.m., and I'm way behind.

Snapping my gaze to my monitor, I read over what I've already written.

The House of Representatives voted to adopt revisions to the North American Free Trade Agreement (NAFTA) on Monday. The bill passed with an overwhelming majority of 391 to 35, signaling a rare bipartisan effort to amend the agreement.

Debate on the House floor lasted under an hour, with only five representatives taking longer than their allotted five minutes.

I need at least another six paragraphs before my editor will call the story complete, and yesterday, every time I tried to research the history of NAFTA, my eyes crossed and the words on the screen stopped making any sense. Grief is a strange thing.

Gil and I weren't even close. But the idea of him in the world reassured me.

Today, it's not Gil stealing my focus. It's Luis Rojas. My birth father. I switch over to Google and enter his name. There are thousands of results, so I start narrowing my search. Venezuela. But when I enter his home town, Calabozo, the first result contains a photo.

My own eyes stare back at me. He's so serious in the picture, and as I read the article, I realize why. "Oh, my God."

Luis Rojas has been jailed for the last six months in The Crypt, one of the most notorious prisons in Venezuela. At least, that's what his youngest brother believed before he, too, went missing.

"Luis tried to expose the horrors of the Farías government's human rights violations, and the secret police wish to silence him. But we will never be silenced. The Democrática Resistencia will fight for the rights of all Venezuelan people until our last breaths. They can torture him and lock him away in The Crypt, but he will never stop fighting for Venezuela!"

My father is a freedom fighter? I glance over at my editor's office across the bullpen. My mind is spinning with everything I'm suddenly desperate to know about this man who shares half of my DNA. But then I stare back at the photo of my family. I can't do anything until I talk to my parents. But once I do...I need to look into this.

Right after I finish my NAFTA story.

A LITTLE AFTER 6:00 p.m., I sling my messenger bag over my shoulder and take the stairs down to the Post's gym. Five years ago, I was on assignment in Darfur, and I had to run from a kill squad that was after my source. I made it all of a mile before I was so winded, I had an asthma attack. Luckily, a family saw my photographer and me and urged us to hide in their home. They saved our lives, and the day I arrived back in the States, I went right to the office and found the gym.

Now, I can run ten miles and barely break a sweat. Two years ago, I started lifting weights and studying Aikido. I lost twenty pounds, and I have abs most women would die for. Nothing seems to trim down my thighs or my ass, but I'm damn proud of my abs.

In the women's locker room, I change into my workout gear, then get on the treadmill. Six miles later, I head for the free weights and spend an hour working my upper body.

The sweat and the burn help me feel alive, and after a quick shower, I head home. Back to my lonely apartment, my dinner of stale pizza and club soda, and a phone call I didn't think I'd ever make.

"Hey, Dad," I say when Steve Pritchard answers the phone.

"Dani? Is everything okay?"

I just talked to them yesterday, and while we're close, I usually only call once a week at most. "Yeah. I just wanted to talk to you about something." I get up to pace my living room, fearing if I sit still another minute, I'll lose my nerve. "Um, right after Gil died, he sent me a letter. Well, scratch that. Right *before* Gil died, he sent me a letter, and I got it the day after the memorial."

"You never said anything." His tone carries the barest hint of pain, and my heart squeezes.

"I know. I'm sorry. But he sent me information on my birth father. A flash drive with his name, date of birth, and last known address on it. I never opened it. I didn't need to. *You're* my father."

"Dani, you know your mother and I love you. You're our daughter, and nothing will ever change that. If you're going to ask me for permission to meet this guy, you have it. Not that you need it."

"I can't meet him. But I do want to find out more about him. I opened the drive last night. I needed to feel closer to Gil, and he obviously wanted me to have this."

"Go for it, sweetheart. Nothing you find is going to make us love you any less. Your Mom and I believe you choose your family. That's why we adopted you and Gil in the first place. Because you needed a home and we had one to give. But what do you mean you *can't* meet him?"

"He's in prison in Venezuela."

"Prison?" My father clears his throat. "Not sure I like where this is heading, squirt. Why is he in prison?"

"I didn't dig into it much yet. I wanted to talk to you first. The rumors are that he was arrested for speaking out against the Venezuelan government's human rights violations. That he's been taken to The Crypt—one of the worst prisons in the world—and is being tortured."

A whistle carries over the line. "You smell a story."

My cheeks heat, and I run a hand through my hair. "I do. And I want to follow it."

The man who lost one son to a black ops mission where his other son was tortured and almost killed sighs. "Be careful, sweetheart. That's all I ask. As far as I'm concerned, the only good thing Venezuela's ever done for our family is give us you and Gil. After that..."

"I know, Dad. I love you."

"Love you too, squirt. Keep me posted."

"Will do." After my father disconnects the call, I sink down onto my couch and stare out the window towards the Potomac. I'm really going to do this. Find my birth father and maybe, get a hell of a story out of it along the way.

TWO DAYS LATER, after almost non-stop research, I have my

pitch ready to go. With my notebook and my favorite pen in hand, I rap on my editor's office door. "Lincoln? Do you have a minute?"

He's leaning back in his chair with his feet propped up on the radiator, a sign he's in full-on idea mode. "Sure. Come on in." Studying me, a gleam appears in his dark hazel eyes. "You have a lead, don't you? Something big?"

"Maybe." After I shut the door, I perch on the edge of his visitor's chair. "I want to do a story on the *Democrática Resistencia* in Venezuela. With a spotlight on one of their leaders, Luis Rojas."

"Who?" Lincoln plants his feet firmly on the floor and slides his keyboard closer before typing in my father's name. "He's in prison."

"It's worse than that. He's in The Crypt. I got confirmation this morning. And...I think I can get in there to interview him." I wish I'd brought my thinking putty with me. I'm so excited about this story I can barely sit still, and I tap my pen incessantly against the top of my notebook.

"Holy shit, Dani. The Crypt's a hell hole. I don't want you down there."

"I'm Venezuelan."

Lincoln blinks at me as if I've just told him I'm from Mars. I don't advertise my heritage. I don't hide it either, but my slightly darker-than-white skin, brown eyes, and black hair mean most people have no idea what ethnicity I am. I prefer it that way. Being American is the only thing I've ever known, so whether my parents were from Venezuela or Antartica never really meant a lot to me. Until now. "My mother was American, and my father was Venezuelan. I was born in Venezuela, just outside of Caracas. The Pritchards adopted me when I was nine."

"Do you have dual citizenship?" Lincoln sits forward and his brows crease.

"No. I qualify, I believe. But I'd need to find proof of my birthplace, and all I have is a small diary my birth mother left for me and Gil when she abandoned us at a church in El Paso."

Lincoln shakes his head. "It's still too dangerous."

Giving him a "you can't be serious" look, I yank up the sleeve of my red sweater to show him the long, angry scar that stretches from just below my elbow to the middle of my forearm. "I got this on assignment in Afghanistan, remember? Embedded with the 82nd Airborne? A stray bullet outside of Kabul. I'm not afraid of a little danger. Not with what's at stake."

"What's at stake? Dani, Luis Rojas is in prison for opposing the Farías regime. There's nothing 'at stake' here."

Anger flares, heat gathering in my chest as I grip my pen tightly. "A man's life is nothing? Luis Rojas is probably being tortured for wanting all of the Venezuelan people treated like *people*. And since *I'm* technically one of those people—or could have easily been one, had my mother not returned to the United States—I think there's a hell of a lot at stake."

Lincoln's mouth flattens, and his hazel eyes darken. "You want to travel to the country with the highest number of kidnappings in the world and interview someone the government would rather see dead—or tortured—than alive. I can't let you go alone and I can't send a photographer with you."

"What if I get my brother to accompany me?" I have to do this. Now that I know where my birth father is, I want this story. More than I've wanted any other story in my entire life.

"Commander Pritchard?" Lincoln's eyes widen. "If you can get him to go with you, I'll approve your travel."

"Fine. Give me a day to arrange things with him and reach out to my contact at the prison. But be prepared to book me that flight." With a grin, I practically skip out of his office and head back to my desk. By tomorrow, I'll have everything arranged.

I hope.

CHAPTER THREE

Trevor

MY DESK PHONE BUZZES, but I don't bother to look away from my computer as I hit the button. "Yes, Marjorie?"

"There's a Dani Monroe here for you, Trevor."

My world screeches to a halt. Dani? Here? Four days after the anniversary of her brother's death? This isn't good. But I can't refuse her anything. Not after all the pain I caused.

"Send her in."

Smoothing my hands down my dress shirt, I blow out a breath, trying to ease the stress of the day, then stand and open my office door.

The woman walking down the hall bears little resemblance to the one I last saw in New Haven more than six years ago. The Dani I knew was soft and curvy with a shy smile that belied her confidence. Long hair used to fall halfway down her back in ebony waves, and her kohl-lined eyes never missed a beat.

But now... My jaw hangs open as she strides towards my office, purpose in her steps. She's lost at least thirty pounds, and the urge to take her out for a steak dinner flares up for a moment until I remind myself I don't have the right to comment on anything a woman does with her body.

Her smile's different too. Instead of shyness, now, there's unease. Like she doesn't want to be here but has little choice. She's cut her hair into an angled bob, and it frames her heart-shaped face in a way that makes her look in command of her entire universe.

"Trevor." Her voice is strong, but not entirely steady as she offers me a firm handshake. Too firm, in fact. One of my knuckles cracks when she squeezes, and she releases my fingers quickly. "Sorry. Kind of a must in my world. Never let a man have a stronger grip than you."

"It's okay. Come on in. Can I get you a cup of coffee or tea?" I don't know how to act around her. Fall to my knees and beg forgiveness for killing her brother? Avoid mentioning it completely? Ask her what she knows? Austin told her some of it, but last I heard, not everything. The air in the room seems to get thinner by the second as she shakes her head.

Dani takes the chair across from my desk and tugs at her black suit jacket. "I wouldn't be here if I had another option."

"Well, that...makes me feel like shit," I mutter to myself as I pull a notepad from my drawer, then meet her brown eyes.

"Dammit." She tucks a thick lock of hair behind her ear and fiddles with a simple, silver drop earring. "I didn't mean it like that. Not exactly. But Austin's out of the country for the next six weeks or so, and I only have one shot at the interview of a lifetime. He sent me to you."

If this woman asked me to fly her to the moon, I'd do it. Even though I've never piloted a damn thing in my life. I owe her that much for what I did to her. Breaking her heart, then killing the only blood family she had? Hell, I owe her the world.

"What do you need?"

"A chaperone." She spits the words out like they're the worst thing she could possibly say.

"Where do you need to go that's dangerous enough to need a chaperone?"

"Caracas, Venezuela."

Oh, shit. The one place I hoped to never see again. "Dani, Caracas is where—"

Anger churns in her gaze. "You don't have to remind me what happened there, Trevor. Gil died, Austin barely survived, and you..." Her eyes shimmer for a moment, and I see a hint of the real Dani. The one she hides from everyone. The one I was stupid enough to walk away from—no, to abandon—all those years ago. But just as quickly as the mask slips, she blinks hard, and it's firmly in place again. She's back to being professional, almost unflappable.

Dani pulls a small tin from her purse, opens it, and scoops a golf ball-sized lump of...something purple into her palm. Her fingers work it into various shapes, and I stare at her hand—the perfectly filed nails with no polish, the soft skin, the way the tendons and muscles flex and dance.

"What is that?" I ask.

"Oh." Her cheeks flush a bit darker, and she unfurls her fingers, revealing the purple sparkling blob. "Thinking putty."

"Huh?"

"Thinking putty. It helps me concentrate. Something about the motion and the feel of it between my fingers helps me see patterns and options I wouldn't normally see. And it helps me when I have to say something...I'm not ready to say."

"Like...?" I don't want to know. Or...maybe I do.

Dani levels me with her brown eyes. "I know what happened, Trevor. The truth. You fired the shot that killed my brother."

"Dani—"

"Don't 'Dani' me." She gets up and starts to pace, her fingers working the putty nonstop. "Austin told me everything. He didn't want to. Hell, it took three years and a lot of cursing. Mostly mine."

I'm so taken aback, I almost laugh. "You cursed out the head of JSOC and got him to spill classified information? He's had so much SEER training, he's unbreakable."

"I cursed out my *brother* and got him to tell me the truth about Gil's death. About *why* he died." Dani's voice cracks. "I know Gil tortured Austin. I know he almost killed both of you. I know his birth father convinced him to turn against the CIA, against the United States, against everything we'd ever known."

"Dammit, Austin," I say under my breath as I stand so we're on the same level. I don't want to look her in the eyes, but I have to own my shit. "Gil was my best friend. Second only to Austin."

And you, once. The thought nearly escapes out loud, but I swallow hard before I continue.

"I think about him every fucking day. I didn't want it to end the way it did, but it was either kill him or let him end up in a CIA black site."

Dani stops, her back to my office door. "I know. Look, Trevor...I won't deny that a part of me hates you for killing him. The part that spent years bouncing from foster home to foster home where the only constant was Gil. But the rest of me..." She squeezes the putty hard enough it makes little popping noises—or maybe that's her knuckles. "I don't blame you for his death. I blame Gil. And right now, I'm staring at a story that could make my entire career and...more. But it just happens to be in the most dangerous city in the world. I need your help."

The vulnerability in her tone only lasts for those four little words, but they play on a loop in my head as I hold her gaze.

I need your help.

This is a mistake. A big fucking mistake. Going back to the place that ended my CIA career with the woman whose brother I killed there? I can't believe I'm even considering it.

I need your help.

I gesture to the chair as I round my desk. "Give me the details. All of them. My boss is on his honeymoon, and I need to run this by Second Sight's co-owner. But even if they expressly forbid me from leaving—I'm in. You're not going to Venezuela alone."

Dani's eyes light up, the relief in them impossible to ignore. "Thank God," she says. "If I had to give up on this now, I'd regret it for the rest of my life."

"So, who are you interviewing?"

Her gaze shifts down to the putty in her hands. "Luis Rojas. He's a freedom fighter for the Democrática Resistencia. The Farías government locked him up in The Crypt for his 'crimes' and the rumors are that he's being tortured until—"

"If he's in The Crypt, he's definitely being tortured."

"Don't interrupt," she says sharply, and I snap my jaw shut. "He's being tortured until he agrees to recant all of his claims that the government is oppressing its citizens and give up information on the resistance movement, so Farías can put an end to them for good."

After a beat to make sure she's done, I arch a brow. "And the Farías regime *agreed* to let you interview him? Why?"

"Because I'm very persuasive." She offers me a challenging gaze, and I shake my head.

Leaning forward, I told my hands on my desk. "Not good enough, Dani. Venezuela is a shit-show. Has been for years. I can protect you from anyone after a quick ransom or a pretty woman to sell into the sex trade. But the entirety of the Farías military complex? We wouldn't stand a chance. No matter how lethal I am."

The words are meant to intimidate her. To frighten her so she won't do anything stupid. Like putting herself in harm's way for a story no one wants told but her.

If she were anyone other than Dani Monroe, I might have

been successful. Instead, she mirrors my position and lowers her voice. "I want this story, Trev. I *need* this story. I've worked fifteen hours a day all week making calls, promising favors, and paying sources to secure this interview. Marcos Farías wants to prove to the world that he's not a monster, and I'm going to expose him for what he truly is."

There's more. Something in Dani's tone tells me she's only giving me *most* of the truth. I should push her. Hell, I should refuse to accompany her completely. Except, she's desperate. That emotion is hidden behind her words and the way she's stopped playing with that sparkling putty and is now squeezing it in a death grip. Dammit. I'm going to regret this.

"When do we leave?"

CHAPTER FOUR

Dani

BY THE TIME I get home, I'm running on fumes. When I'm on a story, I work non-stop and usually end up so exhausted, I feel like I could sleep for a week. Yet, every night when I collapse into bed, sleep comes only in fits and starts.

My quick trip to Boston took six hours, and tomorrow, I have three hours scheduled at my doctor's office getting the required vaccines for Venezuela—typhoid, malaria, hepatitis A, and diphtheria—then another several hours at work handing off my other assignments to the pool reporters, assuring Lincoln that I'll be safe with Trevor with me, and transferring all of my critical information to multiple flash drives. Anytime I travel, I carry at least six of them—some out in the open, some in hidden compartments of my suitcase, my toiletry kit, and, if I'm going somewhere extremely dangerous, my shoe.

One thing you learn when you report from volatile countries? Always keep multiple backup copies of the information you most desperately need.

A little after nine, I place my large duffel bag on top of my dresser. We don't leave for almost thirty hours, but no one has *ever* accused me of being unprepared. Yet, I can't muster the energy to start digging through my drawers.

Not when my thoughts constantly return to Trevor.

He's the last person I want coming with me. I didn't lie. I don't blame him for Gil's death. If Trevor hadn't killed my brother, Gil would be lost to a place where no one could ever find him, his life a nightmare. Or, he would have done something even worse than torturing Austin within an inch of his life. Like killing him. Or many others.

My phone rings, and Austin's name flashes on the screen. "Did you get to Prague all right?" I ask.

"If by 'all right' you mean 'at 2:00 a.m. after the bumpiest flight ever recorded,' then yes."

He sounds tired, and I sink down onto my bed and pull a blanket up over my legs. "How long do you have to stay?"

"Four days. Then on to Berlin. I need to crash soon, squirt. But did you get in touch with Trevor?"

"I hopped a quick flight to Boston this morning. He'll go with me. But Austin, I couldn't admit who Luis Rojas...*is* to me. Please don't tell him, okay?"

"Shit, Dani. Why not? He can't protect you if he doesn't know everything."

The judgement in my brother's voice shouldn't frustrate me, but it does. *He* should be going with me. Not Trevor. But his job helps make the world a safer place, and it's selfish to ask him to put me ahead of his work.

"Because I don't want anyone to know. Hell, I didn't want to tell you either, but Dad didn't give me a choice," I snap. "If anyone in the Farías government finds out...it'll put both Luis *and* me in a lot more danger."

"Don't you think I know that?" A growl rumbles over the long distance connection. "You shouldn't even be *attempting* this."

"I have to!" A deeper sense of anger replaces my frustration. Anger at Gil. At the one person who should have always been there for me. Who should have put his sister above some misplaced loyalty to a father he'd only just met. A father who hated me, who hated everything America stands for.

"Why? Mom and Dad love you. I love you. Why isn't our family enough for you now?"

My eyes start to burn, but I squeeze them shut to stop the mere possibility of tears. "That's a shitty thing to say, Austin. Our family means everything to me. I'm not going to meet Luis because I want a new family. I'm going because...he's part of who I am. And he's making a difference in a country that needs it. Desperately. Maybe if I tell his story, I can make a difference too."

Austin's voice softens. "You make a difference every damn day, squirt. Just by being you. All the stories you've covered? Corruption in Darfur? Embezzlement by private contractors in Afghanistan? The water crisis in Cambodia? People are talking about those issues because of you."

"It's not enough. It's never enough," I whisper.

Neither of us speaks for several seconds, long enough I fear the call has dropped. But then Austin sighs. "Dani? Talk to me. There's more to this than needing to find your roots. Than making a difference. What is it?"

He always could see right through my bullshit.

"Guess all that spy training did you some good." I curl onto my side with the phone tucked against my ear so I can stare out my bedroom window. I live on the top floor of a six-story building, and so I reap the benefits of cathedral ceilings and tall windows. From my bed, I can see almost to the Potomac.

"Good? I'm stuck in Prague on a publicity tour no one believes is actually going to make a fucking difference. Being a *bad* spy would be a lot more convenient right now." The hint of laughter in his voice is tinged with exhaustion, and I snuggle deeper under the blanket.

"Yeah, but you're there because you're the best. Because the President trusts you. I'm proud of you."

"You're evading the question."

If Austin were in front of me right now, I'd throw a pillow at him. Those are my words. The ones I use time and time again when I'm working a story. But I learned them from Austin. When Gil started pulling away from me after we were adopted, Austin was there. Teaching me how to trust. How to be the woman I am now. The one who never gives up.

"Why did Gil send me that flash drive? Why couldn't he just tell me in person? I emailed him every month, begging him to call me, to come visit, to just reach out. He never did. Why cut me out of his life completely only to contact me right before he died? Shit, Austin. He mailed it *after* he'd started in on you."

"There's my little sis." His voice softens, and I hate that I brought up those terrible days he spent in Venezuela. "Hang on a sec, Dani." Muttered words carry over the line. After a moment, a door shuts, and when he speaks again, regret tinges his tone. "I don't know why he did any of it. But I do know Gil was in pain. Those final days, he never left me alone for more than an hour or so. I spent a lot of time with him." He huffs what might be a laugh. "Not by choice, obviously."

"Austin, you don't have to—"

"I do. Because you should know all of it." Rustling sounds overwhelm the connection, and then he clears his throat. "Two months before he died, he'd made a mistake—one call on an unencrypted line, and that was enough for us to confirm he was working for the Loma Collectivo.

"If he'd stepped foot back on U.S. soil, he never would have seen the sun again. And he knew it. So he sent me an email. Only a handful of people in the entire world could have traced that message, but we had one on our team. Gil was counting on it. He wanted to lead us into a trap."

"He *planned* on torturing you?" I choke back my sob as the true horrors of my brother's actions sink in.

"I think so." Austin swallows hard enough I can hear it, then continues. "The three guys he was working with all kept their faces covered. But not Gil. He wanted me to know he was in charge. That he was going to kill me. But he was going to make me suffer first."

A single tear hovers at the corner of my right eye, and I refuse to let it fall as my brother's voice drops to a hoarse whisper.

"That note he sent you? He only told you part of the story, squirt. Everything he did? Turning on the CIA, torturing me, almost killing Trevor? It was all because of what happened between his father and your birth mother."

I don't know that I can handle any more revelations tonight, but Austin's never been this open with me about his days in Venezuela, despite how many times I asked him why Gil did what he did.

"What about her? All Gil ever said was that she left Venezuela when she was pregnant with me. I always knew we had different birth fathers, but he never told me why."

"Are you sure you want to hear this, Dani? It's not a good story."

The hesitation in my brother's tone just makes me more determined to find out the truth. "Yes."

"Gil's father, Jorge Sosa, kidnapped Kate Martinez from a beach resort in Aruba where she was celebrating spring break with friends. She was twenty-one. A creative writing major at Loyola. She wasn't his lover, Dani. She was his prisoner. For six years. Luis Rojas was one of the asshole's muscle men, and he and your mother fell in love. When she got pregnant with you, Luis helped her escape back to the United States."

"Oh, God. So Gil's father blamed *me*. It was my fault..."

"No! Dani, don't go there. You can't be at fault when you weren't even born yet. Jorge Sosa is the one you should blame. A month before that unencrypted phone call, a Special Forces team dispatched to Venezuela to help ensure fair and democratic elections killed him. I think that's what set Gil off."

I can't respond, but I'm pretty sure Austin can hear me lose the battle to keep my breathing steady.

"Gil wasn't stable, sis. Not by a long shot. There's no way he could have held anything but hatred for Luis Rojas. From the little I was able to get out of him while he was...working on me, Rojas stayed with Sosa for another fifteen years after he helped Kate flee, then turned on him and joined the Democrática Resistencia. My guess? Gil sent you that flash drive just to fuck with your head. Don't let him."

"Too late," I manage. "Are you sure? What if you're wrong?"

Pull yourself together, Dani. Now. You have a job to do.

"I'm not." Austin sounds so sure, I believe him, which only makes me more determined to see this through.

"Then I have to do this. I have to meet Luis and tell his story."

A sigh carries over the line. "I know. I wish you weren't going. Or that you'd decided to expose corruption in a slightly safer country. Iraq maybe. Somalia. Afghanistan. Anywhere besides Venezuela. But if you had, you wouldn't be...*you*. You're the best damn investigative journalist I've ever known."

"Hardly," I snort.

"You broke the story of the German Ambassador spying for the Russians. You were the only one who saw the connection between Jessup, Parr, and Caroline Phillips. If you hadn't, Trev wouldn't have been able to find out they were after Ripper. Hell, if it weren't for you, JSOC would have had so much egg on our faces, we'd never have been able to see the frying pan we were in, let alone make an omelet."

"I only broke that story because you gave it to me." I let my gaze soften, the city lights twinkling like little stars.

"Doesn't matter. You're the one who helped me figure out what the fuck those two were doing in the first place. You've always been brilliant, Dani. If you'd listened to me years ago, had come with me to the CIA, you'd be in charge of this place now instead of me."

An uneasy laugh escapes. "Like anyone would have trusted me again after what Gil did." As soon as I say the words, I regret them. "Austin, I'm—"

"Don't. I fought my way back from that shit, and you would have too." His voice takes on a resigned tone. "I've got to go. My wakeup call is at seven. You check in while you're in Venezuela. Every *single* day. And listen to Trevor. He knows his shit. Do you understand?"

"I understand. Thanks, Austin. Love you."

"Love you too, sis."

After we end the call, I still can't muster the energy to get up. Instead, I lie in bed, turning the flash drive over and over in my fingers until my eyelids are too heavy to keep open. I can pack in the morning.

***

Trevor

First thing the next morning, I knock on Ford's office door. Dani booked us two tickets on a flight out of Dulles at the ass crack of dawn tomorrow, and I'm headed down there tonight and staying at the airport hotel.

Assuming Ford doesn't try to stop me from going. Not that I'd listen. I should have talked to him yesterday, but this conversation? It's not going to go well.

"Come on in, Trev," he says with an easy smile. Second

Sight isn't officially accepting new clients again until next week, so everyone's relaxed. We shut down the whole office over the holidays, other than a couple of low-level cases that Clive and Ronan handled while the rest of us took some much needed R&R.

"Heard from Dax and Evianna?" I sink into his visitor's chair with my mug of coffee, figuring small talk, despite my lack of experience with it, is the best way to ease myself into the serious stuff.

"Yeah. They got back to Seattle last night, but they're staying there another two days so he and Ry can work out some of the details of the new teams they're putting together." Ford runs a hand through his hair. Bits of gray dot his temples, but the man's never looked so young...and happy.

"How come you're not out there too, then?"

"Didn't want to be. This is their deal. Now that I have Joey back, I don't want a single fucking reason to leave the country ever again—unless she and I want to take a vacation or her research sends her somewhere."

"You're not going to be involved at all?"

"Dax and I are still going to run Second Sight. Nothing about this firm changes. Except we'll have additional resources if any of our cases involve K&R. The newly expanded Hidden Agenda is *supposed* to let Ryker spend more time in Seattle with Wren."

I snort. "You mean he's not going to go on every mission? I'll believe that when it happens."

Ford nearly spits out his coffee. "It's not going to go well. What's up with you? I haven't seen you since yesterday morning. You disappeared right after lunch."

I stare down at the mug cupped in my hands. "Remember when I told you about Gil? What I did on my last mission for the CIA?"

Ford doesn't say anything. Only nods, then sits back and waits for me to continue.

"Gil's sister came to see me yesterday. She's an investigative journalist for the Washington Post, and she needs a bodyguard to accompany her to Venezuela."

With a nod, Ford sets his cup down. "Makes sense. Venezuela's not exactly known as a safe place for tourists." He taps his keyboard a couple of times to bring up the company calendar. "Your schedule's clear. I'm assuming you're going?"

"Yeah. But, Ford, there's something you don't know."

Arching a brow, he chuckles. "You're CIA. I have a feeling there's a fuckton I don't know."

"*Former* CIA. That's not my life anymore." Jerking up, I start to pace the room. "Dani and Gil were orphans, Ford. Like me. They were raised in the system. Hell, that's where I first met Gil. We were put in the same foster home for a few weeks when I was seven. He watched out for me."

"Shit, man. I didn't know you were adopted." There's an edge to Ford's voice. Hurt that I never shared this part of me with him.

"I wasn't." Pinning him with a hard stare, I admit part of my truth. "I aged out of the system. The day I turned eighteen, I left my foster home and joined the army. But Gil and Dani...they were adopted by Austin Pritchard's parents."

I don't have to wait long for the realization to sink in. "Commander Pritchard. From JSOC."

"Yes."

"Fucking hell." Ford whistles. "So that's why you and Pritchard seemed so...casual with one another at Ripper's thing."

"Part of it." Over the course of the next hour, I tell him everything. How Gil found his birth father in Venezuela and spent weeks down there with the leader of the Loma Collectivo, being brainwashed into becoming a double agent. How Austin tried to bring him home, but didn't know how dramatically Jorge Sosa's death had affected Gil. The night I found Austin tortured and then killed my best friend rather than send him to a CIA black site.

Stone-faced, Ford leans back in his chair. "And after all that, Dani's willing to go to Venezuela with *you*? Does she know that you're the one who killed her brother?"

"She does. Austin—Pritchard—told her a couple of years after it happened." I stare out Ford's window. Snow falls steadily onto the Boston streets, making everything seem fresh and new. Maybe it is. Ford and Dax got married. We have a new junior investigator, a big guy named Tank, Vasquez and Ronan are transitioning to days, and Ford just put out feelers for a couple of replacement overnight guys. Everything's changing. Except me.

Ford's saying something, but I can't look away from the window. When he grabs my forearm, I whirl around and practically knock him to the floor before I realize what I'm doing.

"Trevor! Look at me." He comes back at me, hard, pinning me up against the window with my arms over my head. He's at least six inches taller than I am, and though I'm strong, Ford uses my distraction to his advantage. "What the hell was that?" he growls. "I barely touched you."

"Sorry, man." I relax in his grip once my brain processes the absence of an actual threat. "I haven't slept much the past few nights. The anniversary of Gil's death was Monday."

"Fuck. Really?"

I nod.

"I seem to remember you saying something to me about lack of sleep being dangerous on a mission." Ford releases me and steps back with a small shake of his head. "Bottom line this for me, Trev. When are you going, how bad is it going to be, and what do you need?"

"Tomorrow morning. How bad? No fucking clue. I never

wanted to step foot on Venezuelan soil again. But I don't have a choice. There's nothing I wouldn't do for Dani."

Ford stares at me like he knows I'm still holding back. I'm not going just because I owe Dani for what I did to her brother, but because I'd do anything to make up for the hurt I caused her years before that terrible day.

"And what do you need from Second Sight?"

"Nothing. Just back-up should things go sideways. I'll take a couple of Wren's toys. Two of the GPS trackers Royce designed, an encrypted tablet. It's a simple in-and-out with a one-night stay. Recon of the area the first night, then she'll interview Luis Rojas and take a tour of The Crypt the next day, and we're back on the plane to the States."

Ford sinks down into his chair. "Back-up comes standard with the job, Trev. You know that. Just watch your six and be safe. Because when you get back, I think you, me, and Dax need to have a serious talk about keeping secrets from your family."

<h1 style="text-align:center">CHAPTER FIVE</h1>

Dani

MY KITCHEN TABLE is full of checklists and supplies. Bug spray, water purification tablets, and antibiotics for travelers' sickness. I once spent an entire week in the hospital in Malaysia after accepting tea from a contact and not asking if it had been made with purified water.

One of my little black notebooks has pages and pages of my research on Luis Rojas and his history fighting the Farías government. Marcos Farías took the country in a coup seven years ago, and for a while, the world thought his leadership would bring an end to the Loma Collectivo's atrocities against the Venezuelan people.

But the world was wrong.

As I set my electric kettle to boil, there's a knock at my apartment door. Shit. My neighbor wasn't supposed to come by for another couple of hours. Where did I put that damn spare key?

I throw the door open without even checking the peephole and lose my words. Trevor stands in the hallway dressed in a pair of dark jeans, a light blue t-shirt that stretches over his sculpted muscles, and a gray and black flannel shirt, unbuttoned. A duffel bag hangs off his shoulder.

"What are you doing here?"

He arches a brow. "Is that any way to greet the guy who's taking you to one of the most dangerous countries in the world?"

Dammit. Get it together, Dani.

Flustered, I press my lips together to stop a very unladylike sound—and a few inventive curses—from tumbling out of my mouth. "Well, excuse me," I say as I step back so he can come in. "I thought we were going to meet at the airport in the morning."

"I caught an early flight," he says. "And since our only plan is 'don't let Dani get kidnapped or murdered while she's interviewing one of the country's most famous political prisoners,' I thought we should get on that."

"That *is* the only plan." I huff out a breath and go back to my lists. "I only asked you to go with me because Lincoln wouldn't approve my travel if I didn't have a bodyguard."

"Way to make a guy feel...wanted." He drops his duffel bag and scans the various pieces of paper on the table. After a minute, he nods. "Not a bad packing list. The rest of what we need we can pick up when we get there."

I stop with a pack of anti-nausea pills clutched in my hand. "What else do we need?"

"Weapons."

Staring at him like he's grown a second head, I wait for him to explain. When he doesn't, I march over to him and poke him in the chest. "Listen to me, Trevor James Moana, I've known you more than twenty years. You can't just give me one-word answers when we're heading...where we're heading."

His gaze lands on my finger. "Did you just...?"

"Yes."

"Daniella—"

My heart squeezes, and I back up a step. "No. *No.* You don't call me that. Gil was the only one who called me Daniella, and after what you did…"

Trevor curses under his breath, grabs his duffel, and strides for the door. "I'll see you at 0500 tomorrow." Pausing with one foot in the hall, he narrows his eyes at me. "The moment we get on that plane, *Dani,* you do what I say, when I say, and how I say. *That's* the plan. That's the only way I can keep you safe."

The door slams, and I sink down into my chair. This is not how I wanted to start off the trip. At odds with the lethal spy I hired to keep me safe. The man who grew from the overprotective, outrageously handsome boy who stole my heart the day we met and broke it ten years later.

The man who killed my brother.

"Way too many complications, Dani." I drop my head into my hands. "This isn't going to end well."

I TOSS and turn for hours. This is a mistake. Trusting Trevor with my life isn't the problem. I know he'll protect me until his last breath. But all these feelings I have for him and about him, it's like they're all trying to spill out at once, and that's going to make me sloppy. It'll dull the sharp edge I've honed over years of having to forge my own path.

Sometime after 2:00 a.m., I sink into sleep and immediately find myself trapped in a dream.

"Give it back!" I lurch forward and try to snatch my lunch bag from the tall eleventh grader holding it over her head. "That's mine!"

"Let's see what the little charity case has today!" Bethany cackles as her friends grab my arms and pull me away from her.

Tears shine in my eyes, but I squeeze them shut. I can't cry. Not in front of the mean girl squad at Whispering Pines High School.

*"Peanut butter and jelly. And chocolate milk. That's baby food."
Bethany pulls open the Ziplock bag, dumps my sandwich on the
ground, then stomps on it. When she pours the chocolate milk over
the mushy bread, I lose the battle with my tears and start calling her
every name I heard the worst of our foster parents say over the years.*

*"Hey! Let her go," a deep voice booms, and then one of the girls
holding me drops my arm and runs for the classrooms. "Bethany,
stop picking on the freshmen."*

*I turn and have to look up as the one boy in the whole school I
don't want to see me cry stalks over to us and wraps an arm around
my shoulders. "You okay, Dani?"*

*With a sniffle and a nod, I stare up at my rescuer. Trevor. He's a
junior. On the soccer team. And friends with Austin. He even comes
over to our house some afternoons and hangs out. Though never with
me. The two of them hole up in Austin's room playing video games.
But when he stays for dinner, he always smiles at me.*

*"Oh. Trev," Bethany says, her voice so much higher than usual.
Nicer too.*

*"Get lost." Trevor steps away from me, and the absence of his
warmth makes something inside of me twist in pain. But then he
holds out his hand. "Come on. I have an extra lunch ticket. It's
pepperoni pizza day."*

I wake up with tears in my eyes. Trevor bought me pizza
every day for a week and ate with me at the juniors' table. Even
now, I don't know where he got all those tickets. He was trapped
in the system, just like Gil and I had been. But unlike us, he was
never adopted.

I sigh as I roll over and pull the pillow against my chest.
These are going to be the longest few days of my life.

Trevor

Dulles at 5:00 a.m., even on a Saturday, is a madhouse. Concourse A teems with people, most half-asleep. Or at least that's what it feels like as I'm waiting in line at the security checkpoint. Pretty sure no one in front of me has ever flown before, and even with my security clearance—and guaranteed TSA pre-check—it takes an hour to make my way to a coffee stand four gates from where I'm supposed to meet Dani.

Adjusting my duffel, I reach into the hidden pocket of my jacket for my phone, run it over the scanner to pay for my Americano, and then lean against the wall to wait for my order and scan the crowd. People watching isn't a hobby. It's self-preservation honed over years of covert missions. Eyes, ears, and brain. The three most valuable weapons a spy has.

A couple at the gate in front of me is headed towards divorce. Each carries years of resentment in their expressions and body language. The three twenty-somethings sitting across from them are high as kites. I caught the stench of weed as they passed. And the woman rushing towards the coffee stand dressed in a pair of simple black linen pants, a muted orange tank, and a matching black jacket...is nervous as hell and trying too hard to hide it.

After Dani orders a quad-shot almond milk latte, she turns and startles as she sees me. Her cheeks darken slightly. "Sorry, I'm late. Security had to check every single one of my hidey-holes."

I stifle my chuckle. "That's their job, Danisaur." The childhood nickname slips out before I realize it, and she takes a sharp breath. "What? Did you think I forgot?"

"I...I didn't...no. You just haven't called me that since we were kids." She rummages in her messenger bag for her wallet, but I lean over and run my phone over the reader until it beeps.

That shuts her up until both our coffees are ready on the sideboard. "Trevor? About last night..."

"It was my fault. I don't know why I called you Daniella—except that no one's called *me* Trevor James Moana since my dad died. Though the whole poking me in the chest thing? Don't do that again."

Dani nods as she takes a sip of coffee, then grimaces as she tries to hoist her backpack onto her shoulder while balancing the steaming cup.

"Give me that," I say as I hold out my hand.

"No. You're not carrying my—" But I already have the backpack over my shoulder before she can finish the sentence, and she huffs as she rushes to keep up with me. "I'm not helpless, Trevor. I normally make these trips all by myself. Just like a big girl."

The sarcasm grates along my spine, and I shoot her a look. "Didn't say you were. But you hired a pack mule who can fight. So let me do my job."

"I didn't—" Dani groans. "Never mind. You're not going to listen to me anyway."

"What gave you that idea?" At the gate, we find two seats, and I ease the pack down next to her before dropping my own bag at my feet. When we're shoulder to shoulder, I give her arm a little nudge. "I always listened to you, Dani. Always wanted to, anyway."

Her sigh is a sound I fell in love with back in high school. It usually meant I'd won the argument. And when back in those days, we had some spectacular ones.

"This interview, Trevor...it's going to be the hardest one I've ever done. You're going to have to give me some space here." She peers up at me with so much emotion churning in her eyes, I want to wrap my arms around her and hold her until all that sadness and uncertainty fades away.

Too bad I lost that right years ago. So instead, I nod and

touch my coffee cup to hers. "I amend what I said last night. Caracas is a shit-show. Has been for years. One wrong turn, and you disappear forever." Lowering my head so our foreheads are almost touching, I hold her gaze. "You do what I say, when I say it. Whenever we leave the hotel, you are *glued* to my side. No arguments. But as long as you're in your room, you should be safe. And I won't bother you. You won't even see me unless you want to."

Dani relaxes a fraction and stares down at her feet. Small and delicate, clad in a pair of plain black shoes with neatly tied laces. Good soles too, from what little I can see. She's being smart. She *is* smart, and I need to stop treating her like she's still that bullied, out-of-her-element little girl I met all those years ago.

"Thanks, TJ."

The genuine gratitude in her tone, along with the old nickname, stirs memories of that feeling I used to get whenever we'd race for the Pritchard's kitchen table and I'd pretend to trip on the one loose floorboard and stumble. Just enough to let her win. I felt like fucking Superman those times. Like I could do no wrong in her world.

I want that feeling again. But Dani Monroe won't be the one to give it to me. Not after all that's come between us. She makes that abundantly clear when she pulls a book from her messenger bag, tucks her feet under her, and starts to read.

I guess we're done talking. Probably for the best. The last thing I need is to keep reminding myself how much I once loved her and how badly I broke her heart.

CHAPTER SIX

Dani

Fifteen hours of travel later, the plane touches down at Simón Bolivar International Airport. As we head for Customs, I steal glances at Trevor, but he looks everywhere but at me. I have so many memories of him from my childhood, and none of them line up with the silent, stiff man at my side. We barely spoke on the flight. I made a mistake calling him TJ. I could see the pain churning in his eyes.

After that, I didn't know how to start up the conversation again. So I read a book, watched one of the in-flight movies, and ignored him. The whole damn time.

He carries my backpack until we're forced to get into two different lines to go through Customs. My accreditation through the Washington Post earns me a full ninety minutes stuck in a small, windowless office with two armed officers, and requires multiple phone calls to Lincoln and the Editor-In-Chief, Sarita.

Trevor must have something magical stamped in his passport, because he sailed right through the line and by the time I emerge, has a steaming cup of coffee ready for me.

"Car's ready and waiting," he says as he hauls my bag over his shoulder once more. "We need to get going. The roads between here and Caracas are dangerous after dark."

"I wasn't planning on them detaining me," I retort as I rush to keep up with him. He's a good six inches taller than I am. Always has been. Those long legs can move so much faster than my short ones.

"One more hour, and you can be rid of me for the night." His words carry an undercurrent of sadness, and I want to stop him. To tell him I don't want to be rid of him. But after so many hours sitting next to him, receiving one or two word answers to any question I asked, and seeing him give the flight attendants more consideration than he was giving me have frayed all of my nerves. I just want to get to the hotel and hit the gym. A hard run followed by room service will help.

Our nondescript white sedan has seen better days, and I peer up at him as he stows our luggage in the back seat. "The Post usually reserves an SUV. Or at least something a little more...reliable."

"That'd make us easy marks, Danisaur." Trevor pointedly stares at me until I buckle myself into the stained front seat of the Chevy Spark. The car smells like stale cigarettes with a hint of sweat. Unsurprising since the humidity runs close to ninety percent this time of year.

I've been in worse. The Land Rovers in Darfur feel like they're going to come apart every time they hit a bump in the road. Given how many potholes there are, that's a real possibility. At least the suspension in this car feels solid.

Trevor merges into a line of traffic leaving the airport, both hands on the wheel, eyes constantly shifting between the road and the rear view mirror.

I stare out the window at the slowly setting sun. "I wish I had a chance to know this country. Really *know* it," I say quietly.

"With Farías in charge—just like with the last president—this country is no place you should have ever seen."

"Too late for that." Lush trees sway in the gentle breezes, and with no air conditioning, we both have the windows rolled down. It should smell fresh and clean this close to the ocean, but it doesn't. All I can see are rocks leading down to the sea, some dotted with ramshackle tin buildings that all too often, wash right into the sea, occupants and all. "I came from here, Trevor. I was born here. This country is in my blood, even though I never cared until—"

"Until what?" His voice softens, and he spares me a quick glance as we approach a long tunnel.

The well-lit, two-lane road and the plain concrete walls offer little in the way of distraction, so I reach into my bag for my thinking putty. The one I brought with me is pearlescent pink, and I work it between my fingers as I try to figure out how much I want to tell him.

"Until I started researching this story." It's not a lie. It's just not the whole truth either. "Luis Rojas did a lot of good before he disappeared. The protests he organized were large enough President Farías had to take notice. People were rioting in the streets, demanding better jobs, health care, a *true* democracy rather than...whatever *this* is."

"A dictatorship wearing a democratic wig," Trevor replies, and the corners of my lips tug into a smile.

"Something like that. But after he was jailed, people got scared. He was only one man, but from the few people I managed to talk to when I was still in D.C., he was this larger than life superhero. Always fighting. Always challenging Farías, but doing it in a way that kept him...safe somehow."

With a nod, Trevor checks behind us once more, then

narrows his eyes. "There's a car back there matching every lane change I make. The whole time we've been in the tunnel."

"That doesn't mean anything. It's a *tunnel*. Where are they going to go?" I crane my neck to try to see.

"They're accelerating. Roll up your window, Dani. Now." Slamming his foot down hard on the gas pedal, Trevor pushes the old car to its limit, and I keep watch in the side mirror. It doesn't take me long to spot the car he's talking about. It's almost a twin of this one, only dirtier and with a crack in the windshield. I can't see who's behind the wheel, but they're driving as aggressively as Trevor is, and passing everyone else on the road.

The temperature in the car climbs with each kilometer, and when we burst out of the tunnel, the sun's finally set, and Trevor's words echo in my ears. *"The roads between here and Caracas are dangerous after dark."*

I'm about to ask what he's planning on doing when he cuts across what's now four lanes of heavy traffic and takes a left turn, hard. The wheels under me feel like they almost leave the ground, but as I crane my neck to check behind us, I don't see the other Chevy Spark.

My heart's racing, and until Trevor tells me I can roll down the window again, I don't even know if I'm breathing. "We lost them, Dani. We're okay." Reaching across the small space, he rests his strong hand over mine and gives it a squeeze. "Another fifteen minutes, and we'll be safe at the hotel."

I nod and let my head fall back against the seat. Working the thinking putty faster and faster, I realize what frightened me. It wasn't someone potentially chasing us. It wasn't the possibility we were in danger. I've reported from half a dozen war zones in the past few years. I've covered everything from rioting in St. Louis to the cartel murders in Mexico. Danger doesn't scare me.

Seeing fear in Trevor's eyes? That scares me more than anything.

Trevor

The Hotel Diamonte is a bright, modern space with a view of the El Ávila mountains. Our adjoining rooms are on the fifth floor, and Dani stays by my side as I sweep them both for bugs and cameras. "Clean," I say as I tuck Wren's handheld scanner back into my pocket. Second Sight's tech genius hid the scanner in an electronic, rechargeable lighter. The damn thing's even approved to be carried on an airplane since it uses a plasma arc instead of actual fuel. The Customs agents didn't look twice at it.

Dani relaxes a fraction and sinks down onto the king-sized bed in her room. I'm not ready to leave her. Not by a long shot. Sitting next to her all day...it brought back so many memories.

She still smells the same—jasmine and vanilla—though with her hair cropped, it's harder to catch the scent. The humidity has left a gentle sheen to her cheeks, making her almost glow in the light from the bedside lamps.

I double-check the windows, the closets, and the bathrooms, then hesitate in the doorway between our two rooms. "I have to meet with my local contact. But I need you to promise me you'll stay put."

"If I don't hit the gym, I won't be able to focus at all tonight," she says as she unzips her backpack and pulls out a pair of running shoes followed by her tablet. "After that, it's nothing but research for the rest of the evening."

"No. You're staying in the room with the door locked." I don't want to leave her at all, but I need weapons and intel, and

I can't take her with me. It's way too dangerous for her on the streets at night.

"Trevor, did you miss the big, beefy security guards at every exterior door? The keycard scanners on the elevators? No one's going to come after me here." A pair of running shorts and a sports bra in her hand, she heads for the bathroom and shuts the door in my face when I try to follow her.

"You don't know that. I promised Austin I'd keep you safe, and I can't do that if you're wandering around without me."

"I won't be *wandering*," she calls through the door. "I'll be running. I have your number programmed into my phone. If you want me to check in every half hour, I will. But I'm *going* to the gym."

When she emerges, I have to stop my jaw from hanging open. A small tattoo just above the waistband of her running shorts draws my gaze, which is good, because otherwise, I'd be staring directly at her breasts encased in the tight running bra. Because, fuck. This isn't the girl I crushed on in high school. Or even the woman I'd wanted to make mine in our twenties.

Her abs flex as she huffs out a breath, making the delicate outlines of a compass rose move, almost as if the needle's searching for its true north. And then I realize that's exactly what the tattoo represents. Dani's true north. Coordinates encircle the design, numbers that ping around at the back of my thoughts.

"Mind letting me get a shirt?" Hands on her hips, she tilts her head back to meet my gaze, and only then do I realize I'm blocking her way.

"Sorry." I have to force the word out, then command my feet to move. *Get your head in the game, asshole. You can't protect her if you let your dick do all the thinking.*

The bright red running shirt with Bermuda Half-Marathon printed across the front clings to her curves and does nothing to erase the sight of that damn tattoo from my memory.

Tucking her keycard and phone into her pocket, she heads for the door, but I cut her off, my hand covering hers as she goes for the knob. "Please, Danisaur. I know you're a badass, but this country will eat you up and spit out your bones, and I..."

I don't want to lose you.

"I've been all over the world, TJ." She twists her hand so our fingers intertwine. "Afghanistan, Darfur, Argentina, Russia... I have pretty good instincts, and I know how to fight. Six years of Aikido training." Her full lips curve, and she squeezes my hand. "You don't have to protect me from *everything*."

"Yes, I do." We're so close, the heat of her seeps into my chest, and my dick jerks behind my jeans. In any other circumstances, I'd press her against the wall and kiss her until she couldn't remember why she ever wanted to walk out of this room, but Dani's...off limits.

She levers up on the balls of her feet, then places both hands on my shoulders to steady herself. We're almost eye to eye now, and her gaze holds so much power, I almost step back. "I'll be fine. I'll text you when I'm back in the room."

Her fingers slide down my biceps and tighten on the sleeves of my shirt. Before I know what's happening, she jerks me around, her forearm pressed to my neck, and forces me to the floor. My instincts kick in, and I barely manage to stop myself from sweeping my arm out and taking her down with me.

"Ryo katadori," she says as she offers to help me up. "See? Not so helpless."

"Unfair attack." I ignore her hand and roll to my feet. "Also, dangerous. Don't ever do that to me again." Frustration sharpens my words, and I stalk back towards my own room, pausing at the threshold to give her one last hard stare. "Gym and back here. Text me every thirty minutes. No exceptions."

After my ultimatum, I shut the door with more force than necessary and run my hands through my hair. I can't protect someone who doesn't want to be protected. I hear her slip out of her room, and the urge to follow her, to stay glued to her side, is so strong, I have my hand on the knob before I realize I've moved.

"Enough," I mutter. "Leo's waiting."

In under five minutes, I've hidden two ceramic blades—one under the mattress and another between the folds of one of the bathroom towels—and strung pieces of translucent filament across the windows in both rooms. On my way out, I drape another strand over the top of my door and let it hang down three inches, well above a normal man's eye line.

Repeating the process with Dani's door—I made the front desk attendant give me keys for both rooms—I kick myself for losing my temper. If I hadn't, I could have shown her what to look for.

As it is, I just hope I get back here before she finishes her run.

CHAPTER SEVEN

Trevor

THE HOTEL IS ONLY two blocks from the Plaza Bolívar. Its history doesn't escape me. Political dissidents used to be executed here, and in the dark corners of the square, I can almost see their ghosts.

Locals fill small cafes and line up at food carts. The scents make my stomach rumble. Finding a table at the back of one of the bars on the outskirts of the square, I order a flight of rum and a plate of arepas while I wait for Leo.

A tall, dark-haired man with an eye patch and a long scar running down his right cheek from under the patch to the corner of his mouth picks his way among the other tables, his gait uneven.

I stand as he grabs the chair across from me. He extends his left hand, his right not fully functional these days, and we shake awkwardly. "Trevor Moana. Never thought I'd see you back here again."

"Never thought you would either." I signal for the young woman who took my order, and Leo Basher slides a small messenger bag off his shoulder and shoves it under the table between my feet. "You get everything I asked for?"

He nods, orders his own rum, and then leans closer. "I threw in a couple of new toys as a bonus. Magnetic GPS tracking chip, the CIA's smallest earwigs currently available outside of Langley, and something only the techs have seen." With what I suspect is a wink—hard to tell since he only has one eye—he leans his good arm on the table. "Figured you wouldn't have set foot here without a serious reason, so some extra help would be appreciated."

"Damn straight."

"So? What is it?"

Leo and I never kept secrets from one another unless we were forced to, so I rake my fingers through my hair and wait for the server to drop off our drinks. "To stupid misadventures," I say as I hoist my glass.

"And their consequences," he replies.

The rum is smooth as shit, and I savor the silky burn as it slides down my throat. "Damn. Can't get anything this good in the States without spending a fucking fortune."

"Not going to tell me?" Leo asks.

"Gil Monroe's sister."

Leo whistles—or tries to. The right half of his face has extensive nerve damage. The Loma Collectivo tortured him eight years ago. They wanted the names of all of the CIA's assets in the region. Leo resisted for a week until I located him in a warehouse an hour from here. Those fuckers were my first three kills.

"You're shitting me."

"Nope. She's a journalist. Arranged some big interview at The Crypt." I take another sip of rum and meet Leo's gaze. "You ever hear of a Luis Rojas?"

"Yeah. He and his brothers, Andrés and Franco, have a large following in Venezuela. Luis and Andrés disappeared, and

Franco went into hiding. No one has seen them in months. *El Presidente* confirmed that Luis had been jailed for treason, but Andrés...rumors are, he's dead." Leo wipes a sheen of rum from his lips, then orders a second glass when the server drops off my plate of arepas. "*Doble, por favor.*"

"Spill," I say as I pick up one of the arepas—a messy sandwich with shredded beef and a spicy crema between two crunchy cornmeal discs. "What am I in for that I'm not expecting?"

Tossing back the remains of the first drink, Leo shakes his head. "My friend, I have no idea. But Farías isn't one to forgive. Or admit to any of the shit we know is going on at The Crypt. If Gil's sister—Daniella?"

"Dani."

"If Dani was able to gain access to Luis Rojas, it was only because Farías has some purpose behind letting him be interviewed. You'll be with her?" Concern creases his brow, and he takes a healthy swig from the second drink.

"Yes. I'm her official photographer. As far as the government is concerned." I'm suddenly no longer hungry, but lack of fuel is just as dangerous on a mission as lack of sleep, so I force myself to take a second bite, then a third.

"Trev, The Crypt is an appropriate name. It's nothing but an office building above ground. But below? Fuck. The official prisoners are held on the first sublevel. The cells aren't even half bad. Small, but humane. Go deeper, though...that's a whole different shitshow. Insist on interviewing Rojas above ground. Do *not* let them take you down there."

"I've heard the rumors." Prisoners held for days in stress positions, tied to chairs, forced to sleep bent almost in half in a cell so small, they can't stand up. Freezing temperatures. "As far as I know, Dani doesn't have any details about the interview yet other than the time."

"Find out." He sets his now empty glass down hard enough

the rum left in my glass splashes halfway up the side. "I'm fucking serious."

"You're fucking drunk."

Leo lurches to his feet, then reaches into the pocket of his linen pants. A hundred Bolívar note lands on the table between us, and he grabs my shoulder and squeezes hard enough to send my defenses into overdrive. "Don't judge me, you bastard. You try living like this."

Two seconds later, he's back in his chair with my hand around his right wrist, which is now bent to the point of pain. "Watch yourself, Basher. You don't want to fight me."

"It's better than going to your funeral."

As soon as I release him, he's up again, and this time, I let him walk away. I got what I came for. Firepower and intel. He'll get his shit under control after he sleeps off the rum, and he knows better than to compromise my cover. We're brothers in arms, bonded by blood and pain, and I trust him with my life. But that doesn't mean I won't kick his ass if he touches me again. Or can't keep himself sober long enough to have a fucking conversation.

When the server comes over to check on me, I order a second plate of arepas to go and force myself to clean my plate. I need to get back to Dani and prepare for tomorrow.

Dani

My timer goes off, and I jump onto the side rails of the treadmill and pick up my phone. Though I hate feeling like I'm a teenager checking in with Mom and Dad again, I promised Trevor I'd text him, and I keep my promises.

Close to 4 miles in. The gym's empty. I'm fine.

He replies with a terse: *Stay that way.*

Great. I'm traveling with the world's greatest conversationalist. Hopping back on the treadmill, I push myself faster, trying to banish the demons that have haunted me since I first looked up my birth father's name.

When I hit eight miles, I stagger over to the water dispenser and fill a plastic cup to the brim. Even inside with air conditioning, Venezuela is almost unbearably humid. The run and the icy liquid help focus my thoughts, and I head back to my room, just like I said I would.

Trevor hasn't returned yet, so I lock up, then get in the shower. My muscles ache after so many hours in the air, and when I spill some of my jasmine shampoo into my hands, the familiar scent relaxes me almost immediately.

I can do this. Walk into that prison tomorrow and look Luis Rojas in the eyes for the first time. Will he have any idea who I am? Will he care? Will I?

As I exit the bathroom wearing only a loose tank and a pair of sleep shorts, movement catches my eye, and I lunge for my phone on the bed.

"Whoa. It's just me." Trevor stands in the doorway between our two rooms, a foil-wrapped plate in his hands. "I brought you dinner."

"Oh." Heat creeps up my neck, and I realize how little I'm wearing. Even though more of me is covered now than when I brazenly walked by him in a sports bra and running shorts, I feel so much more exposed. My nipples tighten under the tank, and I turn to my backpack and fumble around for a sweatshirt, only to realize I didn't bring one because we're in Venezuela and it's the middle of summer. Giving up, I turn back and cross my arms over my chest. "Thanks. Did you get what you needed from Leo?"

"Yep." He sets the plate on the little table in the corner, along with a plastic knife and fork, then turns on his heel and heads back for his room.

There's something wrong. He's twitchy, and a muscle in his jaw is working overtime. I'd swear he was chewing gum if I didn't know better. He's close to the edge, but the edge of what, I don't know.

"Trevor?" He stops, and I scramble to figure out what to say to keep him here. Just like every other time he's walked away from me. "This smells great."

"I couldn't remember if you ate meat." He shrugs, but still doesn't face me. "So I got you a shredded beef, a swordfish, and a veggie."

"I like everything but zucchini and SpaghettiOs."

"What do you have against SpaghettiOs?" he asks as he finally turns around.

"One of our foster homes, that's literally all we got for dinner. Every night for six months. I can't stand them anymore." My admission shifts something in his demeanor.

"For me it was Hamburger Helper." Raw emotion flashes in his eyes. Grief, sadness. A hint of shame, maybe. But he blinks, and it's gone again.

"Did you eat?" If I keep asking questions, maybe he won't leave me alone with all these racing thoughts I wish I could ignore. I want to tell him about Luis Rojas before he meets the man tomorrow. But I have no idea how to even *start* the conversation.

Trevor leans against the door jamb and shoves his hands into his pockets. "I ate."

I pick up one of the arepas and take a messy bite, causing a dollop of crema to fall directly onto my chest, just above the tank. Trevor's gaze snaps to my fingers as I hurriedly swipe the mess up with a napkin.

And then he adjusts himself. Oh God. It's subtle—the motion of his hips. But it's there. And now my eyes want to stray below his belt. This is ridiculous. "Will you just sit down? Please?"

It's self-defense. That's what I tell myself. If he's sitting across from me, I won't be able to ogle him.

"I need to get organized for tomorrow," he says, but he doesn't leave, and I angle my head towards the chair.

"Trevor, you are the most infuriating man on the planet."

A dry laugh bursts from his lips. "No, I'm pretty sure that title goes to Ryker McCabe."

"Who?"

"A guy I've worked with a time or two. You'll meet him someday."

Arching my brows, I ask, "Is he going to refuse to talk to me too? Warn me now, because I don't like feeling like a fool for asking."

"Fine. 'll be right back." Two minutes later, he sets two beers on the table, one for each of us, and pulls a bottle opener from his pocket. "The mini-bars here are well-stocked."

"Thanks. I needed this." I hold up the bottle and offer to toast, and reluctantly, Trevor touches the neck of his beer to mine. "You're pretty damn considerate, you know that?"

He chokes on his sip of beer and his hand flies to his nose. Passing him a napkin, I try to hide my smile as he swipes at his face. "Considerate?" His voice is hoarse, and he takes another swig before he manages to speak again. "What does that even mean?"

Leaning forward and resting my elbows on the table, I meet his gaze. "It means you're dancing around me like I'm on fire and you're Frosty the Snowman. I don't bite, Trev. You won't melt if you engage in *normal, human* conversation with me."

He sits back and runs his fingers through his hair. It's so ingrained in him—that motion. Whenever he needs to think. The motion causes his bicep to strain against his t-shirt and exposes a long scar on the back of his arm that I've never seen before. Then again, I've hardly laid eyes on him in almost a decade. Not since he stood me up and left me sobbing at the summit of East Rock.

After he blows out a long, slow breath, Trevor meets my gaze. "I don't know how," he says, his voice almost a whisper. "Dani, I killed—"

"I know!" Shoving my plate aside, I stalk over to the window and peer out a crack in the drapes. The city stretches out before me, a mix of bright lights and patches of total darkness—the division between the rich and the poor. "I'll never forget what happened to Gil, but how many times do I need to tell you that I don't blame you for it?"

"At least a thousand more."

In my periphery, he stands, but before he can reach the door between our two rooms, I catch up to him. This time, though, I don't touch him. Just side step him so I'm blocking his path, cross my arms, and stare up at him. "Count them. I don't blame you. I don't blame you. I don't blame you. That's three. I figure I can get to a thousand in what? An hour?"

"Stop. Don't make me into something—or someone—I'm not. Please, Danisaur. I'm not a hero. I'm not a good man. Or at least I'm not good for…you." The last word escapes harsh and rough, and combined with the use of my old nickname, I can feel myself dancing with the edge of control. My eyes burn, and I duck around him, letting him flee back to the safety of his own space. At the last moment, right before I slam the door, his hand shoots out and presses flat to the wood. "My rules, remember? This stays unlocked and cracked. All night."

"Don't you remember anything from high school, TJ? I never follow the rules." Batting his hand away, I shut the door firmly and flip the lock.

At least he left both beers. I think I'm going to need them.

CHAPTER EIGHT

Trevor

I STARED at the ceiling for two hours before I fell asleep, and my dreams...they left me feeling hollow. Over and over again, I relived the night I broke Dani's heart.

All for nothing. Out of fear and misplaced trust in a man I should have known was no longer my friend.

I can't stop thinking about that tattoo on her hip. The coordinates are burned into my brain, and when I hear her moving around in the other room, I boot up my tablet and enter them into a search engine.

"Oh, fuck."

I expected to see the Pritchard house. But instead, they take me to the summit of East Rock in New Haven. Where Dani always used to go when she was upset. Where I proved her right. Men suck and you can't count on anyone but yourself.

I found her there dozens of times over the years when Austin had been a jerk—as only teenage boys can be—and was too much of a coward to face his little sister. There's a reason I call her Danisaur. That girl could blow the roof off a place with her temper.

The compass had that as her true north. Why? Because that's where she so often found comfort? Or because that's where she learned the world is a shitty place and people let you down? I have to know.

But not today. Today we're heading into the lion's den, and I have no idea what we're going to find.

When I hear the shower in her room, I drop the robe I'm wearing onto the bed and pull on a pair of black boxer briefs. Specially ordered from a guy who used to be a spook, they're tailored with four hidden pockets that are lined with a special material made to foil x-rays and metal detectors.

In the first, at the back of the waistband, I tuck one of the GPS chips. Ford has the ID and frequency it's using, so if things go sideways, he can find me.

Next, one of the small ceramic knives slips into a pocket at my hip. On the other side, I add a flat multi-tool. And next to my dick? A micro-thin lock pick. Adjusting myself, I run my hands over each pocket to verify the lining is thick enough to hide my shit from a standard pat down.

"Trevor—" Dani's gasp makes me jerk. She's standing in the doorway wrapped in her robe. "Oh, God. I'm sorry. The door wasn't closed." Cheeks flushed, she whirls and heads back to her room.

I pull on a shirt and follow her. "Rules, remember? These doors are never supposed to close. You're lucky I didn't pick the lock and open yours last night. And what are you apologizing for? You've seen me in my swim trunks hundreds of times."

"You weren't, um...masturbating all those times."

My laugh surprises her, and she gives me a look of disbelief as I half-double over, my hands on my thighs. "Dani, you need to watch more porn. Or better porn. Most men don't jerk themselves off through their underwear."

She sputters a little, and I pull the ceramic blade from the pocket on my right thigh. "I was making sure this—and a few other things—were properly hidden."

That shuts her up. It also puts a look on her unadorned face I can't quite read. "You're...you really think you're going to need that? The Farías government knows I'm here on assignment for the Post. They're not going to attack me at the prison."

"Maybe not. But I'd be a shit bodyguard if I wasn't prepared for the worst." Sliding the blade back into its pocket, I run my hand over my hip again to ensure I didn't disturb the smooth lines of the underwear. "What can I do for you?"

Her cheeks flush a dark crimson, like I just asked her favorite sexual position, and she folds her arms over her chest. "I wanted to know if you needed help with the camera equipment."

"I'm good."

"Okay. Well, um...I need to get dressed." She stares pointedly at the door, and I take the hint and retreat to my room. Dammit. Without any makeup on, there's a vulnerability to her that's sexy as hell, and after last night, I just want to take her in my arms and kiss her until she forgets her own name.

But, I can't. And twelve hours from now, we'll be on a plane to the States. After that, we'll go back to being strangers. And that's probably for the best.

THE DRIVE to the prison leaves us both on edge. Lane markings in Caracas are suggestions that everyone ignores, and in places, cars fly down the roads five across. Two kilometers ahead, The Crypt looms. The sixteen floors above ground house the Bolivarian Intelligence Service. Windows shine in the late morning sun, though the structure is foreboding with its dark concrete walls and sharp angles.

Dani doesn't say a word the whole time, her gaze fixed on a small notebook in her lap. Before we left, I slipped a GPS tracker into her bag, hidden inside a ballpoint pen.

"You okay, Danisaur?" We're trapped in a long line of cars at a stoplight, and she sighs as she closes the notebook and then rubs the back of her neck.

"I didn't sleep much last night," she admits. "Otherwise, I'm fine. You don't have to worry about me, Trevor. This is my job, and I'm *really* good at it."

"You are." She looks surprised, and I glance over at her, the corners of my mouth twitching into a smile. "I've read every story you've ever published."

"Really?"

"Really." I want to tell her how proud I am of her. How much I admire her. But I don't have the words. At least not ones I'm ready to say. Like how much I worried about her when she went to Darfur or how glad I was to see her byline in the Post once she'd returned.

"You never said anything. Hell, we haven't talked in what? Eight years?" A hint of pain creeps into her voice, though she does her best to hide it. "Why didn't you...?"

"We had this discussion last night. What was I supposed to say to you? 'Hey, Dani. Long time no talk. Sorry I had to kill your brother, but that story you wrote on the Congolese water crisis was amazing'?"

"Point made." She turns away to stare out the window as we make the left turn into The Crypt's gated parking lot. At the entry booth, a man carrying an AK-47 lumbers over to the car.

"*¿Cuál es su propósito aquí?*"

Dani leans over, close enough I can smell her shampoo, and replies, "*Estamos aquí para entrevistar a un preso. Me llamo es Dani Monroe, y él es Travis Lejune.*"

Good. She remembered my alias. Trevor Moana can't step foot in this country ever again, but Wren—Second Sight's tech genius—created half a dozen fake identities for each of us, and this is Travis Lejune's first trip to Venezuela.

"Your Spanish is very good," the guard replies.

"So's your English." Dani passes him our press credentials, and he takes them inside his little booth and picks up the phone.

After a brief discussion with whoever's on the other end, he nods, hangs up, and returns to the vehicle. "Park in the first row. You will be met."

We follow the arrows through the lot and find a space less than a hundred feet from the building's entrance. "Remember, Danisaur," I say quietly, "my rules. You don't go anywhere without me."

She nods, and as soon as we reach the door, a man in a military uniform with close to a dozen medals pinned to the lapels approaches us, flanked by two soldiers carrying pistols and AKs.

"*Señorita* Monroe. I am General Ruben Ochoa. Welcome to *La Cripta*."

Dani

General Ochoa wears a fake smile along with his many commendations.

"Please come with me," he says, and Trevor keeps his hand on the small of my back as we follow the man. His two armed companions fall in to step behind us, and I fight every instinct I have not to look back at them.

Men like this, in countries like Venezuela, expect to be feared. Bullies. All of them. I try to motion to Trevor to drop his hand, but he's not looking at me. He's scanning our surroundings constantly. Likely mapping all of the potential exits and any threats I don't see.

When I quicken my steps to put a few inches between us, he finally pays attention, and I give him a quick shake of my head. His eyes say it all. He's not happy about any of this.

"*Señorita* Monroe, you will be in here," General Ochoa says as he scans a keycard over a door sensor. Two female soldiers wait inside, one heavily armed. The other wears a pair of purple skin-tight gloves. "Señior Lejune, please follow me to the next room."

"We stay together," Trevor says.

"I am sorry." The general shakes his head. "But we cannot have that. You will be searched before you are allowed into the detention facility. I assure you, Señorita Monroe will be fine."

Trevor's about to go apeshit on the general. I can feel the anger rolling off of him in waves, and I step between the two men, placing a hand on Trevor's chest as I stare up at the general. "You'll have to forgive my photographer, General Ochoa. This is his first overseas assignment, and he has this mistaken belief that he has to protect me." Turning to Trevor, I level him with a hard stare. "This is standard procedure for entering most of the world's prisons. Get over it, Lejune. You're here to take pictures only."

"Da—Ms. Monroe, I'm not *quite* as inexperienced as you think," he growls. "And next time, maybe you should brief me on *standard procedures* before I have a chance to make a fool out of myself."

Great. I'm going to get an earful for this later, but at least he turns to the general and says, "My apologies, General. My previous job required me to be much more...protective of my colleagues."

The general chuckles and motions for Trevor to follow him while I enter the first room and set my bag on the table. "*Buenos dias,*" I say to the two women. "*Me llamo Dani Monroe. Y usted?*"

"Strip," the one wearing gloves says to me. I guess niceties are out the window. The name tag on her uniform reads Chavez. The other one is Vidal.

I shed my jacket, laying it carefully on the table, then stoop to loosen the laces on my shoes and step out of them. Two minutes later, I'm standing in front of them in only my bra and panties.

Chavez motions for me to hold out my arms and spread my legs, then gives me the most thorough pat down I've had outside of the interview I did from Fukushima. That one required a cavity search, and I stifle a shudder at the memory.

"You may dress. We will examine your bag now," Chavez says when she steps back, satisfied I'm not wearing a wire or hiding any contraband or weapons.

"*Gracias.*"

"Your accent is quite good," Vidal says, earning a glare from Chavez.

"I was around native speakers for most of my childhood."

By the time I put my shoes back on, Chavez is done checking out my bag, and she steps back, then presses a button on the microphone she wears clipped to her shoulder. "*Esta limpia.*"

The radio squawks once, then the general responds, "Show her out."

He doesn't say a thing about Trevor, and I hope to God he didn't protest the search. If he did...

Relief floods me when I step outside the small room and see Trevor standing just in front of the general. He looks like he's about to lose his shit. Until he sees me. Then, the change in his expression threatens to send heat creeping up my cheeks, but I shove those thoughts somewhere they can't distract me as I return to his side.

"Now that the unpleasantries have been taken care of," the

general says as he leads us down a long hallway, "may I offer you water or coffee, Señorita Monroe? Señor Lejune?"

He opens a door to a lavish office. His, obviously, and gestures to guest chairs as he takes a seat behind his desk.

"No, thank you, General. I'd like to get to the interview as quickly as possible. Our flight back to the United States leaves at 10:00 p.m., and, as you know, security at the airport is very thorough." I keep my tone light but firm. It's the only way to deal with a man like this. One used to having his every order followed. One used to being feared.

"I am afraid we have many rules to go over first, Señorita Monroe. La Cripta is only for the most dangerous of Venezuela's criminals, and we cannot possibly allow you to see Rojas until you understand them all." General Ochoa slides a folder from a stack on his desk and opens it. "Shall we begin?"

CHAPTER NINE

Dani

I'VE LOST count of the number of times I've nodded or said "I understand" in the past two hours. General Ochoa's list of rules is five pages long, and not only did we have to verbally acknowledge all of them, he had agreements drawn up that we had to sign.

Luis Rojas will be inside the interrogation room when we arrive. We're not to touch him, ask him to get up, stand, or move at all. If we leave the room for any reason, we can't go back in. No video recording, and we're only allowed three still images. My voice recorder was approved, but the list of questions I'm *not* allowed to ask takes up two solid pages.

Most of this doesn't surprise me. Interviewing prisoners is always a crapshoot—especially in foreign countries—but I've never had this many restrictions imposed on me.

The two armed soldiers who greeted us escort us down another hallway and into an elevator. Trevor tenses at my side, but relaxes when we ascend to the third floor. Down another hall to the corner of the building, and one of the soldiers scans a keycard. After a beep, the door opens with a loud *thunk*, and the soldier motions for us to enter.

This is it. I'm about to meet my father.

"Dani?" Trevor's hand settles on my shoulder. "You ready?"

I peer up at him, hoping he'll understand without words that this isn't just any interview. Dammit. I should have told him last night. All of it. Even though he was being a jerk.

"You can do this," he says quietly as the soldier holding the door open clears his throat. "You can do anything."

Not this.

"*Señorita* Monroe. *Entrarás ahora*," the guard says and points emphatically.

I take a deep breath, and Trevor's scent wraps around me. It's like the night sky after a summer's rain. Fresh and clean, with a subtle hint of cypress underneath it all. It's home. My home. It always has been.

Yes. I can do this.

Turning, I square my shoulders, adjust the strap of my messenger bag, and push past the soldiers and into the room.

Luis Rojas sits on the far side of a large, metal table. His hands are cuffed to a thick ring welded to the top, and he's dressed in a plain, gray shirt and pants. The difference between the man before me and the last photo of him on the internet is so dramatic, I have to school my face into a mask to hide my shock—and horror. He's lost at least thirty pounds, and his cheeks are sunken. Yet he's freshly shaven, and his hair is neat and clean, combed back away from his face. Streaks of gray thread through the dark brown strands.

Behind me, Trevor stands as still as a statue, and he's so close, I can feel his abs tense at my back. He sees it. How Luis's eyes are the same shape as mine.

"Señor Rojas?" I say as I hand my bag to Trevor and sit across from this man who helped bring me into the world. "*Me llamo Dani Monroe. Encantado de conocerlo. ¿Habla Inglés?*"

"*Sí.* Yes. I speak English," he says. His words are slow and his voice holds a heavy rasp, as if he's not used to talking, and he angles his head slightly as he stares at me. Does he know? Can he see it too?

Trevor sets my voice recorder on the table in front of me, and I flip the switch. A moment later, the camera shutter clicks once. Two more photos before we hit our limit.

"General Ochoa graciously agreed to facilitate this interview and has allowed me to record it. Is that acceptable?"

"Yes." Luis nods. "*El General* is a...reasonable man."

"Señor Rojas, can you tell me why you were arrested?"

Taking a slow, deep breath, Luis flexes his fingers, then starts to work them like he's squeezing an imaginary ball of thinking putty. I wish I could tell him I want to do the same thing. "I lied about *Presidente* Farías in order to incite violence."

It's a canned answer. And not a truthful one. But it's the only one he's allowed to give, I'm sure. "What lie did you tell?"

"I told many, *Señora.*"

"*Señorita.* Can you tell me what they were? These lies?"

Luis looks from me to Trevor, then swallows hard. "I spoke to crowds all over the country," he says. "I convinced many people that Presidente Farías was stealing from funds meant to help them. Using the money for his own gain."

"How did he do this? According to your lies?" My need to protect this man doesn't surprise me, but I also have a responsibility to the Post to get the story I came for.

"He demanded the people pay for social programs he never provided, for health care that was substandard, and for clean water processing plants that were never brought online. Those were the statements I made." Luis's gaze darts to ceiling behind me, and I kick myself for not checking for cameras. He quickly adds, "I have been shown proof all of those statements are untrue."

"Do you wish to recant now?" I ask.

"There would be no point." The resignation in his voice breaks my heart. He doesn't believe he'll ever get out of here. Not under a Farías regime. "I did not understand the repercussions of my actions. How much pain they would cause. Brother against brother, families torn apart...in *feelings*. Those scars will never heal. For that, I am deeply sorry."

"Are you being treated well here?" I'm testing the boundaries of the questions I'm allowed to ask, but I have to. Whatever his answer is, I'll know if it's the truth.

As Luis starts to speak, Trevor snaps the second of our three allowed photos. "I am being treated as I should be."

TREVOR

Change the damn subject, Dani. You're pushing your limits here.

Standing by while this woman I'm supposed to be protecting dances with the very dangerous line General Ochoa drew in the sand is almost impossible. I want to carry her out of here, go right to the airport, and get her back to DC—or Boston—as soon as humanly possible. Because Luis Rojas is more dangerous than I thought. He's not just some random political prisoner.

We're going to have a serious talk when we get out of here.

Dani shifts in her seat, her shoulders relaxing slightly. "Can you tell me about your life before your arrest, Señor Rojas? Did you live in Caracas?"

His gaze softens, and he stares down at his hands. "No. I am from a small town south of here. Calabozo."

"Do you have family there? Children?" Her voice has changed now too. It's gentler. Warmer.

"One daughter," he whispers as a tiny smile threatens his lips. "I do not know her. She was never in Calabozo."

Fuck. Luis knows.

I clear my throat, warning both of them to shut the fuck up with this line of questioning. It's too dangerous.

"Are you married?" Dani asks.

Before Luis can answer, an alarm blares, and bright strobes flash in the corners of the room. The doors behind and in front of us bang open, and guards pour into the room. Two of them grab Luis by the arms while a third unlocks his hands. As they drag him away, I catch sight of his legs. They don't move. He doesn't struggle, doesn't even try to walk. And his shoes? They're brand new. The soles don't have a single mark on them. Not even a speck of dust.

"You must leave. Now," a guard shouts as he wraps his hand around Dani's arm.

"Take your hand off of her." My anger flares, but I can't knock this guy on his ass. If I do, I'll put us both in even more danger.

The guard already has Dani out of her chair, and she lunges for her voice recorder, but can't quite reach it. "Tr —Travis!"

I snatch the device off the table and shove it into my pocket then rush after her before the other guards tackle me. I can see it in their eyes. They'd love to take me down.

The sirens continue to blare loudly, and out in the hall, the overhead lights have cut out and the emergency strobes are the only illumination. Instead of retracing our steps, we're ushered down a different route. But I'm finally able to get to Dani's side and wrap my arm around her waist. I don't care if General Ochoa thinks it's odd for a photographer to hold onto his reporter. I can't *not* touch her right now.

"We're going to be okay," I say quietly as we reach a stairwell and the guards order us down to the first floor.

When we reach the lobby, General Ochoa meets us, his rage barely contained as he clenches his hands at his sides. "I am sorry, Señorita Monroe, Señor Lejune. A small group of prisoners started a fight, and we had to lock down the entire facility."

"I didn't get to finish my interview," Dani says, raising her chin and pulling her shoulders back. "I was promised a full hour with Luis Rojas, and I got less than half of that. When will this lockdown be over with?"

"Not until tomorrow. If you wish to continue your interview then, I will make the necessary arrangements." The general's eyes don't match his conciliatory tone. He's pissed as hell at something, but he's trying to hide it and play nice with the Americans. But why? He could probably have us jailed in a heartbeat and no one would ever hear from us again. If I didn't kill him first.

"I do. What time?" Dani doesn't move, even though the guards are holding the front door open, clearly encouraging us to get the hell out of there.

"Noon. I trust that will be acceptable?"

"Yes. Come on, Lejune. Let's get back to the hotel and change our flight." Without a backwards glance, Dani strides through the open door, and I follow.

CHAPTER TEN

Trevor

THE OLD TIRES squeal as I speed out of The Crypt's parking lot. As soon as we're beyond the gates, I look over at Dani. "Did they hurt you?"

"What the hell happened back there?" she asks as she pulls the voice recorder from her bag.

"Answer the question, Dani. Did. They. Hurt. You?" My fingers are so tight on the steering wheel, two of my knuckles crack.

"Huh? No. I'm fine, Tre—"

"Not another word. Not until we're back at the hotel."

Her eyes widen as realization washes over her face. Yeah, that's right. I'd be surprised if they *didn't* bug the car. After what happened back there, it'll be a fucking miracle if they didn't bug the hotel room, too. At least I'll be able to use Wren's scanner once we're back at the Hotel Diamante.

Dani stares straight ahead the whole way back, but when we get caught at a stoplight, she reaches for my hand and mouths, *"I'm sorry."*

I want to tell her it's okay. But that would be a lie, and I'll never lie to her. Never again, anyway. I did that once, and it ruined everything between us.

No one's following us, so I keep hold of her hand as I maneuver through the slow-moving traffic. I may be angry, but if she needs reassurance, I'll give it to her. No matter what.

The silence has a physical presence all its own as we ride the elevator to the fifth floor, but I wrap my arm around her waist and keep her close until we get to the room. Only then do I let her go so I can ensure the clear filaments are still in place over the doors.

Once inside, I dig Wren's scanner out of my duffel bag and sweep it around both rooms before shoving it into my pocket.

"We're clear. It's safe to talk now. And you'd better have a damn good explanation—"

"Trevor," Dani interrupts, "I didn't mean to keep it from you. I tried...I wanted to tell you last night. But..."

Fuck me. "But I was an ass. You can say it."

She huffs, then sinks onto the bed. "You were. But I should have told you back in Boston."

"What were you thinking, Dani? General Ochoa knows. Luis knows. It was so obvious I'm sure the soldiers know too. You just put a huge fucking target on your back. We need to get out of here."

"No. I have to go back tomorrow—"

"Not an option."

Pushing to her feet, Dani gets right in my face. "Luis Rojas is part of a resistance movement that could legitimately overthrow the Farías government. I need to tell more of his story."

"And get yourself killed in the process? You hired me to protect you." I thread my fingers with hers and pull her over to her backpack. "Grab your stuff. We're going to the airport and getting the hell out of this country."

"I need more time! Luis saved my mother's life, Trev. Didn't

Austin ever tell you about her? About what Jorge Sosa did to her?"

Those two words cut through my anger and frustration. A band tightens across my chest, and I take two steps back. "Jorge Sosa was Gil's father. Obviously I knew your mother had left him at some point, but Austin didn't say anything about Sosa *doing* anything to her."

Dani eyes me like I can't be serious. "Sosa kidnapped my birth mother. He took her from Aruba and kept her prisoner in Venezuela. Luis worked for him for almost ten years. He and my mother fell in love, and when she got pregnant with me, he helped her escape to the United States."

I stagger back until I hit the wall, then sink down to the floor. "Your brother and I are going to have a serious talk when we get back."

"From what I was able to piece together," she says, her voice taking on a strange mix of excitement and pain, "Luis stayed with Sosa until maybe a year before Sosa was killed. Then he disappeared. The next record of him anywhere is in Caracas right after Gil died."

I get up and start to pace, my thoughts pinging from one possibility to the next.

Dani pulls a flash drive from her pack and plugs it into her tablet. After a couple of taps on the screen, she hands me the device showing copious notes she made before we left.

From an interview posted to the Democrática Resistencia's blog:

Luis wasn't always on the side of the resistance. He says he joined when a man he used to work for rose to the upper ranks of the Loma Collectivo. Question: Was this man Gil's father?

Translation of quote from Luis reads: "The Loma Collectivo was not born from hate. Not that I could see. They wanted reform and believed Marcos Farías would be Venezuela's redemption. I fought for them and told anyone who would listen that Farías was the ruler Venezuela needed. After he took power, his actions became militant, and I saw him for who he was. A dictator and a monster. I was branded an enemy of the Collectivo the day I joined the Democrática Resistencia, and they have repeatedly tried to silence me, but the truth cannot be silenced."

"Dani." I clear my throat, trying to ward off the memories of the worst day of my life. "Austin and I—along with a joint CIA-JSOC task force—spent three years of our lives trying to take down the Loma Collectivo. And you're telling me that your birth father was a founding member?"

She doesn't say anything for a long moment, then nods slowly. "Yes." With a sigh, she moves to the window and opens the drapes, but I step in front of her and snap them shut.

"Too dangerous right now."

"Fine." Stalking over to her pack, she pulls out her tin of thinking putty and starts to work it between her fingers. "I never wanted to meet him, you know." Her tone turns wistful, and her gaze is somewhere else, somewhere inside—or maybe even back home. "I have a mom and dad. Steve and Betsy were the only parents I ever needed."

"Until...?" Pulling her back against my chest, I wrap my arms around her waist, trying to offer whatever comfort I can.

"Until this year. The anniversary of Gil's death. I don't know why. But all of a sudden, I just *had* to know who he was. The more I read, the greater that need became until it was all I could think about. The story is about The Crypt and the fight between the Farías government and the Democrática Resistencia, but I came down here because I needed to meet the man who gave me half my DNA."

Dani settles in my arms, and she feels so fucking good there, I keep quiet. Every time I try to talk to her I piss her off, and I don't know how many more times I can get away with that before she cuts me out of her life for good.

"Say something." She tips her head back to look at me, uncertainty and pain swimming in the depths of her eyes.

"We'll stay the night. But no gym time for you. No leaving this room at all. I'll go out and get us some dinner and connect with Leo. He can keep an ear to the ground—try to find out if we're walking into an ambush tomorrow or not."

Do her eyes take on a slight shimmer as she turns in my arms? My Danisaur never cries. Well, almost never.

She releases a shuddering breath, blinks, and the shimmer's gone. "Thank you, TJ."

The long-ago nickname twists my heart and makes me want...more. So much more. "Don't thank me yet, Dani. I'm not agreeing to go back to The Crypt tomorrow. Not yet. You're still my mission. My *only* mission. There's nothing I won't do to keep you safe. Even if that means throwing you over my shoulder and carrying you through customs."

"You wouldn't," she says and tries to wriggle free, but I hold tight, dip my head, and take the biggest fucking risk of my life when I press my lips to hers.

A soft moan comes from low in her throat as she stops fighting and kisses me back. Her lip gloss tastes like watermelon, and I want to go deeper, but I can't. Not yet. Instead, I pull back slowly and hold her gaze. "I would. Because you're more important to me than...well, than anything."

"I'm headed out to meet Leo," I say as I pull the baseball cap over my dark brown hair. Every weapon I have is strapped to my body somewhere—except for the ceramic knife in my hand. Flipping it around, I offer it to Dani. "Keep this close, and don't answer the door for anyone."

She eyes the black, shiny blade, then gingerly wraps her fingers around the handle. "I don't know how to use this. Beyond...aim the pointy end at the bad guy."

A quick glance at my watch tells me I have another few

minutes before I have to leave, so I drop the cap on her bed and gesture for her to stand facing me. "There are two main type of grips you can use with a knife like this." I take her hand and position the weapon with the sharp side of the blade pointing up, towards her thumb. "This is a forward grip. You don't have to get as close to your opponent holding the knife like this."

She flexes her fingers slightly. "What's the other one?"

"Reverse grip." I ease the knife from her hand and turn it over so the blade faces the other way. "You probably feel in more control like this, right?" Dani nods, and I use my free hand to tip her chin up slightly. "If you hold the knife like this, you have to attack using a downward motion. You have to be closer."

Taking her arm, I raise it above her head, then slowly bring the knife toward my carotid artery, stopping an inch away. "Slice if you can. Don't stab. Stabbing can trap your knife in your opponent's body, and you lose your weapon."

"Trevor..." Her voice is nothing but a whisper, and I guide her hand lower as I pivot my body until the knife rests against my inner thigh.

My jeans are unbearably tight with her this close, but the thick material protects my skin from the lethal blade. "Femoral artery."

Finally, I turn the knife over in her hand, back to the forward grip, and skim the very tip of the knife along my upper arm over my light gray jacket. "Brachial artery. Severing any of those three will drop a man in under five minutes."

I need Dani more than I need my next breath. But not like this. Not when I can't give her...everything. All of my focus, all of...me. She tosses the knife onto the bed and wraps her arms around my neck. "I don't want you to go."

Groaning, I pull her against me and bury my face in her hair, the scents of jasmine and vanilla washing over me in calming waves. When I pull back, her lips are parted, and my dick feels like it's being strangled. "I have to, Danisaur. I don't trust room service. They know our names. Who's to say Ochoa hasn't paid off someone at the hotel? Hell, I'd do anything not to leave you here alone, but it's still early, and there are enough people around you should be safe for an hour or two."

"You're not making me feel any better," she says, then snorts softly as she turns back to the bed and picks up the knife, examining it and trying out both grips I taught her. "I won't leave, Trevor. I need to write up my notes from the interview. Start cobbling together something for my editor so he doesn't go batshit when I tell him we're staying another day. But just... hurry back, okay?"

I grab my hat and tug it down low, then reach out and trace the line of her jaw. "Nothing will keep me away from you again, Dani. Nothing."

Dani

He's been gone half an hour, and I can still taste him on my lips, smell him on my skin. And never—*ever*—has being taught how to use a knife been so damn sexy. Something shifted between us when I fessed up to all of my secrets, and I'm desperate to have him back in my arms so we can finally have an honest conversation about this *thing* between us.

Sitting at the hotel room desk with a small keyboard attached to my tablet, I start to cobble my notes together into something approaching a story. What Luis looked like, his quiet voice, his reserved demeanor.

After eight months of imprisonment, Luis Rojas is a changed man. In video shot just before his arrest, he stands tall, shoulders straight, with a fire in his eyes that compelled thousands to gather, risking detainment themselves, just to hear him. The Luis Rojas of today speaks carefully, measuring every word. He says he is "being treated as he should be."

In an interrogation room on the third floor of The Crypt, Luis spoke of growing up in a small town south of Caracas. His two brothers, Andrés and Franco, are younger by five and seven years, respectively. Only one month after Luis was arrested, Andrés was also detained. His whereabouts are now unknown.

I make a mental note to ask General Ochoa about Andrés Rojas if Trevor thinks it's safe to return to the prison tomorrow.

Despite how often I've traveled to dangerous countries for a story, I don't trust myself here. Because this isn't a story, this is someone who risked his life to free my mother from a horrible situation. He's not my father, and I need to stop thinking he is. But we're connected, and he knows it.

I add another paragraph on the Farías regime and the history of The Crypt, then save the draft and upload a copy to the Washington Post's server. After that, I transfer copies to three of my flash drives, and tuck two of them into the hidden pockets in my backpack.

Satisfied for now, I shut down the tablet and start to pace the room. Sunset is less than an hour away, and I don't want to be alone after dark. Not in a country where the police work for a corrupt government and they probably know I'm hoping to expose them.

Picking up the knife, I practice the grips Trevor showed me for several minutes until it hits me. I'm lying to myself. It's not that I don't want to be alone.

I don't want to be without Trevor.

Trevor

I wander the streets of Caracas like a man without a care in the world. Or so I pretend to be. In reality, I watch everything. Everyone. My frequent stops to browse jewelry, sunglasses, and little trinkets in the stalls of an open-air market a mile or so from the hotel? They're all planned. Executed at regular intervals to scan my surroundings.

I haven't seen a tail the whole time, but with Dani consuming my thoughts, I worry I'm off my game. We've turned some sort of corner and there's no going back. We're going to talk about everything once we're back on US soil, and I'll grovel if I need to. Beg. Anything. If she'll give me another chance.

A scarf vendor catches my eye, her racks filled with hand-dyed silks in every color, and I run my fingers along one that bears long streaks of purple, pink, and gold. "*¿Cuánto cuesta?*"

The woman—who looks to be close to seventy—shuffles over and peers at me. My father was Hawaiian. My normally dark stubble is now almost a full beard—intentional to mask my appearance. While there's no way I can pass for Venezuelan, my skin tone and extensive language training don't automatically mark me as American either.

"*Para ti, vendo por doscientos bolívares.*"

"*No. Ciento cincuenta bolívares.*"

Not haggling? That definitely wouldn't help me blend in.

"*Si.*" She gently eases the scarf from its hanger and wraps it in brown paper while I pull out a hundred and fifty bolivars and pass them over.

"*Gracias, Señora.*"

Best to be seen buying something. It's good for my cover. Or so I tell myself. I certainly didn't buy this because it reminds me of Dani and her thinking putty.

The package peeks out of the pocket of my lightweight jacket, and I return to scanning the area. Leo should be here soon, and I head to a bakery a block away. The window's filled with all sorts of local delicacies. The sight of sweet plantains, arepas filled with fruit and dusted with powdered sugar, cakes, and cookies reminds me I haven't eaten since the protein bar I had for breakfast.

Neither has Dani.

At the other end of the shop window, Leo pulls out his cell phone and holds it to his ear as he faces away from me. "Want to tell me why we couldn't just meet at a bar like civilized people?"

"Keep your voice down, asshole. Are you fucking drunk…again? It's not even six."

"That's after five," he says. "And I don't work for you anymore."

"If you're not careful," I say as I stoop to get a better look at the tray of flan on the bottom shelf, "you won't work for anyone soon."

"From your mouth to God's ears. Enough with the lecture. What's so damn important you had to meet like *this*?"

"Luis Rojas." Pausing, I take a step closer to Leo and lower my voice. "He's Dani's birth father."

The phone clatters from Leo's hand, and he scrambles to pick up the pieces. "Fuck."

I can't tell if he's cursing about the phone or Luis, but the ruse is a lost cause, so I mutter, "Follow me but make sure no one's watching when you do."

I stride away from the shop, but keep my pace slow. Still just a guy out for a stroll in one of the most dangerous cities in the world—if you're on the wrong side.

After a few minutes, I find a narrow alley between two buildings. Pulling out my signal scanner, I flick it on and find six different Wi-Fi networks. A second button on the side of Wren's little invention, and all of them go down as Leo ducks into the alley and limps over to me.

"She's his spitting image, Leo," I say as I rake a hand through my hair. "The eyes, the lips... You'd have to be blind to miss it. General Ochoa kicked us out as soon as Luis started talking about his family. His brother was rumored to have been in The Crypt too, but I don't think that's why the general ended the interview. I think it's because he thinks he can use Dani as leverage."

"So get the fuck out of the country," Leo says, giving me a look that says he thinks I'm a complete idiot for still being here.

"I would, but Luis...he was one of the original members of the Loma Collectivo. He worked for Jorge Sosa."

A whistle escapes as Leo shakes his head. "And you want this guy out of prison so you can finally take that organization down."

It wasn't a question, but I answer anyway. "Yep. So I need to know how much danger I'm putting Dani in if we decide to go back there tomorrow."

Leo shoves his right hand into his pocket and leans against the brick wall of the building opposite me. "Gut answer? A hell of a lot. Ochoa's not someone you mess with. He has the president's ear, and if he tells Farías that he has a way to get to the Resistencia...you need to get Dani the hell out of here."

My gut twists, and I finger the scarf in my pocket. Taking down the Loma Collectivo is the biggest failure of my CIA career. They've killed hundreds. Probably thousands. We were so close...and then Gil had to turn and spend the last two years of his life working against us from the inside.

"Make some calls," I say. Leo starts to protest, but I silence him with a shake of my head. "Just do it. I know you're on your way out, man. But you've worked this post forever. You've got to have someone on the inside you can trust."

I don't look away, determined to win this battle of wills, and after a full minute, Leo swears under his breath and stares down at his scuffed shoes. "Fine. But you owe me for this one."

"And you owe me for getting you out of that warehouse while you still had one good eye. Do this, and we're even." Glancing at my watch, I continue. "At this point, there's no way we'll make it through Customs in time for our flight. So we're staying until tomorrow. If I can get in touch with my former SSO, maybe he can arrange some backup. Or at least start working on a plan to get Luis out of The Crypt from the States."

"Your mobile secure?" Leo asks.

I snort. "When have you ever known me to take a chance on an open line?"

"Never. Sorry. Long day. Stupid question. I'll touch base tonight." Leo holds up a piece of his broken phone. "Once I get this taken care of."

"Stay safe, Leo."

"Yeah, right. I'll do my best." He limps out of the alley, and I'd bet the thousand bolivars I have hidden in various pockets that he's going right to the bar. I shouldn't trust him, but even a drunk Leo Basher was once better than half the spooks in the world stone cold sober.

I hope he still is. Our lives depend on it.

CHAPTER ELEVEN

Dani

BY THE TIME the electronic door lock disengages, my stomach is in knots and I think I might have actually destroyed this batch of thinking putty. It's so warm, it's practically liquid, and bits of it keep sliding between my fingers and down the back of my hand.

After dropping the putty back into its tin, I rush for the door and practically launch myself at Trevor.

"Dani, what the hell? If I'd been a hostile...where's the damn knife?" Trevor flicks the lock, then the deadbolt, before scooting around me to deposit two plastic bags on the table by the window.

A hint of shame flushes my cheeks, and I glance over at the desk. "I kept it with me while I was working. And I like the forward grip better."

Trevor freezes, then slowly turns towards me. The heat in his gaze makes my core clench. "You...practiced?" he asks.

With every step, I'm hyperaware of the shrinking distance between us. "The first time I went to Afghanistan, I knew nothing. I don't think I could have thrown a punch to save my life without breaking my fingers."

Taking my hand, Trevor runs his thumb over my knuckles, and I try not to let him see how that simple touch is about to reduce me to a puddle of highly aroused goo.

"The guys I was embedded with showed me a few tricks. How to break a choke hold." I bring the heel of my hand up towards his face, but stop short, my palms itching to feel the stubble on his cheeks. "How delicate a man's nose really is."

Trevor threads our fingers and brings our joined hands to his side. "Good men."

"They were." We're so close, his breath warms my face, and I inhale the subtle scent that always lingers on his skin. It's so light, I never realized it was as ingrained in him as his voice, the intelligence behind his eyes. "When I got back from that assignment, I signed up for an Aikido class. The first time I took a guy to the ground...I was hooked."

His laughter...it's rare. Like he doesn't *let* himself enjoy many things in this life.

"Why don't you do that more?" I ask as I skim a light touch over his cheek.

"Do what?"

"Laugh. Relax. Can't you stop thinking all the time and just...be?"

He takes a step back, and the moment shatters. A string pulled past its breaking point. My brother wasn't the only casualty five years ago. Something else died along with him. And I'm just now seeing it—the missing piece. Joy. The emotion no longer lives in Trevor's eyes.

"*Pabellón Criollo*," he says as he pulls a Styrofoam container from the first bag. His words are rough, and a muscle in his jaw ticks as he sets two plastic forks on the table, followed by two bottles of water. "It's the national dish, apparently. You said you ate everything."

"Except—"

"Zucchini and SpaghettiOs."

The hole left by the piece of my heart I gave him so long ago aches. "You remembered."

"I remember everything you've ever told me, Dani." He sheds his light black jacket, and the pistol secured in his chest harness draws my gaze. Followed by the knife under his other arm. As I stare, my mouth slightly open, he looks away. "Sorry. I should have...I don't know."

Before I can reply, he escapes to his room, and when he returns without the chest harness, he sets the pistol—now in a holster—on the table, then moves to my mini-fridge.

"Want a beer?" he asks as he crouches in front of it.

"Sure." I'm not much of a drinker. Hell, before last night, I don't remember the last time I had a beer outside of work events, but Trevor is pushing every one of my buttons, and I don't know how much longer I can go without jumping him and begging him to fuck me or losing my patience with him completely.

Tonight, he only pulls a single beer from the fridge. "You're not having one?"

"Don't want to compromise my judgment. Or my aim. I'll stick with the water."

"Trevor James... Are you calling this," I gesture between us, "compromised judgement? Because you kissed me before you left this afternoon, and now, you're bouncing between sexy as fuck and annoying as shit."

"Danisaur—"

"Don't call me that. I haven't been into dinosaurs since I was nine." Wedging my hands on my hips, I keep the table between us so his amazing scent and all those muscles can't compromise *my* thinking.

This time, his laugh doesn't appear to shock him, but it sure as hell shocks me. "What?"

"Dani, I never called you that because you were into dinosaurs." When he gets himself under control, the heat in his eyes could melt lead. He circles the table, and when he stops right in front of me, I hold my breath until he pulls me against him and slides his fingers into my hair. His lips are so close I can feel their warmth against my ear. "I call you Danisaur because when you get angry, baby, you roar just like that T-Rex in *Jurassic Park*."

Slapping my hands against his chest, I try to shove him back, but he's too strong, so I huff, which probably doesn't do much for my case. "I do not."

"You do." He slants his lips over mine, and all of my indignation, fear, and frustration fly out the window. For this one moment, all I want to do is feel and pretend that I can have everything I want. With him.

Trevor

If the last kiss left me off balance, this one knocks me on my ass. Dani's hands flutter over my sides to the bottom of my t-shirt. I'm about to let her pull it off when my phone rings, and she jerks.

"This better be fucking important," I growl at Leo when I answer.

"You asked me to keep you updated on the weather forecast," Leo says, an edge to his voice. "Or do you *want* to be caught with the world's worst sunburn?"

Shit. He's talking in code, so he's somewhere he can be overheard. Or he's in trouble.

"Did you bring your sunscreen?" I ask as Dani's brows furrow and she presses closer to me so she can hear his response.

"Got my SPF 50 right here. But you're going to need something stronger. Those storm clouds you saw earlier are over Miraflores now, and I don't know what's going to happen when they move on. Tomorrow's not going to be a good day to be outside."

"Message received. Find yourself some shade and stay there, man. Thanks."

I drop the phone on the table next to the food, then pull out a chair for Dani. "Eat. I'm calling Ford to see how quickly he can get us out of here."

I dig an earbud from my pocket and sit next to her. I don't want to hide anything from Dani. She can handle the truth. At least, I hope she can.

"Ochoa went to the presidential complex at Miraflores. That's what Leo was trying to tell me—if you didn't pick up on it. So it's fair to say he knows who you are and thinks you'll be good leverage to get Luis Rojas to talk."

Dani swallows hard, her eyes a mix of too many emotions for me to name. "He's going to kill him, isn't he?"

I lay my palm up on the table and wait for her to take my hand. "Not if Luis is as strong and as smart as I think he is. Did you see him when they took him away?"

She shakes her head, a whiff of her shampoo wrapping around me. "I was too focused on the asshole dragging me out of the room."

Tightening my grip, I meet her gaze. "He can't walk, Dani. Or hasn't, in a very long time. His shoes were brand new. Not a single scuff of dirt on them—not even the soles. And he didn't move his legs at all. He's been in custody for what? Eight months?"

"Close to that, yes." Her voice drops to a whisper. "Why let me talk to him at all?"

I shrug. "Couple of options. First, they knew who you were before we even got on the plane. Though I don't think that's it.

More likely, they dangled a press interview in front of him like a carrot to try to get something out of him. 'Just tell us this one thing and we'll let you see the world above ground.'"

Dani sucks in a sharp breath and yanks her hand away. "And now that they know about me? What will they do to him?"

"Probably nothing until they confirm your DNA and can get you in front of him again. Then...all bets are off. That's why we're getting the hell out of here. Ford can arrange a flight for us on a private plane. We'll have to take the long way home—probably through two or three other South American countries, but it's the safest thing to do." I nudge one of the plastic forks towards her. "Eat something. Tomorrow's going to be a long fucking day."

I take my own advice as I dial Ford's emergency number. We all have 'em. Forwarders that will reach us no matter where we are in the world—and our phones are more secure than any other piece of tech on the market today.

"Trev, what do you need?" Ford asks. A television blares in the background, and I think I hear an announcer call a thirty-seven yard field goal.

"Exfil for me and Dani, ASAP. She's in danger here, and I don't want to wait for our commercial flight tomorrow afternoon. Too many risks."

Dani picks at her shredded beef and fried plantains, disappointment and uncertainty written all over her features, and I reach over and cup her cheek, holding her gaze and hoping I can convince her that everything will be okay if we get out of here quickly.

She gives me a short jerk of her chin towards the phone, then pulls away and stabs a plantain.

"Roger that," Ford replies. "You have safe transpo from the hotel? Or do I need to send someone?"

"I'll get us wherever we need to go." I don't trust our rental car—not anymore—but *borrowing* another won't be a problem.

"Give me two hours and I'll have a plan for you. Dax is home, and he can make some calls if I run into any resistance. Just stay safe in the meantime."

"We're not leaving the hotel until I know exactly where we're going. Ochoa might be desperate, but he isn't stupid. We'll be fine until we hear from you."

As the call disconnects, I pray I'm right.

CHAPTER TWELVE

Trevor

DANI and I finish our meal in silence. I don't know what to say to make things better. To reassure her that I'll protect her, that I won't let anything happen to her.

Because I can't make that promise. We're only two people against a dictatorship that could easily make both of us disappear forever. I can't tell her that I lied to Ford—for her benefit *and* his.

We're not safe here.

"So what happens now?" she asks as she polishes off her beer and then cracks the seal on the bottle of water. "We take turns on watch or something?"

A chuckle threatens to escape at the idea of Dani patrolling the hotel room while I sleep. "No. You rest, work on your article, or just watch TV. *I* keep watch. And wait to hear from Ford."

"Trevor, I'm not a child." There's a petulance to her tone I remember well from high school. "Tell me what's going on. What's *really* going on. One minute we're kissing, and the next...you close yourself off and go all 'Liam Neeson I have a particular set of skills' on me.

"You hired me—"

Dani's growl of frustration shouldn't send heat shooting straight to my dick. Or make me wonder what she'd sound like if I planted myself between her thighs and tasted her.

"You're fired," she says as she stalks over to me and arches those perfect, dark brows. "That excuse is no longer valid. Try again."

I can't find the words to explain the reasons I'm still heavily armed, locked in a Venezuelan hotel room with a woman I'm pretty sure I've loved since high school, and *not* tearing her clothes off. Because they don't exist. I should be worshipping her body right now, not listening for footsteps out in the hall or checking my phone every five minutes hoping for a message from Ford.

"I'm right here, Trevor. Waiting. Like I've been waiting since that night you...the night I wanted...shit." Swallowing hard, she lifts the hem of her shirt to reveal her tattoo. "Do you know what this is?"

My mouth goes dry, and I reach for the bottle of water and take a long swig. "Yeah. Your true north."

"Do you know where the coordinates lead?" Her voice is softer now. Almost hopeful. How can I tell her we can't do this here? For over a decade, we've avoided this conversation, because once we have it, there's no going back.

"The summit of East Rock," I whisper. Dani's eyes widen, and I trace the compass rose with my thumb. "Couldn't sleep last night. Looked it up."

"When did you—?" Her cheeks tinge a dusky rose, and she clears her throat. "Oh, God. Sports bra. Tiny shorts."

"Also known as Hell," I mutter.

"Excuse me?" Anger replaces her embarrassment, and this

time, I can't control my laughter. "Trevor, I have worked damn hard at the gym every single—"

She falls silent when I run my hands down her sides to her hips and then curve my fingers over her ass. "Dani, you're gorgeous. You've *always* been gorgeous. There is no size or shape you could ever be that I wouldn't want. That's why this is hell."

"I don't understand. You walked away. All those years ago, you didn't want anything to do with me. You never showed up." The confident, take-no-shit reporter is gone, and in her place is a woman I fear I made doubt her own worth.

I want to hit something. Go find a punching bag and beat the shit out of it. Or even better...find someone to beat the shit out of *me* for ever giving her that impression. "I was scared, baby. Fuck that. I was terrified." I lead her over to the bed and pull her down so we're sitting hip to hip.

With her hand in mine, I stare at our linked fingers. "Gil and Austin were my best friends. Both of them were overprotective as fuck where you were concerned."

"Like you were any different," she scoffs.

"No, I wasn't. Gil and I...we got into more than one fight over him ghosting you."

"You never told me that." She peers up at me like I just gave her the world, and I don't know how I'm supposed to go on without shattering that hope, that light.

Smoothing a lock of hair behind her ear, I frown. "I never told you a lot of things, Dani. And that wasn't right. Hell, Austin doesn't even know everything."

She shoves at me—gently, but still with displeasure. "We're family..."

"No." That word...it stings. Even though I've come to think of Second Sight as my family, that took almost losing them to accept. Standing, I start to pace the room. "You and Austin and

Gil were a family. I was always the poor foster kid who inserted himself into your lives because he didn't have anyone else."

"You were *never* that," she snaps. "How could you think any of us felt that way?"

"Shit. How did I never see it?" My voice isn't much above a whisper as the realization takes hold and I stop, my back to her, every single interaction I had with Gil after he joined the CIA now suspect.

"See what?" Dani's close enough for me to feel her warmth in the chill of the room's air conditioning, but she doesn't touch me. Just waits for me to make the next move.

"Gil. He..." I shake my head. I don't want to do this to her, but it's either this or let her think she did something—anything—wrong all those years ago to make me not want her.

I turn to face her, my hands on her waist. I don't know if I'm holding her for my benefit or hers. "I didn't show up that night because Gil called me. He said he'd talked to you and you were sorry you ever got me involved. That you should have kept your problems 'in the family.'"

Dani's brows shoot up, then she sucks her lower lip between her teeth and closes her eyes. "I never said that. I never even talked to him." Her body shudders, and the sound that escapes is almost a sob. "I wanted you. Needed you. And when you didn't show up, I thought you didn't want me."

"I know, baby. I know *now*. And I'm...fuck. I was an idiot." Wrapping my arms around her, I hold her close and breathe in the scent of her hair. "I loved you, Dani. That night...walking away from you...that was the hardest thing I've ever had to do, and the biggest regret of my life. And if I had it to do all over again, I never would have let you go."

Dani's voice is muffled against my shirt, but every one of her words hits me right in the heart. "So fix it."

"What?" Drawing back, I smooth my hand over her hair,

relishing the way the silky strands feel between my fingers. We shouldn't be doing this now.

"Fix. It." Dani offers me a weak smile. "We're both here. Now."

I cup her cheek. "Dani, when we fix this—and it will be when, not if—we're going to be safe. Every moment we spend this close is a moment I'm not at the top of my game. A moment I could be distracted. A moment that could get one of us killed. I'd never forgive myself if I couldn't protect you."

Dani swallows hard and takes one step away. Then another, and crosses her arms over her chest. "Promise me you won't pull another disappearing act when we're back in the States."

"I won't. I promise."

ONE THING you master both in the army and the CIA? How to fall asleep in seconds. Wherever you are. Because even a few minutes of sleep can save your life. What I wouldn't give for all the tricks I learned back then to work now.

Two hours of staring at the ceiling is enough, and I head to my mini-fridge for a bottle of water. After I crack the seal, I check on Dani through the crack in the adjoining doors. I want to be next to her. Sleeping soundly after long hours spent making up for lost time.

But when she got into bed and patted the mattress next to her, I had to turn her down. "When we spend the night together, Danisaur, it's going to be just the two of us. Safe. Alone. For as long as we need for...everything."

And now, she's curled on her side, holding a pillow to her chest. Her skimpy tank leaves little to the imagination, and those tiny pink shorts? Fuck. They were almost enough to make me lose my resolve right then and there.

I can't keep watching her sleep like a creepy stalker. And the stress of the day—and of the phone call I had with Ford a few hours ago—are starting to take their toll. Setting the bottle down on the nightstand next to my gun, I climb into bed and stretch out on my back.

Just five more hours. At 7:00 a.m., we can find a clean car and start driving. Two hours later, we'll be at the General Bartolomé Salom airport, where Dax managed to wrangle us a flight to Belize. Once we're there, we should be safe enough to take a commercial flight back to Boston.

My lids are too heavy to keep open, and as I fade into sleep, my sluggish mind sets off warning bells I can't ignore, but also can't seem to muster enough energy to care about.

A HIGH-PITCHED SOUND ROUSES ME, and I struggle to open my eyes. Something's wrong. I roll over, my muscles sluggish. The clock on the nightstand reads 3:04 a.m. I've only been asleep for forty-five minutes, and I can't fully wake up. Another sound—this one I recognize as Dani whimpering—and I try to stand, but my legs catch in the sheets. I hit the ground and yank open the nightstand drawer to reach for my emergency medical kit.

My fingers are slow and unwieldy, but I manage to extract the syringe of adrenaline and fumble for the cap. It lands silently on the carpet, and I jab the needle deep into my outer thigh.

Within seconds, my heart rate spikes, and sweat prickles the back of my neck. But my thoughts start to clear, then ping wildly.

The water. Dani and I both had a bottle earlier, but those came from the store. Not the fridge. When we got back...I checked the doors. I didn't check the windows. Fuck. There's only one reason to drug me. To get to her.

Pulling my gun from the holster, I lurch to my feet. The

room tilts on its axis, but I will it to stop and head for Dani. A thud from beyond the adjoining door is followed by a muffled cry, then a muttered oath—in a male voice.

The part of me that's falling in love with her wants to tell her I'm coming. The trained assassin? He doesn't make a sound. Creeping forward, I let out a controlled breath, trying to slow my heartbeat. Adrenaline doesn't make for steady hands, but it's better than being too drug-addled to see straight. My bare foot touches the cracked door, and I nudge it open another inch.

Fuck. In the slight glow from the desk lamp, two men flank Dani's bed, one of them holding a rag over her mouth as she struggles not to breathe. Her lids are heavy, despite the panic flooding her eyes.

Training takes over. I brace my shoulder against the wall and fire. Four shots. Head, center mass, head, center mass, and both of the men collapse without a sound. Dani manages to shove the rag away, but when she tries to push the sheet off of her body, her eyes roll back in her head and she moans quietly.

I clear the room, scanning every corner and the bathroom before I step over one of her attackers, grab her arm, and drape it over my shoulder. "We have to get out of here, Dani. Right fucking now."

CHAPTER THIRTEEN

Dani

MY HEAD POUNDS like someone used it to play basketball, and I want to throw up. The stench of blood—harsh and coppery—is all I can smell, and as Trevor lifts me to my feet, I realize why.

It paints the wall behind me. Dots my forehead and chest. I think there's a drop in my eye. And, oh God. What's that on my cheek? It's...sticky.

"Trevvvvv." My stomach pitches, and I push away from him, fall to my knees, and vomit.

"Dani. Sweetheart." He's next to me, brushing my hair away from my face. "We can't stay here, baby. I'm going to pick you up now, okay?"

"I...donnn...can't..." I retch again, but push up and grab Trevor's arm. "T-tabllllet.

Shit. My words don't even make sense to me, how the hell is he supposed to understand? He scoops me into his arms and carries me out of my room and into his where he sets me on the bed. "I'll get your stuff. Sit here and do not move."

My vision is hazy, but I reach for a bottle of water on his nightstand to rinse out my mouth, and he slaps it away. "No!"

"Trev...?"

Warm hands cup my cheeks, and I smell gunpowder. "It was drugged, Dani. I barely made it in there in time. We have maybe five minutes before the National Police show up. I need to get you some clothes and then we're getting out of here. But I can't do that if I have to worry about you moving from this spot."

"I can help." My mind's starting to clear slightly, and my words are sharper. Still slow, still hard to force out, but adrenaline is taking over.

"No." He doesn't give me a moment to argue, instead rushing back into my room where I hear him shoving stuff into my backpack. Wiping the back of my hand over my cheeks, I come away with streaks of blood, and my stomach roils.

He just shot two men. Two men who were going to take me somewhere I might never have escaped from. The horror of our situation settles over me, and my eyes start to burn. But I can't cry. I won't. I have to pull myself together so we can get out of here.

Trevor's jacket is draped over a chair, and I shrug into it, letting his scent replace that of the blood and calm me. Shoes. I need shoes. Well, pants too, but definitely shoes.

"Come on, Dani," he says as he crosses back into the room to find me halfway to the adjoining door. "Shit. I told you—" Shaking his head, he mutters something I can't quite hear, then shoulders his duffel bag. "We're heading for the service elevator, then to Leo's place."

His words are coming so quickly, they almost blend together, and he takes my hand and leads me into the dimly lit hallway. We jog to the stairwell, and as soon as the door closes behind us, Trevor pulls out a small tool—almost like a screwdriver—and jams it between the door and the frame. "This will slow them down," he explains, then drops my backpack and rummages inside before finding a pair of pants and my running shoes. "Put these on."

As I do, he shoves his feet into boots and straps on his chest harness, then pulls a linen button down shirt from his bag to cover up his weapons.

"Look at me, Dani."

I do, and he takes the edge of the black jacket I'm wearing and swipes it over my left cheek, then my chin.

"Okay. That's most of the blood. Did they hurt you? Can you run?"

"I can rr-run," I say, though I don't know how he can understand me as my teeth have started to chatter. The stairway is air-conditioned, but it's not warm, and in the back of my mind, I know this is shock setting in.

Keep it together, Dani.

Trevor cups the back of my neck, pulls me close, and kisses me with such fervor, for a second, I forget someone just tried to kidnap me. "You're okay, baby. I promise. And I'm going to keep you that way."

Before I can respond, Trevor hoists my backpack and his duffel bag again, takes my hand, and leads me down the stairs and out into the warm, humid night.

Trevor

The hotel backs up to an alley, and we rush alongside the building until we come to the corner, then I pull Dani against my left side and scan the street. At the far corner of the hotel, a white van idles. All of its lights are off, but the street lamp illuminates the exhaust coming out of the tail pipe.

"Other way," I whisper, and we hurry south. This street is

busier, even at 3:00 a.m. I don't see any obvious threats, but my racing heart and the impending crash I know is coming don't leave me very confident in my own abilities. "Keep watch for anything or anyone who stands out. I need to find us a car."

Ten minutes later, we're in a ruddy brown pick-up heading for the outskirts of Caracas. Once I unlock my phone, I toss it to her. "Find Leo's number and put it on speaker."

"This better be a goddamn emergency," he slurs when the call connects.

"Sober up, asshole. Someone just tried to kidnap Dani. We're on the move. I need somewhere safe for us to hole up for a few hours. I won't make it to Puerto Cabello without sleep."

"I'm not drunk," he mutters, then rattles off an address. "You bring the National Police to my doorstep, and I'll kill you myself."

"Fuck you too," I say and then nod at Dani to end the call. Before I can open my mouth again, she's entering the address into the GPS.

"Make a left at the next stoplight." I do, and she pulls her knees up to her chest. "Are you sure you can trust Leo?"

"As sure as I am about anything right now."

"That's not an answer." Clutching the phone in one hand, she uses the other to hug herself tightly. The uncertainty in her voice leaves me completely off balance—or maybe that's just the epinephrine shot wearing off. Or both.

"I know. We'll be back in the States in eighteen hours, and then we'll be safe."

"And what about Luis Rojas? He won't be safe." With a quick glance at the phone, she adds, "Take the next right and then keep going for another six kilometers."

"There's enough on the tape from the interview for me to contact my former handler. Taking down the Loma Collectivo would make his entire career." Bitterness creeps into my tone, and I shake my head. Big mistake. Pain lances through my temple, and I wince.

"What's wrong?" Dani scoots closer on the bench seat and touches my arm.

"I'm fine, baby. It's just the epi wearing off." I realize my mistake as soon as the words escape my lips. Her eyes widen, and I shift my grip on the steering wheel so I can take her hand. "Someone drugged the water in my fridge—yours too, probably. They were careful. Must have come in through the window or the air vents, because my tripwires were all in place over the doors when we got back. Luckily, I didn't drink much of it. But when you screamed and I woke up, I knew. Gave myself a shot of adrenaline."

"Oh, God." She pulls her hand from mine and shrinks against the seat. As if the memories of the attack are finally registering, she starts to shake. "You...killed them."

I can't apologize for shooting those bastards. I won't. I kept her safe. Alive. But the horror in her voice...if I've lost her...

"I'd do it again," I say quietly and ease the phone from her hand to check the GPS. Only another two kilometers, and we can both rest. There's no one else on the road with us right now, so at least I know we're not being followed. "Nothing matters to me but you, Dani."

We don't speak again until we reach a little house in a quiet neighborhood on the west side of Caracas. Leo's sitting on his front steps and pushes to his feet when the truck starts to slow. He directs me to pull between his house and the neighbor's, then park in a tiny backyard full of dead grass.

I almost fall when I get out of the truck. My head pounds and my legs feel like they're about to give out, but I force myself to keep moving and grab our bags, then head around for Dani. She's unsteady on her feet as well, but she doesn't protest when I wrap my arm around her.

"I set you up in the basement," Leo says as he leads us

inside. "Water, protein bars, a full med-kit, blankets, and an air mattress."

Just past the kitchen, he kicks a rug to the side to reveal a trap door. I reach down and pop the metal hasp, then raise the wood panel. A set of stairs leads to a brightly lit space that clearly doubles as his communications center. A laptop, widescreen monitor, and weapons locker line one wall. In the opposite corner, there's a small bathroom, and Dani makes a beeline for it, not saying a word to me.

"You aren't here," he says as he takes the last two steps with a grunt and then heads for the laptop. "If you need to contact your people, you can use my setup, but make goddamn sure you're masking your signal."

After writing down a fifteen digit password, he presses the paper into my hand. When I meet his gaze, I realize he was telling the truth. He's sober.

"Thanks, man." I stop him when he starts to turn away. "Leo, I'm sorry. I shouldn't have jumped to conclusions. I owe you for this one."

"I made it pretty damn easy for you." With a lopsided grin, he shrugs. "I'm getting the hell out of here, Trevor. Two weeks. Maybe less. I'm too old for this shit, and the chances of Ochoa *not* putting the pieces together and tracking me down eventually are slim to none. So you owe me nothing. Just get the fuck out of here and back to the States safely and we'll call it even."

He claps me on the shoulder once, then limps back up the steps and shuts the trapdoor.

Dani

In the tiny bathroom, I take one of the hand towels and start scrubbing my face as hard as I can. I want the memory of the blood and bits of—oh, God, is that brain matter?—off my skin.

Trevor knocks softly. "Dani? Are you all right?"

I scrub harder. "Yes. I'll be out in a minute."

I'm not okay. Not by a long shot. But I can't tell him that. I have to keep it together.

When I open the door, he's sitting on the air mattress, his elbows resting on his knees and his head in his hands. His boots sit unlaced, ready to go, and he's put the pistol right next to the pillow.

My body aches, and I sink down next to him. "Are *you* all right?" I ask.

Trevor eases my running shoes off my feet. "I am now. Just wiped. But I'm not letting you out of my sight. Not for a minute."

"You're going to have to if you want to sleep." I wriggle until I'm stretched out on my side, then wait for him to join me. "Unless you sleep with your eyes open. Which, if you do...tell me now so I can turn over, because that would scare the crap out of me."

"I don't." Trevor skims his knuckles along my reddened cheek, and something inside me threatens to shatter into pieces. "I almost lost you," he whispers. "I need to know what happened. Before I woke up."

I don't want to. I'm barely holding it together. But he's so close, and the stress pushes me over the edge. Burying my face against his shirt, I breathe him in and find a hint of calm. Not enough to stop me from shaking, but enough for me to speak.

"I think I woke up when they came into the room. The door locks...they beep." A shudder runs through me, and Trevor wraps his arms around my waist and pulls me almost on top of him. "They each grabbed an arm, and then I couldn't breathe. Something...something was over my..." Not even Trevor's scent can keep me grounded now, and my voice rises half an octave. "It hurt, and I took a breath before I could stop myself. But then I got so dizzy, and I knew I couldn't inhale again or I'd..."

"You're safe, Dani. Know that. You're safe with me."

I want to believe him. I need to believe him. But I can't. Not anymore.

"I tried to fight," I manage, "but they were too strong. And they had my arms." Shaking my head makes the room spin for a second. "I said that already."

"Stop." He shifts so he can cup my cheek. "I don't need to know the rest. I was wrong."

"They...said..." I have to tell him. I wanted to back at the hotel, but I was too out of it. "I kicked one of them." A hiccupping sob escapes, but I can't cry. I don't know how to let my tears fall. They just burn the corners of my eyes. Trevor brushes one of them away with his thumb, and I blow out an uneasy breath. "The bigger one told me to stop fighting. That no one was coming to save me."

The noise that rumbles in Trevor's throat is almost a growl. "I will *always* come for you, Dani. When we get back to the U.S., you're staying with me for a couple of days, and we're going to talk about all of this." His lids droop, and his shoulders relax slightly. "Never letting you go again."

I can see the fight he's waging with his body to stay awake, to stay present. All for me. But exhaustion has me in its grip as well, and I rest my head on his chest so I can listen to his heartbeat. "You're sure you can trust Leo?" I ask again as my eyes close and I snuggle closer.

"Yeah." The single slurred word is enough for me, and I let myself drift in his arms, ready to get the hell out of Venezuela and land somewhere we can finally figure out what this is between us.

CHAPTER FOURTEEN

Trevor

Something tickles my cheek, and for a moment, I forget where I am. Until Dani moans in her sleep, and I'm instantly awake. We're in Leo's basement, the only lights coming from his laptop and a single bulb over the stairs.

Glancing at my phone, I relax. We still have an hour before we need to leave for Puerto Cabello, and I'll spend every minute of that I can with her in my arms. Why didn't I insist on sleeping with her earlier?

Because you were scared.

The inner voice that's kept me alive through years of covert operations isn't happy with me right now. Can't say I blame it. If I hadn't woken up in time, she would have disappeared into the bowels of The Crypt.

I want Luis Rojas out of there with everything I am. He's the key to taking down the organization that put Gil on the path to destruction. The organization that forced me to finish the job. I rest my cheek against Dani's forehead as memories threaten to drown me.

"The Loma Collectivo wants the resistance eliminated completely by the end of the year," I say as Oliver sends a map of Caracas from his laptop onto the wall screen. "And they're willing to kill anyone who stands in their way."

The briefing room deep underground offers few distractions, and we've been going over and over the intel Austin and I gathered the last time we visited Venezuela's capital city.

"You're certain they have Pritchard?" Ollie asks.

I pull a thumb drive from my pocket and plug it into the laptop. "See for yourself."

The video shows Austin tied to a chair, shirtless, blood dripping from dozens of cuts all over his torso. He's blindfolded with duct tape over his mouth, and his chest stutters as he struggles to breathe.

As Ollie stares, gaze riveted to the screen, a dark-clad figure enters the frame. It takes the camera a moment to focus on Gil's face, but when it does, he's smiling. "You shouldn't have sent him, Trevor. I know all of his secrets. I grew up knowing them. Just like yours. You can't stop me. La justicia está de mi lado!"

A knife flashes for a split second before Gil stabs Austin in the thigh. He screams and thrashes weakly, but he's lost too much blood, and Gil was always a master of inescapable knots.

"Pull all of your American agents out of Venezuela by the end of the week, or I'll send Perfect Pritchard back to you in pieces." Gil leans close to the camera to shut off the recording, and I see it. His eyes. He's lost all hold on reality, and if I don't get down there in the next twenty-four hours, Austin's as good as dead.

"Trevor?" Dani's soft voice brings me back to the present, and I open my eyes to find her staring up at me. "You were somewhere else. Where?""

"It's nothing you want to hear about. Not right now." I offer her a weak smile, then check my phone again. "We should get up. The faster we get to Puerto Cabello, the better. If I know Dax, he'll have the plane there at least an hour early."

"Who's Dax? You mentioned him last night."

"He runs Second Sight. Well, he and Ford are partners. But he's the majority owner. Special Forces for years until..." I shake my head. Dax's pain is his own. "He was injured—blinded—in the line of duty, but he's one of the strongest, most capable men I know."

Dani sits up and presses her palms to my chest. "When we get back to Boston, will I meet him?"

Her warmth seeps into me, and I realize what I've been fighting for more than ten years. I love this woman. I've *always* loved this woman. I want her to meet everyone at Second Sight. My family. I want to wake up with her every morning. Fall asleep with her every night. Hell, we've never even been on a date, but I still know there's no one else for me and never will be.

"Yes. You'll meet him." I slide my hand up to cup the back of her neck and pull her close enough to touch my lips to hers. "You'll meet everyone, Dani. And we'll have time to talk. Really talk. About us."

She nods and lets me help her to her feet. Ten minutes later, we're back in the stolen pickup truck, on our way to safety.

The sun paints Puerto Caballo in warm colors as the truck sputters to a stop at the edge of the airfield. Dani fell asleep halfway through the drive, curled against me with my arm around her shoulders.

Now, I dip my head so my lips are close to her ear. "Dani? We're here." She startles awake, and her jacket falls away, revealing the deep, purple bruises on her upper arms. "Fuck, baby. Why didn't you tell me these were so bad?" I take her hand, then trace the edges of one of the worst of the marks.

"Because there's nothing you can do about them," she says. "I'm *fine*, Trevor."

"You're always fine." I release her and hop out of the truck, rush over to the passenger side, and open the door. "Come on. We're exposed out here, and I don't like it."

As soon as we're on the plane—a private Cessna a good five levels above my pay grade—Dani turns in her seat. "What did you mean when you said I'm 'always fine'?"

The question throws me off balance, and I strap in as the Cessna starts its taxi. The only crew member outside of the pilot and copilot is one attendant with a Beretta strapped to his hip.

"Mr. Moana?" the man says from the jump seat by the cockpit. "We're executing a short field takeoff with a quick climb. There will be a fair bit of pressure. There's gum in your seat pocket."

He's not kidding. Within two minutes, the pressure in my ears ratchets my headache up to eleven, and Dani leans forward, chewing her gum as quickly as she can and squeezing her eyes shut.

When my hand rests on her thigh, she relaxes slightly and links our fingers. "You're not off the hook," she manages as the plane continues to climb. Five minutes later, it levels off and we both relax, sinking into the plush leather seats.

The attendant brings us both bottles of water, sandwiches, and Cokes, then disappears into the tiny galley. Whoever he is, Dax trusts him—or paid him enough for his silence.

Dani pulls her tablet from her bag and sets it on the little table that extends from the wall. "Trevor? I'm still waiting for an answer."

"Can we talk about this when we get to Boston?"

"Not this. No." Crossing her arms over her chest, she sits back in her chair and waits for my answer.

I glance out the window at the clouds below. This is one of those moments where I could easily fuck everything up. But I'll never lie to her. I can't.

"In twenty years, Dani, I've seen you cry exactly once. Austin...he thinks he heard you one night, but he can't even be sure—"

"He did. The night you stood me up."

Why couldn't I have kept my mouth shut? I rake my hands through my hair. What I wouldn't give for a shower and a change of clothes. And to start this conversation over again. My frustration prickles along my spine.

"Two men tried to kidnap you last night, Dani. They were planning on torturing you to make Luis Rojas talk. And you're sitting there like we're on our way home from a beach vacation."

"You need me to be okay, so I'm okay," she replies. "Your job is to keep us alive. Mine is to not make that any harder than it already is."

This is horseshit. I unbuckle my seatbelt and skirt the table between us. Before she realizes what I'm doing, I have her belt off and she's in my arms.

"Trevor—"

"No." I settle back into my seat with her held firmly in my lap. "We're talking about this. Right now. We have another seven hours on this plane, and I won't spend the entire time worried about you."

"I told you, I'm—"

"Fine. I know. Except you're not." I run my thumb over one of her dark brows. "When you're mad, there's a tiny muscle right here that ticks." Pressing my lips to the spot, I let my hand trail down to the side of her neck. "And this tendon, right here?" Another kiss, and I draw back to find heat and an emotion I can only describe as overwhelm churning in her eyes. "It tightens whenever you want to cry."

She starts to argue, but I hold my finger to her lips. Her gaze threatens to stop me, but dammit, I want a future with this woman, and that means we both have to stop being afraid to let the other in.

"I get it, Dani. You're one of the few people who understands how I used to let myself hope every time I moved to a new foster home. And how all that hope would vanish a month later when I'd be too much trouble or something would go wrong with the adoption paperwork or I'd do something stupid to get myself kicked. You go through that shit enough, you start hiding your feelings from everyone."

That tendon starts to tense—just a bit—and there's a shimmer to her eyes that wasn't there when we sat down. "I'm not going anywhere, baby. I'll never break your trust again."

Gently, I slide my knuckle up and down the side of her neck, trying to massage away the tension and tell her that I *see* her. The real her.

"Let me in."

"I don't know how," she whispers, and the dam that was so close to breaking repairs itself in a single heartbeat. "This is who I am, Trevor. I'm always okay. If you can't accept that..."

The rumble in my chest sounds almost feral, and surprises me as much as it surprises her. Surging forward, I claim her lips, and the passion that meets my kiss makes my entire body ache with desire. "I'll take you..." I say as I come up for air, "any way I can have you."

Dani grinds her hips against me, and fuck, I wish these seats offered a little more privacy. Her hands move to the hem of my t-shirt, and a little bump of turbulence reminds me where we are.

"No." I take her wrists and pin them behind her so she's forced to look at me. "Not here. Not like this. The first time I get you naked, we're going to be in my bed. Not at thirty-five thousand feet with an armed flight attendant ten feet away."

"Who says we have to be naked?" Dani's hooded gaze almost destroys my resolve, but I shake my head.

"I do. There's no halfway with me, Dani. It's all or nothing."

With a huff, she relaxes, and I loosen my hold so she can go back to her seat, hating how much the absence of her warmth affects me. After she's buckled back in, she meets my gaze. "I trust you with my life, Trevor. I hope you know that."

"I do. But if this is going to work long term, you have to trust me with your heart too."

Her lips purse, then curve into a frown, and as she pulls her tablet closer, she says quietly, "I know."

Dani

Curling my legs up in the plush, leather seat, I read over the draft of my article. Trevor's staring out the window, and has been since our little fight. Hell, I don't even know if it *was* a fight. I want to go to him and apologize, except, I don't know that I'm sorry. Every boyfriend I've ever had—not that I've had many—has ended things with me when I refused to "open up."

But I don't have anything to open up about. Nothing that anyone wants to hear, anyway. The dozen foster homes Gil and I rotated through until I was in the sixth grade? The last one where he got a beating for failing to turn his homework in on time? Or what about his death? How he chose his birth father —a man he'd never met who *raped* our mother—over me? Over everything?

Trevor knows all of that. Hell, he knows more about me than anyone—except maybe Austin.

I study his profile. After five days on the road, his thick stubble is now a full beard, and it makes him look older, more distinguished. His brown eyes have always carried a hint of sadness—or maybe resignation. Whatever the look, it comes from spending so long in the system. Despite his confidence, his skills, his quick mind, I don't think he ever believes he's good enough. We have that in common, at least.

Returning my focus to the tablet in front of me, I work a ball of thinking putty between my fingers. The pink sparkles catch the sunlight from time to time, and I go over everything my birth father said to me in the short time we had together.

"What did Luis mean when he said 'I did not understand the repercussions of my actions. How much pain they would cause. Brother against brother, families torn apart in feelings. Those scars will never heal. For that, I am deeply sorry'?"

Trevor sits up a little straighter and rakes a hand through his hair. I wonder if he even knows how often he does that when he's thinking. "Maybe nothing. It sounds like he was saying what he thought he needed to in order to avoid a beating."

"No, TJ. *Listen.* 'Families torn apart *in* feelings.' His English was so good. Doesn't that seem like an odd mistake for him to make?"

"Fuck me." Trevor slams his hand down onto the arm of the chair. "*Sensacíon.*"

"Well, yes. That's the Spanish word for feelings. How does that help explain anything?"

"When I rescued Austin...the night I..."

"The night you shot Gil. I don't blame you. Pretty sure that's number five. So only nine-hundred-ninety-five to go." I'm so tired of him constantly apologizing for something that can't be changed. Like he's been sentenced to atone for his mistakes for the rest of his life. "Go on."

Trevor's staring into the clouds, lost in his memories, but his back is so stiff, he's practically vibrating. "The abandoned office building where I found Austin? It was across the street from a half-finished construction project. The sign on the fence was broken, half of it missing, but the first half read '*Sensacíon de.*' "

"Luis knew about...Austin? About Gil?" I press my hand to my heart. "And he was trying to give us something we could use to get him out of there."

Nodding, Trevor leans forward, steepling his fingers. "Maybe. Dani, you can't publish this story. Not yet."

"Why not? My editor isn't going to be happy with me if I can't produce a story to back up the expense of sending me—us—to Venezuela. He's not a patient man."

His dark eyes hold mine. "Just give me a few days. Let me see if my CIA contacts see the same clues in Luis's words as I do."

"I can put an embargo on the story. Lincoln won't be happy, but he'll honor it. He has to."

"Do it. Otherwise, I'm worried Farías will hide Luis Rojas so deep, no one will ever be able to find him."

Disbelief mixes with gratitude and what I think is love as I realize what he's saying. "You...you're going to get him out."

"Not me." Trevor shakes his head, reaches across the table, and waits for me to put my hand in his. "I don't ever want to set foot in Venezuela again."

CHAPTER FIFTEEN

Trevor

By the time our last flight lands in Boston, it's well after 2:00 a.m. My body aches with every step. At my side, Dani stumbles as we get off my apartment building's elevator and crashes into me. "Whoa, baby. You okay?"

"I feel like I've been awake for a week," she says, but when she meets my gaze, it's not exhaustion I see in her eyes. It's need.

We both slept over half the trip from Belize, waking only when the First Class flight attendant offered us hot towels in preparation for landing. Having her curled against me felt like the most natural thing in the world. Like she'd always been there and always would be.

I open the door, flip on the light, and invite her into my private space. I don't bring anyone here. Not even Ford or Austin.

"How long have you lived here?" Dani asks as she runs her fingers over the spines on my bookcase.

"Eighteen months." I drop our bags at the foot of the bed

and kick off my shoes before arranging them precisely in their assigned spot in my closet. I need a shower. Badly.

Dani leans against my bedroom door and tucks a lock of hair behind her ear. Haloed in the light from the living room, she looks like an angel. "Is there anything of *you* here?" Scanning the room, her gaze lands on my dresser. On the only items I care about in this whole damn place.

"Oh. There you are." Dani lifts the center photo and cradles it in her hands. In the picture, she and I stand on either side of Austin at his graduation from the Air Force Academy. "I have this same picture."

She takes the sleeve of her jacket and cleans a smudge from the glass before returning it to its spot between a picture of everyone who gathered at Dax's wedding last month, and the last photo I took with my dad before he died. We're fly fishing —or trying to—and we look like we're on top of the world. For all I know, we were, but though I look at that picture every damn day, my actual memories of him? They've faded so much, I can't even remember his voice.

"You need to get a life, Trevor." Though she's smiling, Dani's eyes are filled with pain, and she slides her arms around me and settles with her cheek against my chest. "Or at least...start living the one that's right in front of you."

The silence grows between us, so big and heavy it's hard to breathe. "I need a shower."

"Oh, God. So do I." Dani tips her head back to look up at me, and her cheeks tinge bright red. "We could, um...?"

I'm simultaneously hard as a rock and terrified. Dani's starred in more than one of my dreams over the years, but the reality of having her all to myself, all night... "Yes. Hell, yes."

"I just need to get my toiletry kit," she says as I make a beeline for the bathroom. "I won't feel...like me if I don't have my toothbrush." Her nervous laugh reassures me. At least I'm not the only one scared as fuck about this.

I strip out of my t-shirt and pull off my socks, dumping them in the hamper. Dani knocks timidly, then slips into the room wearing only the tank from last night and her panties. "Do you have...I mean of course you do. Can I borrow some toothpaste? Err. Have some toothpaste? I'm not planning to give it back."

She's so beautiful when she's nervous. Or confident. Or anything in between. "Left drawer."

Side-by-side, we lean against the sink and brush our teeth, like we've done this every night for years. When we've finished, I open the shower door and turn on the water.

"I can...go after you. If you want."

With a roll of her eyes, Dani finds the button on my jeans and flicks it open. "Trevor? Get naked."

She doesn't need to tell me twice. I shove my jeans down to the floor, and her gaze lowers to my erection straining through my boxer briefs.

"Um, how many weapons do you have in there right now?" As soon as the words leave her lips, she covers her face with her hands. "Oh, shit. That's like...the *worst* thing I could have said."

"Or the best." My voice is rougher than I intend, but when Dani laughs, nothing else matters but her. "Serious answer?"

"Please."

I remove the ceramic knife from my hip pocket, then the GPS tracker, followed by the multi-tool. "That's it."

She eyes the hard bulge below my waist. "Prove it."

"You're going to pay for that one, Danisaur." Pulling the tank over her head, I stop breathing. She's not wearing a bra, and her nipples tighten. When I hook my thumbs in the waistband of her panties and look for permission, she nods.

And then she's bared to me. All five-foot-five inches of toned muscles and generous curves. Fair's fair, so I ease the black briefs over my dick and let them fall to the floor.

She inhales sharply, and I hope to God that's a good thing.

Taking her hand, I guide her under the spray, and she moans as the hot water hits her shoulders. "Don't take this the wrong way," she says as she tips her head back and smiles, "but I'm not sure I've ever felt anything as good as this shower."

I snag the bar of soap from the shelf as she lathers up her hair. "Just wait."

"Not too long, I—" My thumbs skate over her nipples, and her voice catches in her throat. "Trev..."

"Relax, Dani. Just...let me take care of you for a while."

IF I DON'T GET inside this woman soon, I'm going to lose my damn mind. But more than ten years of longing leaves me completely unsure of what to do now. Until she takes my hand and leads me to the bed.

"When did you get this?" she asks as she traces the lines of the tattoo on my left shoulder. Stars tumble down my arm, both in tribute to my country and in memory of the friends I'd lost during my years with the CIA.

"Four years ago." I cover her fingers with mine, needing to maintain this closeness as long as possible.

"And this?" Dani presses a kiss to the thick scar left from Gil's knife. I can't tell her. Not when we're mostly naked and she's looking at me like she wants to eat me for dessert.

"That's a story for another time, baby. Tonight... I just need you."

I pull back the blankets, then stand frozen as she sheds her towel and stretches out on her side with her head on my pillow. Her breasts are perfect handfuls, something I tested multiple times in the shower, and the trim black curls covering her mound are glistening. "Dani, I..."

"Don't tell me you're suddenly shy, Trevor." She leans up on an elbow and grabs the towel around my waist to pull me closer.

"No." I rip the towel away and climb into bed next to her, my hand tangling in her damp locks and angling her head so I can claim her mouth. She moans into the kiss, yielding when my tongue traces her barely parted lips, and if I weren't so hard and desperate for more, I think I could do just this for hours.

Her deft fingers skim down my back, and then I'm on top of her, grinding my dick between her thighs.

"Shit, Trev..." Dani digs her short nails into my ass, and I almost lose control and come without even tasting her. "Inside me."

"Not yet." My lips travel to her jaw, back to her ear, and down the curve of her neck. "I've waited years for this. I'm not rushing it."

A few drops of my precum already coat her thighs, and the scent of the two of us together is enough to make me wish I'd rubbed one out in the shower so I wouldn't feel so close to the edge. But this is Dani. The woman I'm falling in love with—the woman I've loved for as long as I can remember—and we're going to do this right.

Her nipple tightens into a hard nub when I score my teeth over the tender flesh, and she moans and writhes under me. "Do that again."

"Liked that, did you?" I oblige, moving to her other breast, and her moan turns to a whimper. Her muscles tremble, the scent of her arousal fills my nose, and once my lips travel over her taut stomach to her mound, she inhales sharply.

"Trev? What are you—?"

"I'm going to taste you, baby. What's wrong?" My heart shoots into my throat. If she's changed her mind...

"I'm not...it's never worked for me...like that." Her voice trembles, and her eyes shimmer for a moment until she squeezes them shut. "You don't have to..."

I slide back up and roll onto my side so I can gather her into my arms. "I want to. If you trust me."

"I trust you," she whispers, but the uncertainty in her eyes kills me. "What if I can't...?"

With a gentle brush of my lips to hers, I try to reassure her. "If you can't, we find another way. Simple as that. There is nothing about you, Dani, *nothing*, that will make this night anything other than perfect."

She nods, and I start exploring her body all over again, spending extra time lavishing kisses to her true north tattoo. "I will never stand you up again, baby," I say with my lips pressed to the latitude and longitude inked just above her right hipbone.

"You'd...better...not," she says between gasps and tiny mewls.

A part of me wants to stop all of this so I can stare deep into her eyes and promise her with everything I am that I'll never leave her. That I'll be the man she wanted all those years ago— and more—for the rest of her life. But I've seen enough death and destruction, enough good men and women break those promises to their loved ones, that I can't. I won't.

I'll just love her for as long as I can. Every chance I get.

The first dip of my tongue between her slick folds sends her back bowing and her hands twisting in the sheets. The taste of her... Holy fuck. It's as wild as the ocean, as sweet as honey, and as fresh as a spring storm. I could live off of her—just her—for the rest of my days.

Spreading her thighs, I find her clit, and it's like she comes alive for the first time.

"Trevor! Oh, God. Oh...what are you...yes!" Dani's pleas dissolve into helpless whimpers as she begs and pleads without words for me to keep going. One hand slides up to capture a nipple between my thumb and forefinger, and the other spreads her lower lips and sinks deep inside her.

"I can't...I can't...I can't...don't stop..." she cries when I swirl my tongue faster and add a second finger.

That's it, baby. Give in.

My fingers thrust in time with my lips and tongue, and when her entire body tenses, I know she's ready to fly.

Biting down gently and sucking on her clit sends her over the edge, and she screams and bucks, dissolving into endless waves of pleasure.

Dani

I've never... No one has ever made me feel like I do right now. Treasured. Accepted. Safe.

Trevor draws a blanket over us as he holds me close. My body is nothing but Jell-O. Everything but my heart. That's steadier than it's ever been.

I meet Trevor's gaze, and my entire world shifts on its axis. How could I have ever thought he didn't care? "That was...amazing."

"We're not done, Dani. Not by a long shot." Trevor's voice rumbles in his chest and warms my whole body. "I'm going to make your toes curl more than once tonight."

A shudder runs through me, and against my thigh, the press of his cock ratchets up my own arousal. "Promise?"

"Hell, yes." Trev twists his fingers in my hair, and so many emotions swirl in his eyes, I can't pick out just one. "I want all of you, baby. All night."

Arching my back, I offer him everything. Anything he wants. "I'm yours, Trevor. I've always been yours."

The noise he makes—it's a growl. Almost feral. He pins my wrists to the bed and straddles me, kissing me until my lips are swollen and all I can taste is my own release on his tongue. My body aches in the most delicious way, and my nipples tighten and tingle. Warmth gathers in my core all over again.

The room takes on a slight shimmer, and I blink hard, confused at the tears brimming in my eyes. Until Trevor's hands slide down my body, caressing everywhere with such tenderness, I can't hold in my sob.

"Daniella." Trevor's expression shutters, and he curses softly under his breath. "I'm sorry. I didn't mean—"

The use of my full name...it does something to me I can't explain. All of a sudden, this isn't just fulfilling a fantasy. It's something more. Something so perfect, so right, every emotion is magnified.

"Say it again."

Trevor's dark brows furrow, and he holds himself over me, braced on his elbows. "What?"

"Say it again. As many times as you want. With you...I can be Daniella. I can be...me." I swallow hard, and a tear trails down my cheek until Trevor kisses it away. "I understand now," I say quietly. "What you meant on the plane when you said I needed to trust you. And I do."

"Daniella Monroe, I'm going to make sure you never doubt who you are again," he says as he lowers himself down on top of me and his cock nudges my entrance. "You're brilliant and smart and beautiful. You're the only woman I've ever..." He shakes his head and kisses me again, and I wrap my arms around his neck and hold on tight.

"Make love to me, Trevor. I want you inside me. Now."

He leans over and rummages in the drawer of his nightstand before tossing a foil packet onto the pillow next to me. "What do you like, *Daniella*?"

"You." I reach down and wrap my fingers around his cock, and its girth...my eyes widen and I tip my head up so I can look him in the eyes. "It's been a while for me. More than a while. And you're...um...a lot bigger than my usual toys."

Trevor chuckles. "Toys? When we go back to DC, you're going to show me these toys of yours, baby." He shifts onto his side, grabs the condom, and rips the packet open.

I'm mesmerized as he rolls it over his length—and a little scared, but I trust this man more than I trust myself.

"Look at me, Daniella Rosa. You are mine, and before we're done here tonight, you're going to know it better than you know your own name." His eyes darken, his voice drops, and pleasure gathers between my thighs. "And in case it's not clear..." He takes my hand and presses it to his heart. "I'm yours as well."

HEAVY POUNDING WAKES ME, and Trevor groans. "Whoever that is needs to go the fuck away. Right now." After he presses his lips to mine, he rolls to his feet, then snags a pair of boxer briefs out of his top drawer. "I'll be right back. I want at least another few hours with you in bed before we have to face reality."

His eyes, though still bleary with sleep, hold the promise of so very many things. I glance at my phone to check the time— barely 8:00 a.m.—and find two dozen messages waiting for me. Emails, texts...oh shit. Shit, shit, shit.

"Don't move!" a gruff voice commands. "Trevor James Moana, you're under arrest for the murder of Arturo Velasquez, Roberto Cordova, and Gilberto Sosa in Caracas, Venezuela. Turn around and lace your fingers behind your head."

"What the hell is the meaning of this?" Trevor asks. A dull thud sends my heart shooting into my throat, and he groans, "I'm not resisting, but I want to know who's accusing me."

Oh God. I scramble out of bed and grab the first thing I see —one of Trevor's t-shirts from his duffel bag—and pull it over my head.

"Above my pay grade, asshole. But that article in the paper

this morning was pretty damming," the first voice says. "Orders came from Washington. You're in a shitload of trouble."

"Trevor! I didn't—" I cry as I race for the living room.

"Freeze!"

My eyes zero in on the barrel of a pistol, and the snap of handcuffs makes me flinch. Three police officers stand in a semi-circle around Trevor, and a fourth—the one pointing his gun at me— is only a few inches away.

"Daniella Rose Monroe, you're named as a person of interest in the murder of Arturo Velasquez and Roberto Cordova. Hands behind your head, lace your fingers together."

"I don't understand. They came—"

"Dani, don't say another fucking word," Trevor snaps as two of the officers muscle him towards the bedroom. His hands are already cuffed behind his back, and he twists his head to stare at me, his eyes dark and cold as steel.

"Tell me what clothes you want," the cop on the left says to him, "and we'll get 'em. Try anything, and you're going down to the station wearing nothing but your briefs."

"I want my goddamn lawyer."

"Last chance, asshole. It's fifteen degrees outside. You want to be taken out barefoot?"

Trevor grumbles something I can't hear, and the other two cops focus on me. "Hands. Now, Ms. Monroe. We'll take care of clothing for you when Moana's done."

I don't have a choice. They have guns, and Trevor's right. Anything we say now won't do either of us any good.

As one of the officers takes my right hand from behind my head and twists it down to the small of my back, I swallow hard. The cuff is cold and tight, and my shoulders start to ache as he snaps the second one around my left wrist.

Trevor doesn't meet my gaze as the two officers lead him towards the door. He's wearing a pair of sweat pants, sneakers, and a flannel shirt. The look on his face...he thinks I lied to him. That I published the article even though he asked me not to. I have to tell him I didn't. That my editor must have done it while we were asleep.

"Trevor! I…"

"Not a word, Dani. Not one word. How could you?"

"Get a move on," one of the officers says to Trevor and prods him in the back.

"I didn't—"

Trevor cuts me off, his voice hoarse, and anguish written all over his face. "I don't want to hear it." And then he's gone, and I'm being guided into the bedroom that smells of us. The lump in my throat feels like it's the size of a baseball, and the rest of me is numb as I direct the officers to my backpack. At least I put on panties after the last time we made love, so they don't have to dig too deep to find my pants and shoes.

While I dress, they read me my rights, and when I'm cuffed again and we're on our way to the elevator, I look from one cop to the other.

"I want a lawyer."

CHAPTER SIXTEEN

Trevor

It's cold in the back of the squad car, and despite the cops' *generosity* in letting me get dressed, I don't have socks or a jacket to keep me warm.

Or Dani, apparently. Knowing she published the story after I asked her not to crushes the hope that I'd finally found someone who would stick. Who'd stand by me no matter what.

The same sinking feeling I got every time a caseworker came to move me to another foster home chokes me, and it's hard to keep breathing.

It was always going to happen. You're not someone's forever.

If I could drive a blade through my inner voice's throat, I would. Too bad the asshole's all in my head.

The cops don't bother to hide their disdain for me, and they're gossiping about the story in the Washington Post.

"This guy pissed off someone big down there in Venezuela," the driver, Paverelli, says as he glances back at me in the rearview mirror. "Didn't take more than an hour after the story broke for the warrants to come down."

His partner, a younger kid named Doyle, pulls out his phone and taps the screen a few times. I sit up a little straighter, but I don't have to. He starts reading out loud.

"The interview with Luis Rojas was cut short when he started talking about his family," Doyle says. "Then there's an editor's note at the end of the article. 'Two members of the national police attacked the Post's reporter in her hotel room. She only escaped after a heroic effort by her bodyguard, a former intelligence officer with knowledge of the local area.'" Doyle tosses a gaze over his shoulder. "That'd be you, igit."

The Boston slang for idiot ratchets my anger up another half a dozen notches, and I clench my jaw hard enough my molars start to ache. Venezuela is one of a handful of countries allowed to extradite suspects in capital crimes from the United States. I'm fucked if I can't get in touch with Dax or Pritchard.

Dani might be okay. She's only a "person of interest."

Why do you care?

This time, I imagine kicking my inner voice in the balls. I can't stop loving her no matter how angry I might be. Worry twists in my gut. She couldn't have known how bad it would be. For either of us. But how could she put her career ahead of whatever we were building together?

I stare out the steel mesh-covered window at the early morning traffic. This city is my home. It's where I found a family again. Where I made love to Dani for the first time and invited *her* into my family as well.

If I don't play this exactly right, I'll be on a plane by nightfall, and my family? Everyone at Second Sight? Dani? They'll never see me again.

Two hours later, I've been strip searched, photographed, fingerprinted, and processed. The dark red jumpsuit marks me as an extremely dangerous offender, and I sit in a solitary holding cell in leg irons with my hands cuffed in front of me and attached to a chain around my waist.

Fuckers even decided they had to secure a cover to the handcuff locks. I have no idea why since the cavity search guaranteed I don't have anything on my person I could use to pick the damn things.

Every time someone speaks to me, I demand my phone call. But so far, all my requests have been denied. I'm not surprised. If Farías has friends—or worse, spies—in the United States government, I'll be on a rendition flight before dinnertime.

A uniformed guard passes by the small cell, and I push to my feet. "Hey. I still haven't gotten my phone call."

He stops, arches a brow, and snorts. "The van to take you to the airport is already on its way. I don't know who you killed, Moana, but they have some powerful friends. There's no phone call for you."

"Wait," I say as he turns to continue down the hall. "Look, can you at least tell me what happened to Daniella Monroe? She has nothing to do with this. She's not being extradited as well, is she?"

"Don't know anything about her," the guard says. "Sorry."

Sorry? If I could spread my legs more than the seventeen inches of chain running from ankle to ankle, I'd kick the metal bench I was sitting on. Though in these soft, canvas shoes, I'd also break more than one toe.

Sinking down, I let my head fall back against the concrete wall. Years of training on micro-expressions and body language tell me that the guard was honest with me, at least. He doesn't know anything about Dani.

A strange ache forms deep in my chest and spreads until it's all I can feel. For years, every time I got on a plane, someone died at my hand. Enough kills under your belt and you stop caring about the preciousness of your own life. Too many enemies.

But for the past few days, I had a reason to want to live again. Someone who wanted me, who didn't care about all the darkness I carry inside. Or so I thought. Was I wrong? I'd give anything to talk to her. To ask why. But I'll never get that chance. Once they force me onto that plane? I might as well stop fighting. I'm as good as dead.

Dani

The interrogation room is all one color. Dark gray. From the steel table to the walls to the uncomfortable chairs. Even the cement floor is gray, covered in that slick kind of paint nothing sticks to. Not blood or tears or...things I don't want to think about.

I'm no longer handcuffed, and I was able to call Lincoln—or leave him a message, anyway—but a female officer brought me in here what feels like ages ago, and no one's checked on me since.

The two-way mirror I face inspires visions of screaming and throwing this hard metal chair, just to get someone to talk to me. For all I know, half the officers in the precinct are watching me. When they first locked me in here, I paced, flexing my fingers again and again as I tried to imagine I had my thinking putty with me. But now, I'm too tired. The cuffs have my shoulders tense and strained, and a headache is splitting my skull.

How could Lincoln do this to me? To us? Before they let me call him, I saw a copy of the article. He took my unfinished piece, and despite the message I sent explicitly stating we could *not* publish it yet, added an editor's note and did it anyway.

If I weren't locked in this room, I'd kill him. Or make him wish he were dead.

Every time I blink, I see the betrayal on Trevor's face. He thinks I broke my promise and no one let me tell him I didn't.

I rest my arms on the table, hoping for a way to cradle my head, but it's so awkward and painful, I don't think I can stay in this position long. Lincoln better come through. Trevor's in trouble. If he gets returned to Venezuela, they'll kill him.

The loud *thunk* of the lock startles me awake. I don't remember falling asleep, but I do remember the dream I was having. I was back at The Crypt interviewing Luis, but this time, when the alarms went off, it wasn't Luis the guards dragged away.

It was Trevor.

I sit up straighter and try to calm my racing heart. Until I see Lincoln. "You fucking asshole!" I scream as I push to my feet.

Two officers—one male and one female—sidestep him and block my path, and I try to see over them as the woman warns me to sit back down.

"Dani, hear me out, okay?" Lincoln says with his hands raised.

"Not unless you have a lawyer with you who's going to get me out of here right now." I stalk back to the chair and sit, dropping my cuffed hands onto the table and pointedly staring off into the corner of the room rather than at him.

"That's why I'm here. To get you. The Post's lawyers have been on this for two hours, and the judge has already agreed to drop the warrant for your arrest. You need to stay in the city for another day so they can process all the paperwork, but you're not being charged with anything."

"And Trevor?" A tiny spark of hope doesn't have time to catch before Lincoln shakes his head.

"He's already on a plane to Caracas."

"No!" The word escapes on a wail, and I drop my head into my hands. "They'll kill him!"

"Dani, come on. Let's get out of here." As Lincoln touches my arm, I jerk away. "I didn't mean—"

"I don't care what you *meant*, Lincoln. I'm done trusting you. The only thing I want from you right now is a ride to Trevor's office. And I wouldn't even take *that* if I had any other way to get there."

He nods, and the regret twisting his features is obvious, but I can't think about that now. I need help, and only a couple of people in this world are in a position to give it to me.

CHAPTER SEVENTEEN

Dani

LINCOLN DRAPES a Washington Post jacket over my shoulders, and it takes everything in me not to throw it back in his face as we walk side by side from the precinct to his rental car. He came for me, made all the right calls for the Post's lawyers to have the charges dropped, and I *know* he's sorry for what he did.

I'm just too worried about Trevor to acknowledge any of that.

"Where is this place?" he asks once we're in the car with the heater on full blast.

"Houston Street." I hold out my hand for his phone, and when he unlocks it for me, search for the exact address and bring up driving directions. It's after 2:00 p.m. in Boston, and just after 10:00 p.m. in Turkey, where Austin is.

"Give me your backup phone," I say as Lincoln pulls out of the parking lot and onto the highway.

"My what?"

"You know you have one. I need it. Mine's still at Trevor's apartment, and we don't have time to get it now."

Lincoln sighs, then digs into his jacket pocket and comes up with a flip phone. "What?" he says as I look at him in disbelief. "It's a hell of a lot harder to hack."

"And probably almost as old as you are."

Austin's number—the one that's only for family to use—goes to voicemail. "It's Dani. I'm okay, so are Mom and Dad, but something's happened and I need you. I'm on my way to Second Sight. I think you probably know the number—or can find it. I don't have my phone and probably won't for a few more hours, so call me there as soon as you get this, please."

Disconnecting, I press the heels of my hands to my eyes and curl inward, trying to hold on to the scent of Trevor's shirt and the memories from the night before.

"Dani?" Lincoln's tone is full of regret, and I swallow hard before I drop my hands to look at him. "I'm so sorry. The story was too good. A reporter nearly killed just for interviewing a political prisoner? The front pager we were scheduled to run today...a judge delivered an eleventh-hour injunction right before we went to press, and...it was chaos. Sarita was yelling at me to come up with another option, and your writing is always polished, always perfect. I knew it wasn't finished, but I figured we could do a follow up piece at the end of the week."

Every word comes out faster and fainter than the last, and a small part of my anger fades. "I know you didn't mean for all this to happen." Letting my gaze wander to the steadily falling snow outside, I choose my next words carefully. "Identifying Trevor as a former intelligence officer who knew the area? That was the worst possible thing you could have done. I can't tell you why. Even if I *could*, I wouldn't. Because I can't trust you anymore, Lincoln. As soon as I don't need the Post's lawyers anymore, I quit. And if you try to stop me or give legal one inkling that I'm not planning on returning to my position? I will go public with what you did, and no news outlet will ever trust you again."

He nods, his shoulders slumping as he flips on his blinker and eases the sedan towards the offramp. "I won't say a word. If there's anything you need to get your friend back, you'll have it. Any of the paper's resources I can give you...just ask."

I clench my hands inside the warm jacket pockets. "What I need now is a miracle."

***

SECOND SIGHT'S offices look a lot like I feel right now. Worn down, beaten up, and frantic. The woman at the front desk—Marjorie, I think—is on the phone, her voice totally at odds with her kindly face and white hair. "Well, you tell him Mr. Holloway is expecting a call back in the next twenty minutes. Otherwise, our next call will be to WBZ."

She jabs a button on the phone and then finally notices me. "I'm sorry, but Second Sight is closed to clients today."

Suddenly, the hours in the police station, the lack of sleep, and the fact that I haven't eaten in almost twenty-four hours collide with her impatient tone, and the walls press in on me. I brace both hands on the desk to keep myself upright. "I need to talk to Dax. He's the owner? It's about Trevor Moana. He's...he's—"

"What do you know about Trevor?" The deep voice with a hint of a Southern drawl commands attention, and halfway down the hall, a man with glasses, a cane, and a commanding presence that fills the space stares at me. Or...in my general direction.

"I'm Dani. Daniella Monroe. Austin Pritchard is my brother. I was with Trevor when they arrested him. He's already headed to Venezuela, and I think...I think they're going to kill him. I need your help. Please."

My knees give out, my hands slip off the desk, and I land on my ass with a very undignified grunt. "Shit."

Footsteps pound towards me, multiple sets, and then I'm on my feet again, a strong arm around my waist as another man—taller than Dax and with hints of gray in his brown hair—guides me down the hall and into an office with Dax at our heels.

"Here," the man says as he pulls out a chair and deposits me onto the soft leather seat. "Do you need a doctor?"

"N-no. I just...haven't eaten today. It's not important. Who are you?"

"Ford. Ford Lawton."

Beyond the window, half of Boston spreads out in front of me, beautiful and quiet and serene as the snow continues to fall. But inside, papers are strewn about, some littering the floor, a filing cabinet has one of its drawers hanging open, and there's a dent in the wall to my right that's decidedly fist-shaped.

Ford sticks his head into the hallway. "Marjorie! Get us a couple of pizzas? And some coffee? Please?"

I flinch as he shuts the door forcefully, then look between him and Dax. I don't know where to begin, and even though I need their help, I worry once they find out it was my article that led to Trevor's arrest, they'll kick me out and I won't be able to help find him.

"The Feds showed up two hours ago," Dax says as he takes a seat across from me. "They had a blanket warrant for anything even remotely related to Trevor's cases, which, I reckon in this place, covers Hell's half acre. Wouldn't tell us a single fucking thing about where he is. How do you know he's already headed to Caracas?"

"M-my editor. The article in the Post? It was mine. I told Lincoln it wasn't ready, that it couldn't go out until I gave the okay, but he went behind my back and published it anyway," I rush to say before the angry expressions on the two men's faces turn lethal. "He's the one who outed Trevor as former CIA."

"Still doesn't explain why they put him on that plane so damn quick," Dax says, and before I can explain, Ford clears his throat.

"I didn't want to tell you when the Feds were here," Ford says.

"Stop."

Dax touches his ear, and Ford curses under his breath. "Hang on."

As he strides out of the office, Marjorie enters carrying a tray with three steaming mugs of coffee, a sugar and creamer set, and a granola bar. "Pizza will be here in half an hour," she says as she passes me the granola bar. "In the meantime, I got this out of the vending machine for you, dear."

I tear into the wrapper, and across from me, Dax lets Marjorie take his hand and guide it to his coffee cup. "Thanks. Unless it's food or our lawyers, we're not to be disturbed."

"Of course. You ring me if you need anything." She passes Ford on her way out, and he sets a small metal box on the desk, then presses a button on the side. It flashes red twice, then green.

Ford blows out a breath. "Clear. They didn't leave anything behind."

"Anything?" I ask.

"Bugs. Get on with it, Ford."

The granola bar gone, I suck down half the mug of coffee while Ford summarizes some of the worst parts of Trevor's past —and mine. Gil's betrayal, how Trev had to rescue Austin from Caracas after Gil tortured him, and his final operation for the CIA—killing his best friend.

"Fuck. So what? Farías wants revenge for Trev killing one of his double agents? That wouldn't be enough for the government to just hand him over with no appeal."

"There's more." The two men turn to me, and I suddenly feel so very small and alone. Trevor trusts them, so by extension, I do as well. But the way they're looking at me...it's like I just killed a member of their family.

Oh God. Maybe I did.

The realization threatens to suck me under. Barring a miracle, I'll never see Trevor again, and everything that happens to him now. It's my fault.

I CAN'T EAT when the pizza comes, even though Ford and Dax have reassured me a dozen times that they don't blame me and neither will Trevor. "You didn't see him when they took him away," I protest.

"Trevor's one of the smartest guys I know," Ford says.

"Excuse me?" This, from Dax as he tucks a napkin into the collar of his shirt and then carefully feels around for the paper plate in front of him. "You know I'm still in the room, right?"

"I said 'one of.'" Ford snags a slice of pepperoni from the box and returns his focus to me. "Dani, this is going to sound... indelicate, but they arrested the two of you at 8:00 a.m., at Trevor's place, and it's pretty obvious you were in bed together when it happened."

A flush creeps up my neck, but there's no use hiding anything. If it would get Trevor back, I'd strip naked and let them check me for hickeys without batting an eye. "We...were."

"When Trev told me about this trip, he left out the part about being in love with you. But it was so damn obvious, a neon sign couldn't have been any clearer."

I suck in a sharp breath. "We hadn't seen each other in years."

With a chuckle, Ford holds up his left hand and twists the obviously new and shiny ring on his finger. "I proposed to my wife more than twenty years ago. And then lost her until this past June. We got married right after Christmas. Love isn't beholden to the ravages of time."

When tears start to burn the corners of my eyes, I want to let them fall, but I can't. I don't know how.

"Call from...Ryker. Call from...Ryker," a computerized female voice announces as Dax's phone vibrates on the desk next to his paper plate. He tucks an earbud into place and taps it.

"How fast can you get to Caracas?" He asks without a single word of introduction. A moment later, he continues, "I'm going to put you on speaker. Ford's here, along with Dani Monroe. She's Austin Pritchard's sister. Voice Assist, transfer call to speaker."

"Transferring."

After a crackle, a rough voice bursts from the phone. "Inara and West are somewhere in the middle of the Everglades for an off-book SERE training refresher. I can't even reach them for another two days. But Graham and I can be in the air as soon as I find a plane willing to take us. You gonna tell me why?"

Dax pulls off his glasses and pinches the bridge of his nose. "It's Trev. He's been extradited to Caracas. They going to try him on multiple counts of murder."

"No. They're not," Ryker says with a grave finality to his tone that leaves me cold. "They're going to kill him. No one escapes The Crypt."

CHAPTER EIGHTEEN

Trevor

UNITED STATES MILITARY aircraft aren't designed for comfort. Or quiet. But compared to this piece of shit I'm currently on, they're like flying first class.

When the transport van arrived at an airstrip half an hour south of Boston, the two MPs who walked me up to the plane both gave me looks that said they'd be shocked if we didn't crash halfway there.

And that was the last bit of sympathy I'm likely to ever receive. The four angry Venezuelan soldiers, two of whom had to carry me up the boarding stairs—the chain between my cuffed ankles too short for me to manage on my own—shoved me to the ground at the back of this rust bucket and locked my wrists to a metal bar welded to the floor behind me. I can't get comfortable. The plane isn't much bigger than the one Dani and I took to Belize, and every time I stretch my legs, I earn a kick from one of the two soldiers sitting in the rear seats.

I don't have any way to tell time, but if I had to guess, I

haven't had any food in more than twenty-four hours, and nothing to drink in at least six. But these fuckers don't care.

My head is pounding, made worse by the not-quite-pressurized cabin of this death trap. If I lean back, the vibrations from the plane's hull threaten to give me a TBI. So I try to sit up as straight as I can.

Once you land, you're dead. Probably won't hurt so much if you're already concussed.

The only thing keeping me going? Dani's not on this plane. The MPs tried to find out what had happened to her. They weren't total dicks. Even apologized when they couldn't get an answer for me.

"Listen, I'm former CIA, but before that, I was army. My boss was Special Forces. Call him. Dax Holloway at Second Sight. Tell him where I'm going. Please. And get him to find Dani Monroe."

"We have our orders, sir. I'm sorry."

The rumble of the engine changes, and pressure builds in my ears. We're descending. I flex my fingers, trying to dispel the numbness that set in hours ago. Whatever comes next, I have to be ready.

It's not going to be good.

By the time the wheels touch down, I can almost make a fist. The soldiers work quickly, freeing my cuffs from around the pipe and locking my hands to the waist chain in front of me. They don't give me a chance to stand on my own—not that I think I could. Instead they drag me off the plane, letting my knees hit each one of the metal steps.

Headlights blind me for less than a minute before someone shoves a hood over my head, cinching it around my neck tight enough to override my brain's control over my limbs. Panic sets in, and, unable to calm myself down, I thrash and shout obscenities at the men holding. me.

And then they let go. My legs won't hold me, and my palms scrape against blacktop before my head hits, and I see stars against the dark hood. Boots and fists and pain. That's all I feel until I give in and let unconsciousness take me.

Dani

One of my favorite sights? New snow on the sidewalks. When the Pritchards adopted us and moved us to New Haven, I'd never seen snow before.

Ford offers his hand to help me out of the car, but I wave it away. I'm not exactly speaking to the men of Second Sight at the moment.

"Dani."

"Don't 'Dani' me. You need me down there." I stalk through the fresh snow, then have to wait until Ford talks to the building security guard before we can head for the elevator and up to Trevor's apartment.

"It's too dangerous." Sliding a key into the lock, Ford pauses. "If Trevor finds out I didn't do everything I could to keep you safe, he'll kick my ass six ways from Sunday."

"No." I lose my words when Ford opens the door. The apartment smells like Trevor. Like sunshine and warm sand at the beach. Like strength and ocean breezes and...*home.* I make a beeline for his bedroom and find myself standing in front of his dresser.

Three photos.

"My dad always showed up. Until he didn't. Until he couldn't."

"I didn't want to go to Seattle. Weddings...they just aren't my thing. But family shows up. I wish...I wish I'd figured that out before you needed me and I failed you."

"Dani, if we don't get out of here, we're going to disappear, and no one—not one single person—is going to come to look for us."

Ford stands in the doorway, his hands shoved into his pockets. "I've worked with Trev for more than three years now, and I've never been here."

"Trevor doesn't let anyone in." But staring at the picture of him from the wedding, I realize how badly he wanted to.

I point to the photo. "What do you see here?"

His lips curve into a slight smile. "Everyone who matters to me."

"And when you look at what Trev keeps in this room, right here, what do you see?" Stepping back, I let Ford peruse the three frames, then watch as he takes in the rest of the spartan space.

His smile falls away, and he scrubs his hand over his chin. "Those photos are everything that matters to him. The only things in this room that matter to him."

"Bingo." I sink down onto the bed, dig into my bag, and pull out my thinking putty. The familiar feel of it between my fingers helps me gather my thoughts into something I think Ford will understand. "Trevor was never adopted. Gil and I were. After his dad died, no one ever came for him. Supposedly, he had some extended family. A second cousin, a great-aunt. But no one wanted him."

"He told me he aged out of the system, but why the fuck wouldn't his family want him?"

I don't say anything. Just watch and wait for him to put the pieces together. When he does, the harsh realization pales his eyes. "We're his family now."

The room takes on a shimmer as I blink back my tears. "So am I."

"We called everyone in for Ripper. But for Trev... We need more than just Ry and Graham."

"That's not it. You don't need an army." With a small shake of my head, I sigh. "An army would just attract more attention. But you do need me. Because if I'm right, he's already been sent to The Crypt, and I can get us in there. General Ochoa is after *me.* Hell, I wouldn't be surprised if he only took Trev to get to me. I can contact him and offer myself in trade."

"No fucking way," Ford says, almost on a growl. "You think Trev would ever want you to put yourself in danger for him?" He straightens, standing up a little taller, and if I don't figure out the right thing to say in the next few minutes, I'm going to lose any shot at this.

But God—or whoever's in charge up there—must be looking out for me, because I pick up my phone to give myself a minute to collect my thoughts and find a text message waiting for me. Along with a photo that threatens to stop my heart from beating.

"Ford? You need to see this."

I angle the phone as I tap the screen, and Ford swears loudly. The text is from an unknown number, but Ochoa isn't fooling me.

We have Señor Moana. If you wish him to remain alive, you will surrender yourself to La Cripta in the next twenty-four hours.

In the picture, Trevor lies on his back under a bright light. His eyes are closed, and blood trickles from a split lip and a cut on his cheek. The dark red jumpsuit is stained with dirt and sweat, and his wrists and ankles are chained.

"Ford, you can't stop me. Either put me on a plane to meet up with Ryker and Graham, or I'll find my own way there. Trevor isn't alone anymore. He has at least one person who will *always* show up." I tap my chest, right over my heart. The heart Trevor owns. "Me. I'll *always* come for him. So either help me or get out of my way."

RONAN, one of Second Sight's guys, parks outside a small public airfield thirty minutes north of Boston. "I don't like this," he says as he pulls a large duffel bag from the trunk of the car.

"I don't either. Let's get that straight right now." An hour ago, Ronan showed up at Trevor's with a whole complement of tactical gear that's *mostly* my size, a small arsenal, a laptop, batteries, comms units, and multiple GPS trackers. One of which is now embedded in my right ass cheek, thanks to Ford's handy little dart gun.

I rub the sore spot, then sling the new rucksack over my shoulder. It's at least thirty pounds, and I stifle my grunt. I can't show weakness. I won't.

"I know the drill," I reassure Ronan, who continues to eye me with skepticism. "Do exactly what you, Ryker, or Graham say, don't go off alone—at all—and don't get captured or killed."

"At least you know how to fight," he mutters as he approaches a man in brown fatigues. "Sergeant Smith?"

"To you, anyway. If anyone finds out where we're going, I might as well be named Sergeant Fuck-Up. Strap in. Ear protection's in the locker under the bench. We're flying high and fast, so if you've got anything warm in those bags, get it out now."

This isn't my first military transport plane flight, but most of the others were in full daylight, officially sanctioned, and involved a bunch of guys who—once they found out I was an Aikido expert—became overly protective of me. Tonight? My partner's a red-haired, green-eyed kid who looks like he's closer to his twentieth birthday than his thirtieth. But his gaze is steady and deathly calm, and he handles himself with a confidence all of the Second Sight guys seem to have in spades.

"I hate to fly," he says as the plane's engines start to spin up for takeoff. "Don't make me regret this."

I give him a saccharine-sweet smile. "Don't fuck up, and I won't."

Ronan's eyes widen, and he chuckles as he leans back and closes his eyes. "Yes, ma'am."

CHAPTER NINETEEN

Trevor

Rough fabric scrapes against my cheek as I try to raise my head. It's dark. I'm still wearing the hood. But it's no longer strangling me. My senses return slowly without the use of my eyes. How the hell Dax does this every damn day, I'll never know.

Then again, it's not like he has a choice.

My whole body aches. I'm sitting up, that much I know. And I'm barefoot. Rough stone or concrete under my toes. Ropes secure my ankles to whatever they have me sitting on. A metal chair, I think. As I try to twist my legs back and forth, the thin, rough bindings abrade my skin.

My wrists are similarly bound, and I give up trying to free myself quickly when I realize there are more ropes at my elbows and knees.

I don't know how long it's been since they dragged me off that plane. Hours? A day? I don't feel side effects from any sort of sedative, so it's probably only been a few hours. My head pounds, dehydration leaving me feeling like my tongue is two sizes bigger than it should be.

Listen.

If I have any hope of getting through this, I need to rely on my training.

Don't panic. Assess the situation. Make a plan. Bide your time. Execute with conviction.

A dull, low noise around me starts to coalesce into sounds I can recognize. Human suffering on a mass scale. Quiet moans. The occasional scream or curse—in Spanish.

No footsteps. Very little movement. Scuffing noises, like an arm or a leg sliding over the rough concrete. I try to recall the few photos and online rumors I was able to find about The Crypt.

Think.

My thoughts feel sluggish. Five underground levels. The first isn't rumored to be all that bad—for a prison. Standard six by eight foot cells, each with a toilet, sink, and cot. But those are largely for show only. Those the Farías government only want to receive "a slap on the wrist."

Each level below gets progressively more...inhumane.

I don't know how long I sit quietly, controlling my breathing, counting the different pitches of coughs and moans. There could be up to thirteen separate prisoners within earshot. Maybe more. For all I know, some aren't making any noise at all.

I can't go much longer without water. My muscles are starting to cramp painfully, and with no ability to move, every time they do and I jerk, the ropes cut deeper in to my wrists and ankles.

"Hey, assholes! Some food and water would be nice! Unless you flew me all this way just to let me die on day one! Seems like a waste of jet fuel."

Several voices call out, urging me to stay quiet.

"Silencio."

"Cállate."

"No los hagas venir."

The last one—don't make them come—is exactly what I *want* to happen. I need information. I need to see what's on the other side of this hood and face the shitstains who think torturing a former CIA assassin is a good idea.

"You want me dead? Ignore me, then. I'll just sing the national anthem until you come shut me up."

Too far, Trev. Too far.

But I'm committed now. And possibly fucked in the head.

"Oh, say can you see, by the dawn's early light. What so proudly we hailed at the twilight's last gleaming?"

My throat is so parched, it seizes up on me, and after I cough hard enough I probably would have thrown up had there been anything in my stomach, I continue.

"Whose broad stripes and bright stars through the perilous fight, o'er the ramparts we watched were so gallantly stream-ing? And the rocket's red glare, the bombs bursting in air—"

I'm shouting so loudly, I don't hear a thing. Until someone punches me in the gut, and I double over, unable to breathe.

Before I can recover, my head snaps back, the hood is pulled tight, and water drenches my face. *Fuck!* I can't stop myself from inhaling when my diaphragm stops spasming, and the lukewarm liquid floods my lungs.

"You wanted water, *sí?*" a man asks, and the water stops.

Coughing and pulling at the ropes tying me down, I fight my body's reflexes until I can rasp, "Yeah. Thanks. Next time... ice it...will ya'?"

I'm ready for the second round, and manage to get a healthy swallow in before I have to hold my breath and try to convince my body I'm not really drowning.

"Look," I manage after the third bucket empties over my head, "I can do this all day. Or night. Whatever the hell time it is." Another coughing fit leaves me out of breath, but I don't stop, even though it's only going to earn me more pain. "I'm... former CIA...fuck face. You keep...waterboarding me...you'll either...kill me...or make me think...it's a day at the beach."

My captor says something that might be "fucker" in Spanish, then rips off the hood.

Bright lights burn my eyes until a shadow falls over me, and I squint up at him. One of Ochoa's men. The one who manhandled Dani.

Footsteps approach from behind me, General Ochoa's chuckle smooth and full of confidence I'll use to strangle him with if I get the chance.

My chair is spun around to face him, and his lips twist into an insincere smile as he leans down to meet my gaze. "Señor Lejune. Or should I say Señor Moana? You are enjoying your stay with us?"

Now that my eyes have adjusted, I scan my surroundings. I'm in one of the cells on the first level. It's small, but with enough room for Ochoa and the guard to stand inside the door. Concrete walls. Low ceilings. A drain in the center of the floor next to me. A metal electrical pipe runs the length of the cell with a single bare bulb in the center. There's no cot. No toilet or sink. "Yeah. Barrel of laughs. Five-star accommodations, too."

"That...will change soon."

Of course it will.

I say nothing, challenging him.

"You were not my target, Señor Moana. Merely my way to get to Daniella Monroe. However, the lawyers for her newspaper were able to get the charges against her dropped. You, on the other hand, murdered two members of the Venezuelan National Police. Not to mention Gilberto Sosa and half a dozen others five years ago."

Dani's safe. Still in the United States. Thank fuck. I'll die here, but Dani won't.

"I thought your only use would be as leverage against Daniella. But then I realized there is so much more you can assist me with."

I snort, the motion tearing at my split lip, and I taste blood. "You obviously don't know me at all, asswipe. You might as well just kill me."

He wants to break me, he's going to have to work a hell of a lot harder than this. I have nothing left to lose. Dani's safe, and while Dax and Ford might want to launch a rescue mission for me, they'd figure out pretty damn quick it would be suicide. Not even Ryker and his team are good enough to get *inside* The Crypt. They'd need a fucking army.

"All in good time." Ochoa whistles sharply and three other soldiers loom on the other side of the cell door. "Show this *pendejo* the finest accommodations La Cripta has to offer."

I don't fight as one of the men slices through the ropes. He nicks both of my arms and one leg in the process. I'm in no condition to best anyone at the moment. Instead, I let them cuff my hands in front of me, then drag me out of the room, past three other cells with prisoners huddled under blankets, and into a rickety elevator. With one man holding each of my arms and the other two watching me, their backs to the door, there's no hope of escape. But I take in everything.

A service weapon at each hip. Slight bulges close to their ankles—backup pieces, likely. Billy clubs. One of the two in front of me pulls a set of keys from his front chest pocket. Do they all carry them? Or just him? I have to find out.

The elevator jerks to a stop, and we're moving again. Where it was hot and humid on the first level, now it's freezing, and my thin prison garb is still soaking wet.

The tops of my feet scrape along the rough floor, but my legs are too weak for me to even try to walk. I must have been in that fucking chair for at least five hours.

Another bright hallway. So bright, the soldiers pull

sunglasses from their pockets. Squinting, I think I can make out bars. Cells. The occasional hint of movement.

At the end of the row, the soldier with the keys unlocks a cell, and the two dragging me suddenly let go and shove me inside. As soon as I hit the floor, I start to shiver uncontrollably. It's like lying on a block of ice.

The door slams, and I raise my cuffed hands to shield my eyes. A set of bars has been cemented three feet above me. There's no way to stand. The most I'll be able to do is get to my knees. The toilet is just a hole in the floor, and light floods the entire space, making it impossible to tell if it's day or night.

"You make noise, you starve," one of the soldiers says before he slides a cup of water and two small cornmeal cakes through the bars, then stalks away.

My stomach twists in on itself as I grab one of the cakes and shove half of it in my mouth. It tastes like shit. Stale, crumbly, and...is that mold on the edge? But I don't care. I have to keep up my strength as long as I can. If I'm going to die, it'll be on my terms.

Dani

A gentle hand shakes me, and I force my scratchy eyes open. The thin wool blanket covering me is surprisingly warm, but my cheeks sting as hot, humid air fills the belly of the plane. We're on the ground in Venezuela, and Ronan stands over me, his rucksack already slung over a shoulder.

"Time to go." Holding out his hand for the blanket, he gives off an obvious air of impatience.

"You could have woken me when we started our descent," I say sharply. Taking the blanket in both hands, I fold it in under three seconds, then shove it back into my own bag. At his scowl,

I arch a brow. "My dad served for more than twenty years, my brother's still serving now. You think I didn't pick up a thing or two?"

"I like her." The rough, raspy voice is familiar. Ryker. I push to my feet and turn towards the lowered cargo ramp. The man clad in all black is taller than anyone I've ever seen. He didn't look *that* tall in the photo on Trev's dresser. He's in front of me in four steps and grabs my rucksack. "Ryker."

"Dani. And I can get my own pack." I draw up to my full height, which still puts my eyes level with the center of his sternum.

"Didn't say you couldn't." Ryker jerks his head towards the ramp. "Let's get this shitshow on the road." He strides out of the plane, followed by Ronan, and I stalk after them, my memories playing on a loop in my head.

"You are the most infuriating man on the planet, Trevor Moana."

He chuckles. "Pretty sure that title goes to Ryker McCabe."

"Who?"

"A guy I've worked with a time or two. You'll meet him some day."

A black van sits at the edge of the runway with another man loading metal storage boxes into the rear cargo area. He's built...that much I can tell, even at 6:00 a.m.

"Peck, this is Dani," Ryker says.

"Graham Peck," the younger man clarifies. "Graham, I mean."

Graham and Ronan exchange greetings, and I get my first clear look at Ryker under a light from the hanger fifty feet away. Half his face is scarred, his left eye doesn't open as wide as the right, and the corner of his mouth turns down slightly. I try not to stare. After all, I saw some of the devastation in the photo from the wedding. But apparently, I don't succeed, because Ryker's expression hardens.

"You don't want to know, Dani. But if we get out of this country alive, I might tell you."

With a nod, I climb into the back of the van and turn on my cell phone. Nothing from Ochoa, but one new message from Austin. "You got my brother's ETA?" I ask Ryker as he slides behind the wheel.

"Yep. He'll meet us at the safehouse at oh-nine-hundred. Just about exactly when we'll get there." The van accelerates smoothly, and once we hit the main roads, Ryker scans the rear view mirror and locks gazes with each of us in turn. "If you can manage to sleep in this no-shocks-piece-of-shit, do it. Because once we arrive, we've got a fuckton of work to do."

CHAPTER TWENTY

Trevor

GRITTING my teeth so I don't groan, I let myself collapse onto my side under the constant blinding lights. One of Ochoa's soldiers stomps towards my cell, banging his Billy club on the bars as he goes. They patrol regularly—every fifteen minutes or so—keeping us all awake.

Training taught me how to sleep in short bursts, but if I've gotten more than an hour in the past six—hell, in the past twenty-four—it'd be a miracle. I'm still shivering, thank fuck. It's when you stop you have to worry. Frigid air blows into the cell, and I have to curl into a ball to try to protect my fingers and toes.

The footsteps recede, and I force myself up to my hands and knees again. I have to keep moving as much as I can. Keep my muscles from locking up completely.

I know every one of Ochoa's tactics. I've used them. One more reason I quit the CIA. Sometime in the next few hours, he'll pull me out of here. Take me somewhere warm. Offer me food. Water. Some sort of carrot to get me to *help* him.

Fat fucking chance.

I inch closer to the bars and press my face against them. *"¿Cuales son tus nombres?"* I whisper. No one answers, so I repeat my question. I need to know the names of the others down here with me in case I ever get out of here. *"¿Cuales son tus nombres?"*

"¡Cállate! Los guardias nos harán daño."

The voice is weaker than my own, older. Warning me the guards will hurt us if we keep speaking. But I think...it might be Luis.

"Me llamo Trevor. Estaba con Dani Monroe."

"Dani? ¿Está segura mi hija?"

Is his *daughter* safe? He knows. Of course he knows.

Two other prisoners tell us to be quiet, and I won't risk drawing the soldiers' attention to them. They've been here longer. They don't have my training. But I have to reassure Luis, so I chance one more word. "Yes."

ANOTHER THREE PATROLS PASS BY, and I can feel myself getting weaker by the minute. Two cornmeal cakes and a single cup of water isn't enough to keep me alive for long, and the world spins when I push myself up.

Keys rattle from just outside my cell, and the door bangs open. Fuck. They were quiet, and now that they know I've been moving around, things are likely to get a lot worse for me. Rough hands fasten around my upper arms and drag me down the hall.

Back into the elevator, where they drop me in the corner and start kicking me. Curling my arms around my head, I twist until my back is against the wall and let all of my muscles go limp except for my abs. Liver, kidneys, head, dick, and balls. Those are the most vulnerable spots.

As the elevator jerks to a stop, the soldiers stop their assault and grab me again, and before I can get my bearings, I'm in another room. This one's bigger. Emptier. No chair. No bars. Just concrete walls and floors with old stains I recognize. Bodily fluids. Blood.

With nowhere to strap me down, the soldiers keep hold of my arms. My bent knees are just touching the ground, and I keep my head bowed, hoping Ochoa will believe I don't have the strength to raise it.

"Señor Moana. How was your first night with us?" Using a fistful of my hair to yank my head up, he slaps me across the cheek with his other hand.

"Peachy," I manage. "Three stars. You're spending way too much...on air conditioning."

I expect him to order the soldiers to beat me for my sarcasm, but instead, he laughs. "Oh, Presidente Farías subsidizes our power. We are not concerned. But you should be, my friend."

"Not your fucking friend."

This earns me a quick punch to the stomach, but I'm ready for it and tighten my abs just in time. Ochoa stifles a grunt at the unexpected resistance, and his eyes narrow. "You are a strong man, Señor Moana. I respect that. So I will give you another chance to help me get what I want." He releases his grip on my hair, and I stop pretending, lifting my head to stare him in his cold, brown eyes.

"And what's that, dickwad?"

"Names."

"Tom. Dick. Harry. That good enough for you?"

Anger twists his expression for a brief second, and then he schools his features into a mask of calm. "Those are not the names I am interested in. You will tell me all of the American assets in Caracas."

"Did you miss the part where I'm *ex*-CIA? That information's well above my pay grade now."

Even if I knew, I wouldn't tell him. And he knows it.

The warm air in the room is playing on my exhaustion, dulling my senses and my reaction time as my body yearns to sleep for even a few minutes. The next two punches hit soft tissue, and I retch, spitting blood and bile onto the floor at Ochoa's feet.

"For every name you give me," Ochoa says, stepping over the bloody mess, "I will allow you one hour of sleep. For every five names, a hot meal. But only if you tell me the truth."

There it is.

He's practically following the advanced interrogation and torture handbook to the letter. Every time he drags me out of my cell and into this room, I'll be colder, hungrier, and more exhausted than I am right now. Self-preservation will kick in, and I'll have to fight my base need to *survive.*

The lights never go off. Not even here. I'm already losing track of time. Soon, I'll forget what the sun looked like, how it felt on my skin. And Dani. I won't be able to call up her scent. The sound of her voice. The feel of her body against mine.

"One name, Trevor. Just one and you can sleep for an hour. Up here, where it is warm." Ochoa's voice is calm and reassuring. I can still see through his act. But for how much longer?

Raising my head, I spit in his face. "Fuck you."

He pulls a square of linen from his pocket and casually wipes his cheek, but when he speaks again, his voice is hard and cold, his anger barely contained. "Take him back to his cell."

Dani

It takes us an hour longer than expected to get to the safe house, and I have two messages from Austin that he's stuck in the same terrible traffic we are.

Ronan is snoring in the seat across from me, with Graham and Ryker keeping a constant watch for any car that might be following us. We've taken half a dozen detours because Ryker "had a bad feeling" about something. Only one because of Graham.

I have so many questions. What's the plan being the most important one. But Ryker cut me off when I tried to ask with a terse "no distractions while we're out in the open."

Ronan jerks awake with a loud snort, and Ryker mutters, "About damn time. You're sleeping in the van tonight."

"Give me a break, will ya'? I broke my damn nose two weeks ago and it's not healed properly yet." Ronan's voice carries just a hint of an Irish accent when he's pissed off—which seems to be most of the time.

Ryker turns down a short dirt driveway and blows out a breath when he pulls the van around the side of a squat, dilapidated house. "We're here."

I check my phone. No update from Austin. At least I know he landed. But if they're watching for me, they're also watching for him.

Twenty minutes later, everything's unloaded, and Ryker and Graham are setting up a command station of sorts in the house's sparse living room. Ronan is going through a metal crate full of weapons and taking inventory.

I find a seat at the small kitchen table with the encrypted tablet Ford gave me before we left. Ryker asked me to sketch the layout of the upper floors of The Crypt, and I replay our time there, trying to remember as much as I can.

A new message dings my phone, and I grab it, expecting to

see Austin's name. Instead, I freeze and the device clatters to the floor. "Ryker." I can barely hear myself, but he's on his feet in a split second and headed towards me.

"What is it?" He scoops up the phone, and as he taps the screen, his multi-hued eyes turn almost an icy blue-green. "You have less than twelve hours," he reads, "to keep him alive. I do hope you are on your way."

In the attached photo, two of Ochoa's soldiers hold Trevor up by the arms. His head is bowed, he's unbelievably pale, and blood spatters the floor in front of him.

"The bastard's baiting you," Ryker says. His very large fingers fly over the screen with a deftness I don't think he should be capable of, and after another minute, he passes the phone back to me. "This sound enough like you for Ochoa to believe it?"

I need more time. Even the Post can't get a Visa application approved this quickly. One more day. Please.

"Y-yes. But...we can't leave him there another day. They're torturing him." My stomach is in knots, and my hands start to shake.

Snatching the phone back from me before it falls again, Ryker sends the message, then pierces me with his hard stare. "There is no fucking way we can get him out without recon-naissance and a shitton of luck. Going in there today is suicide. This whole mission is suicide."

"Then why did you come?" I stand, holding on to the back of the chair to keep myself upright. "If you're so sure this is going to fail, why even bother?" He doesn't answer right away, and my anger flares hotter. "You know what? Maybe you should just go home. I don't trust Ochoa for a second, but if I have to, I'll let him have me on the *chance* he'll let Trevor go."

"Not happening." Austin's voice startles me. Everyone else too, apparently, as he has three guns pointed at him before I can blink.

"For fuck's sake, Pritchard. Don't you know how stupid it is to sneak up on me?" Ryker asks as he holsters his weapon.

"Wasn't trying to. You were all distracted." Austin pushes through the wall the three other men made around me and folds me into a bear hug. "I'm sorry, squirt. I never should have let Trevor do this. I should have been the one to go with you."

The tears I haven't let fall since I discovered my birth father's name soak into his shirt, and I cling to him with all the strength I have left. "We can't leave him there," I say between sobs.

"Everyone in the living room. Now," Ryker snaps, and I flinch in Austin's arms.

"McCabe, watch your tone," my brother says as he guides me into the main room.

"You should know me well enough by now, Stars and Bars. This *is* my nice voice. Sit down and shut up while I explain how this is going to go."

Anger radiates off Austin in waves, and he works his jaw back and forth. I've only seen him this tense two or three times in my life, and when we sit, I scoot out from under his arm in case he blows up.

"Dax called me because this is what I do," Ryker says, his hands on his hips and his gaze fixed on me. "You don't know me, Lois—"

"Lois? You're supposed to be the best but you can't even remember my name?"

"Lois Lane? You *are* a reporter. Outside of this safehouse, we use codenames. You're Lois."

Graham, who's seated in an old wooden chair next to me, leans over and cracks a smile. "Guess that means I'm Jimmy Olsen."

Ryker shoots him a look, and he snaps his mouth shut.

"If the peanut gallery's done?" No one responds, and he

nods his approval. "*Dani*, you don't know me. But that story I said you didn't want to hear?"

I nod. His scars. He stripped off his jacket when we got inside, and his forearms and biceps are covered in them—along with numerous tattoos.

"Fifteen months. The Taliban tortured Dax and me for fifteen months. Ripper, the only other member of our Special Forces team to survive, went missing before I broke out, and we only found out back in June that he'd been held for six fucking years by an asshole who tried to erase everything about him. Broke him in more ways than I thought a man could break. When we found him, he was down at the bottom of a goddamned well. And he'd been there for days. Trevor helped us rescue him. So when I tell you that I will *die* before I leave another man behind, know that I am fucking serious. We are not leaving Venezuela without him and every single person in this room. But we also can't go in there without a plan, and my tactical specialist is somewhere in the middle of the Everglades, unreachable. So we're going to set up comms and connect with Dax, Ford, Wren, and whomever else we need to get this shit done, and all of you are going to follow *my* orders here."

He scans the room, making eye contact with each person in turn. "Anyone have a problem with that?"

One by one, we all shake our heads.

"Good. Now let's get to work."

CHAPTER TWENTY-ONE

Dani

Four separate laptops are spread out on a coffee table, and I'm pretty sure my mom's knitting projects had fewer strands to them. Austin's been on the phone for over an hour trying to track down sources who might know the layout of The Crypt's underground floors.

I can't do more than pace and force down the terrible MRE Ryker handed me a few minutes ago. It's supposed to be beef stew, but I'm pretty sure those chunks of "meat" are made of leather and the carrots? They're so orange, they have to be radioactive.

"Dani?" Ryker angles his head towards the bank of computers. "Need you over here."

The man doesn't use a single extra word if he doesn't have to, and a part of me wants to snipe at him for it. But if he can get Trevor out of The Crypt, he can communicate in hand gestures and charades for the rest of this trip and I won't give a shit.

Dax's face takes up one half of the screen and on the other, a petite redhead who looks vaguely familiar flashes a smile as I sit down. "Hi. I'm Wren." She turns her computer slightly to reveal another woman with black hair and features a lot like mine. "This is Cam."

"Dani." I glance over at Ryker, and the look in his eyes as Wren's face fills the screen again...it's like he's a different person.

"My...my wife," he says, and his lips twitch like he wants to smile.

"Oh! From the picture."

"What?" Ryker asks.

"Trevor has a picture on his dresser from the wedding. All of you. Cam's married to...West?"

"Yep," Cam says from off screen. "We're your tech support."

Dax snorts. "They're a hell of a lot more than that."

Wren's smile fades, and she's suddenly all business. "Dani, I need your full name, date of birth, and social security number. I could find it, but it'd take me time we don't have."

"Why?" Quickly shaking my head, I continue, "Never mind. I don't care why. You want to steal my identity when this is all over with, go ahead. As long as Trevor's safe." I rattle the information off and Wren's fingers make dull clicking noises over the connection as she takes it all down.

"Short answer?" she says. "We need to fake travel records for you. There are only a couple of countries left in this world that don't computerize customs records, and if General Ochoa figures out you flew down on a private plane, he'll probably assume you have help with you. I need your brother's info too."

"I didn't come through customs," Austin says. "Why do you—?"

"To make sure you're easily traceable somewhere else. I'm putting you on a commercial flight to New Zealand that leaves Ankara in three hours."

"You can...do that?" I ask. Dax was right. She's a hell of a lot more than tech support. She's amazing.

"She can do just about anything," Ryker says with obvious pride in his voice. "You put her and Cam together, and they're fucking unstoppable."

"Can it, soldier. You're going to embarrass me," Wren says, and the video's so clear, I can see her cheeks flush almost the same shade as her hair.

After she has Austin's information, she returns her focus to Ryker. "Ready for the GPS readings."

The giant next to me picks up a handheld scanner. "Where'd they put it? The chip."

"Um, right ass cheek." I don't hesitate to twist in my chair, but Ryker stops me when my hand goes to the waistband of my pants.

"Not necessary. This'll read through fabric."

Thank God. Ryker calls Austin over and pulls the sadistic dart gun from a duffel on the floor. "You're next, Stars and Bars."

"I have a name, you know. And you're not touching me with that thing."

Standing, Ryker looms over Austin. "You wanna try that again?"

"No."

"Listen, Pritchard, I'm about two seconds from knocking you on your ass. You expect to go into the field with me, you're gonna be tracked. Because if you get yourself caught and taken into the bowels of The Crypt, or anywhere else, we have to be able to find you."

"Just because I'm holed up in this shack with you, McCabe, doesn't mean you get to—"

Ryker grabs Austin's arm, spins him around, and shoves him against the wall. Without missing a beat, he tosses the dart gun to Graham, who pulls up my brother's black t-shirt and injects the chip just above his waist.

"You fucking piece of shit," Austin growls as Ryker lets him go.

On screen, Wren shakes her head and mutters something that sounds like "Men."

"Yep. That I am. A fucking piece of shit who can now rescue your ass if you need it. We don't have to like each other, Pritchard. I know you only let Rip go because Trevor asked you to."

"What the fuck?" Austin shoves Ryker, but it must be like pushing against a brick wall. "I didn't let Richards—"

"Ripper." The word escapes on a hiss, and Austin rolls his eyes.

"Fine. I didn't let *Ripper* off the hook because Trevor asked me to. I did it because it was the right thing to do. And as for the rest of you," he sweeps his hand around the room, encompassing Graham and the comms equipment where Wren and Dax are listening in, "I looked the other way and buried all evidence you were even *in* Afghanistan last summer. Not because of Trevor. Because the world needs people like you. Your team can go places I can't. Do things I can never do and never *want* to do."

Silence fills the safehouse for a long moment, until Ryker arches a brow and looks over at Graham. "Sounds like the head of JSOC just endorsed Hidden Agenda."

Austin slams his palm down on the table, and Ryker takes a step towards him, hands clenched into fists at his side. "That is *not* what I said, McCabe. And if I hear you repeat that to a single fucking soul, the next time you need help you better come asking dressed in a fluffy pink tutu."

The tension in the room is suffocating, but a second later, Ryker sputters what might be...a laugh? On screen, Wren's mouth hangs open. Dax shakes his head with a smile tugging at his lips, and Graham looks at Ryker like he's never heard the man make that particular sound before. Austin's just as confused until Ryker slaps him on the back hard enough to make my brother stumble. "You know, that just might be worth it. And it's Ry."

"What?" As quick on his feet as my brother is, he can't quite process the sudden shift in Ryker's mood. Neither can I.

"My name, Stars and Bars. My friends call me Ry." He pins me with those odd, multi-colored eyes. "That goes for you too, Dani. That one," he says as he jerks a thumb towards the back door where Ronan's setting up a perimeter alarm, "is still on probation."

For the first time since the police took Trevor away, I smile. This whole plan could go sideways in a hurry, and if it does, any one of us could pay the price. But I have family with me. Not just Austin, but everyone in this room and on comms. I haven't even met half of them, but that doesn't change how I feel.

I'm not alone.

It takes Wren and Cam a bit to work their magic, and while they do, Ryker sets up a little mini-projector connected to one of the other laptops. "On the left, the streets around The Crypt with traffic cameras marked. On the right, all we've been able to gather about the building's layout. We work in teams tonight. Ronan, you're with me. Graham, you, Pritchard, and Dani are on point to meet with Leo."

"Leo?" I ask.

"He's been in country for almost fifteen years. Can't beat that kind of knowledge. You're meeting him at Plaza Bolivar at nineteen hundred."

I stare at the diagrams of The Crypt. Austin's hours of phone calls—many of them made while he was on a plane over the Atlantic—yielded transcripts of interviews with two survivors who'd been released from The Crypt after giving

Ochoa the information he wanted. They couldn't remember anything but the bottom floor. The transcripts of their interviews haunt me.

That is where the worst happens. The cells are too small to stand or even sit up. It is cold. All the time. The elevator requires a keycard, and there are cameras every three meters. The guards came often to beat or taunt us.

We were not allowed to sleep, to move, or to speak to one another. I was only released when I gave Presidente Farías the information he desired. I refused as long as I could, but after three weeks, I was dying. I told his men everything and I was moved to the top level. To a cell with a cot and hot meals. I was allowed to sleep. Before he ordered my release, Presidente Farías demanded my family sacrifice their home, all of their possessions, and their livelihoods for me. We had to leave Venezuela and can never return.

"We don't know Trevor's down there," I say as Ryker tells Graham where to park and how to approach the plaza.

Ry pauses mid-sentence, passes Graham off to Wren online from Seattle, and flips off the projector before he motions for me to follow him towards the back door.

Outside, the sun is still shining brightly, and the warm breezes ruffle my hair. "Dani, there's nowhere else Ochoa would put him."

"You can't be sure."

Ryker presses his lips together for a long moment, then lowers himself down to the back porch steps with a quiet groan. "Arthritis," he says when I sit next to him and ask if he's all right. "Too many beatings, broken bones, and months spent in caves where the temps weren't much warmer than down in The Crypt. I tune it out most of the time. Bury it so deep I don't feel it."

I nod, understanding all too well. My pain isn't physical, but it's buried all the same. "Kind of surprised you'd show it to me."

He makes that same hoarse sound from earlier, and now, I recognize it as a chuckle. "You're not the only one."

"How can you be sure Trev's down...*there*?"

Ry rubs his bald head, his fingers tracing the scars from more torture than I think one man could ever survive. "Because Ochoa knows who Trevor is. What he did. What he wants to do. And how well Trevor was trained to do it."

The realization hits me hard, and I drop my head into my hands. "Because of Gil."

"Yeah. Or..." He sighs, and I think I know what he's going to say.

"Luis."

I can't...I need to run. But there's no time and nowhere that's safe for me to go. "We can't leave him down there until tomorrow. Please, Ryker—Ry. Isn't there some way we can get him out tonight?"

"No." His growled answer makes me flinch, and he softens his tone. "Wren's almost done faking your travel arrangements. After that, things are going to move fast. Too fast for any of us." He pauses, then adds, "Except Trevor."

"That's what I'm afraid of." I don't cry. I won't. Not until Trevor's out of that place and safe. Back with me. But I sniffle once and swallow hard. "What if he isn't..."

"The same?" Austin joins us, taking a seat on my other side and nudging his shoulder against mine. "He won't be, squirt. You won't be either. But Trev was trained for this. To survive. To send his mind somewhere nothing can hurt him. He'll come back to you."

For a few minutes, no one says a word. We just sit quietly, staring at the cloudless sky, breathing free air, and praying for a miracle.

CHAPTER TWENTY-TWO

Trevor

NOTHING GIVES me reprieve from the bright lights and the endless cold. The soldiers brought out the belly chain and connected wrist cuffs when they dragged me back here, and now, I can't raise my hands high enough to cover my eyes. I've stopped trying to roll over and curl into a ball, but I still force myself to my hands and knees every few hours.

Conserving my strength and ability to move are both equally important now. It'll be another half a day or more—probably—before Ochoa sends for me again. He'll wait until I'm delirious from lack of sleep, then try to trick me into giving up the names he wants.

But he doesn't know how well I've been trained. Not truly. Every other time the guards leave, I let myself fall asleep. Fifteen minutes isn't near enough time. Deep, restorative sleep only happens when you can manage a solid hour. But these micro-naps should keep me from going insane. For a time.

The heavy footsteps come again, followed by the slamming of the Billy clubs against the bars. "*¿Quién quiere cenar?*"

Dinner. It's probably nothing but cornmeal cakes again, but anything's better than this endless twisting and cramping in my stomach. Cell by cell, they slide the water cups through the bars, and I count. Six, each taunted in Spanish about their crime or their family or their smell. Until the soldiers stand in front of my cell and shove two cakes and a plastic cup inside. "The American does not look so good," one of them says, then laughs.

I squint up at them. "You're no GQ model either, shithead."

"You will not be joking much longer," the other soldier warns. "General Ochoa wants you to know how useful you have been."

What the fuck is he talking about? I haven't given them anything. Unless... No. God, no. Not Dani. "*El general es estúpido*," I manage. "Never going to help him."

"The woman is on her way. You and the *salvador de la resistencia* will both give up your secrets when the general locks her down here."

With that final threat, the soldiers retreat, and an all-consuming, burning pain starts deep in my heart. She can't give herself up. Not for me. Not for anyone. She's the toughest woman I know, but she hasn't been trained. There's no way she'll last more than a couple of days down here, and then...her death will be on me.

The door to this level bangs shut, the lock engages, and then, it's eerily quiet. Everyone who can still move at all is eating, but I don't have the strength.

The enemy of survival? Despair. I can't save her. Not from here. When they first threw me in here, I felt all around the bars, hoping to find a weak spot. There isn't one. My two trips upstairs? They've told me nothing I can use.

The urge to give up presses down on me, but only for a moment, because then...

"Trevor." The hoarse whisper cuts through the silence, and I freeze.

"Luis? *¿Eres tu?*"

"Yes. You must keep Daniella safe."

I drag myself closer to the bars. He's across from me. But not directly. Not that it would matter. The lights are too harsh for me to see anything.

Another prisoner tells us to be quiet, and for a time, I close my eyes and let the memories of my time with Dani comfort me. I'll never be with her again. Not like we were. I'm almost asleep when Luis calls out for me.

"Tell me about Daniella? I will never know her."

What can I say in just a few words? Dani's life—the parts of it I got to share—plays out like a movie in my head, and for so much of it, Austin's there with her. I jerk up so quickly, I hit the bars overhead. Austin. He'd *never* let Dani turn herself over to Ochoa for me. She wouldn't let up on him either. It's not in her nature. She'd force him to do something. And that something... would likely involve Ryker, Dax, Wren...

A spark of hope flares to life, and I roll onto my side and fumble for one of the cornmeal cakes. The belly chain digs into my back, and the handcuffs cut into my wrists as I strain to bring it to my lips. Fuckers shortened the chain on purpose in the hopes I wouldn't be able to eat.

After two bites, I drop the cake onto the rough concrete and reach for the water. It's lukewarm, and I wouldn't be surprised if the soldiers spit or pissed in the cup before they filled it, but I don't care. Not with how dehydrated I am. I've only pissed once since I've been in this hell hole, and now...I have a reason to fight back.

First step is establishing a communications protocol with Luis that won't get us beaten or killed.

Tapping my knuckle lightly on the bars, I try Morse Code for *listen.*

Nothing happens for so long, I don't think Luis understood. Closing my eyes, I feel around for the half-eaten cake in front of me, and wash it down with another few sips of water. I'm about to risk saying something when I hear scratching. In a pattern I recognize. Dot-dot. Dot-dash. Dash-dash.

"I am."

MORSE CODE IS EXHAUSTING. CIA requires eight separate dots and dashes. Fight is fourteen. The sounds are barely audible, but I can't be sure the soldiers aren't listening. We speak slowly. In one or two word phrases, careful not to reveal too much. Another three patrols come and go. The second cornmeal cake is drier than the sand in Afghanistan, but I can feel myself getting stronger. As much as I can, I work my muscles to keep limber and stave off the intense shivering from the constant flow of frigid air.

Think. How long has it been?

There's no way to mark time here other than the soldiers' visits. Sometime in the late afternoon? Ry wouldn't come in here guns blazing without a plan. Neither would Austin. I have to hold on at least another twenty-four to forty-eight hours. By then...maybe.

I tell Luis that Dani's happy. That she was adopted and has a brother who will always protect her. He tells me that the floor above us is where Ochoa interrogates him. Every three days. Tomorrow is the third day. He's too weak to walk or fight, but he observes, and he knows the soldiers' patterns.

After several hours, I tell him to rest. *"Keep hope."*

He sighs and then spells out *"Si."*

Dani

With a scarf to cover my hair and a flowing black sleeveless jacket that lets me hide a knife strapped to my thigh, I climb into the backseat of Austin's nondescript sedan. It's not much different than the car Trevor and I used when we were here, and now that it's dark outside, my worry for him has skyrocketed. They've had him for almost twenty-four hours.

Graham slides into the passenger seat. "I'd feel better if you let me drive," he says.

"Tough shit. Who's been here before, Jimmy Olsen?" Austin turns the key, and the car roars to life. It might look like the world's oldest beater, but the engine has definitely been upgraded.

"Not you, too. I get enough of the nicknames from Ry and West. What's wrong with Graham anyway? Or Peck?"

"We're headed into the field, remember? She's Lois, you're Jim, and I'm Perry."

Graham rolls his eyes as he looks back at me. "Doing okay...Lois?"

"No. We still don't have an actual plan, do we?"

Over comms, Dax mutters, "Working on it. Though the wisdom of having a *blind man* orchestrate your infil is definitely questionable."

"Until West gets in touch, you're the best we have," Ryker says in my ear. He and Ronan are driving the streets around The Crypt while Wren creates a backdoor into each traffic camera they find. When they infiltrate the building tomorrow night, they don't want anyone to see them coming. Austin, Graham, and I are going to Plaza Bolivar to find Leo.

"What happened to code names?" Graham says. "I want my own name back."

"Comms are secure for now. Once we get out in the open, it's codenames only," Ryker replies.

"Found something." This is a new voice.

"Who the hell is that?" I ask.

"Ripper, ma'am." The voice with a hint of Texas to it is kind and a lot less gruff than Ryker and Dax's tones. "I found a money trail."

"How much?" Ry asks.

"Millions. Maybe close to a billion. Still tracing. I'll upload it all to the share when I figure out where it ends. Going dark to focus."

I lean forward and touch Austin's shoulder. "Why is he looking for a money trail? A trail to...or from where? How is that going to help Trev?"

My brother checks the mirrors as he accelerates onto the poorly maintained highway. "We're not doing this halfway, squirt. The Loma Collectivo is going to end here and now. The CIA has been trying to bring them down for ten years. It's what Trev and I were working on when Gil captured me. We were close too."

"He told me that much."

"If we can prove the Farías government is as corrupt as we know they are, we can stop them."

"Won't getting Trev out of The Crypt do that? And Luis...if he's still alive? If I publish the truth of what happens there..."

"That's not enough. We have to cut off their funding and expose how much they've stolen from the Venezuelan people over the past decade. It's the only way to get the people on our side."

"And how exactly are you planning on telling the people how corrupt their government is? He controls all the broadcast television in this country. All the radio stations. The newspapers." Sitting back, I stare out the window as the lights of Caracas grow brighter.

"Leave that to Ripper and Wren," Graham says. "Trust us, Dani."

I do. Despite Ronan and Graham looking like they're fresh out of college, Ryker's scars and tattoos, Wren's easy smile, and the fact that Dax can't see, there's a serious undertone to every word, every movement, every thought this team has.

They'll get Trevor out or die trying.

Plaza Bolivar is filled with people, and a part of me wishes Trevor had felt comfortable bringing me with him when he went to meet Leo the first time so I could have seen this under happier circumstances.

Graham links his arm with mine, and every few minutes, he leans in and tells me to smile or laugh or just look affectionately at him. Austin follows a few feet away, occasionally skipping ahead of us so we don't look like a group.

"You're doing great," Graham whispers in my ear.

"Just keep your hands to yourself," Austin says over comms.

"Dude, I'm gay. Back off." The muscles in Graham's arm tense, and I lean my head against his shoulder with a huff. "Sorry. He's always been overprotective."

Austin's voice in my ear is getting more strained by the minute. "You do realize I can hear you, right?"

"We can all hear you," Ry says from wherever he and Ronan are. "Keep the chatter to a minimum."

We spend another ten minutes milling about the square, and Graham and I even take a picture in front of the giant statue of Simon Bolivar riding a horse. It goes straight to Wren so she can put any faces she can identify into her facial recognition program. Austin's wearing a bodycam, and that footage feeds directly to her too.

"Contact spotted," Austin says. "Two o'clock."

Graham steers us through the crowd and into a small restaurant at the far end of the plaza. As we pass the bar, I see

Leo nursing a drink and leaning a hip on a stool. He nods towards the back of the dimly lit space.

"On your six," Austin says, and Graham and I push through the rear door and emerge into a quiet alley. We can still hear the music from the plaza, but there's no one else around, and Graham drops my arm to withdraw his pistol and drape his jacket over his right hand.

"I'm clean," Leo says when he joins us. "Been watching the crowds for an hour. Where's flyboy?"

"Right behind you," Austin says. "Never thought I'd see you again, man. Give me some good news."

"I found the third brother. But he won't talk."

"Wait, as in...Franco Rojas?" My gaze pings between Leo and Austin, and both nod. "Did you tell him who I am? I mean...to him?"

Leo's lips pinch into a thin line as he shakes his head. "He hung up on me before I got a chance."

"Give me his number." I pull out my phone and unlock it as the other three men stare at me. "This is what I do, guys. Convince people to talk to me."

"It can't hurt." Austin shrugs. "Do it."

Annoyance flashes in Leo's one good eye—probably over Austin's tone. He's very much in "JSOC Commander" mode, and it's almost scary how forceful he can be compared to the guy he usually is with me. After a blink, Leo seems to get himself under control and rattles off Franco's number.

"It's okay to call from here?" I ask.

Leo nods. "I'll keep watch." He limps slowly to the mouth of the alley and leans against a wall, casually pulling a candy bar from his pocket and tearing off the wrapper.

My stomach growls, but I ignore it for now and take a deep breath. Focus.

"Who is this?" Franco asks in Spanish when the call connects.

"I'm your niece. Luis's daughter. Don't hang up."

"Luis does not have a—"

"He fell in love with Kate Monroe when she was Jorge Sosa's prisoner, and they had a daughter. My name is Daniella, and I need your help."

CHAPTER TWENTY-THREE

Dani

THE HOUSE MAKES odd settling noises throughout the night, and each one wakes me up from a dead sleep. The guys take turns on watch.

After ten minutes, I managed to convince Franco to help us, and before I stretched out in this sleeping bag in a back room, he spent two hours giving up everything he knows about the Loma Collectivo.

I check my phone. No new messages from Ochoa. Wren worked some magic and fabricated a photo of me on a commercial airplane that I'll text to the general at 4:00 a.m. with the message, *I'm on my way. But before I get on my connecting flight, I want proof of life.*

My final flight will land at 2:00 p.m. local time. Wren will take care of the electronic customs records, and then Ryker expects the general's soldiers to be waiting for me.

"You should get some sleep." Ryker leans against the door jamb with a cup of coffee in his hand.

"I tried. Managed maybe three hours. I just…I don't know how to do this."

"Do what?" Ryker takes a sip of coffee and studies me.

"Exist knowing that Trevor's…where he is because of me." I sit up and wriggle out of the sleeping bag, then draw my knees up to my chest.

Ryker gestures out to the main room. "Get yourself a cup of coffee, and I'll tell you how."

I scramble up and follow him, grabbing a cup out of the metal French press. "You brought a French Press on a rescue mission? Who *are* you people?"

"I live in Seattle. And West—Cam's husband—is a little militant about his coffee. No one fucks with the SEAL. Not even me." Ryker eases himself down in a chair next to the bank of laptops and taps a few keys. "Wren? Going dark for a few minutes, sweetheart. Doing a system restart. Nothing to worry about."

"Roger that," she says, obviously distracted by something on her own machine. She barely even looks up.

After another couple of taps, the camera light turns off and Wren's image disappears, but Ryker doesn't make a move to restart the system.

"She's my everything," he says. "And the day I realized that was the day she was captured by the head of the Nevsky Bratva—Russian mafia. He beat her, drugged her repeatedly, and would have killed her if she hadn't found a way to escape."

"She escaped?" I can't hide my shock. She's looks like she's all of a hundred pounds after a good downpour.

"Yep." Obvious pride relaxes his features, and it's like he's a different man when he talks about Wren. He rubs his hand over his scalp and gets a faraway look in his eyes. "When she was taken, I shut down. If it hadn't been for West and Inara…" With a shake of his head, he focuses on me. "Keeping it together when the person you love is in danger is the hardest thing you'll ever do. But you do it because they need you."

He reopens the connection with Wren and she glances up at him with an impatient look on her face. "Took you long enough. Cam and I have been trying to crack the firewall on this Venezuelan contractor's server for five hours."

"And?" Ry leans forward, a gleam in his eye. "Tell me you found what I think you found."

"Yep." The screen splits in two, Wren giving Ry an exhausted but triumphant smile on the left, and on the right?

"Blueprints for The Crypt," Ry says. "I love you, little bird. You just gave us the advantage that'll let us take these fuckers down."

"You know what to do," Austin says as he wraps his arms around me in a maintenance closet at the Caracas airport and holds on tight. "We'll be there at shift change. Not a single minute later than 5:00 p.m. Wherever you are in that place, we'll find you."

"Get Trevor out first."

My brother's body goes rigid. "No. If we do that, he'll kill me. You first, then Trev. If you can find a way to get to him, do it, but be careful. I mean it, squirt."

"Love you," I whisper. Before he can stop me, I pull away and rush into the women's bathroom. Once I throw the black floppy hat, sunglasses, and bright pink coat into the trash, I scrub my hands over my thighs. They're suddenly damp and shaking.

I can do this. For Trevor. Whatever the general is planning on doing to me, he won't kill me in the first twenty-four hours. Anything else, I can survive. As long as it gets Trevor out of there.

All I have in my small messenger bag is my wallet, phone, passport, and one of my tins of thinking putty. Or...what looks like a tin of thinking putty. The odds of me being able to keep it are slim to none, but Ry has so many contingencies built into this plan, I'd consider it ridiculous if my life weren't on the line.

Before I open the stall door, I unlock my phone and stare at the video of Trevor the general sent me a few hours ago. My proof of life. He's lying on the dirty floor of a cell, handcuffed, with his eyes closed. Until a booted foot jabs his hip and he tries to curl away from the assault. His eyes never open, and he never makes a sound. But he's alive. Or was. According to Wren, the video was recorded twenty minutes before it was sent.

"I'm coming, Trevor. Hold on for me," I whisper as I touch the screen. With a final deep breath, I push through the door and head for the sink to splash some water on my face.

There's a tiny comms unit sewn into the lining of my bag at the seam. Graham did the sewing, and the bag had to pass inspection by Ry, Austin, Leo, and Ronan. None of them could find the unit.

"Here I go. Let's hope the general got the memo about not killing me."

Joining a line of people emerging from Customs, I breathe deeply. My heart's pounding so hard I can hear it in my ears, and I feel like I just got off the treadmill after doing sprints.

That sensation ratchets up another hundred levels when two soldiers approach me, one with his hand on the butt of his gun. "Daniella Monroe, you will come with us."

They don't give me a chance to respond before taking my bag, spinning me around, and cuffing my wrists together. One of them starts to pull me towards the exit by my upper arm, but I plant my feet and jerk free of his hold. "I can walk on my own. I came here voluntarily, and I'm not going to run."

Whatever the soldiers see in my eyes must convince them, because the one on my left gestures for me to keep moving. Five minutes later, I'm locked in the back of a police car that's speeding away from any semblance of safety.

No one speaks for the forty-minute drive to The Crypt, and when we arrive, General Ochoa meets us inside the doors. The experience feels eerily similar to the visit I made here with Trevor, except for the handcuffs and my worry for the man I love.

"Señorita Monroe, thank you for joining us," the general says with his plastered-on fake smile and overly solicitous tone. He's dressed to show off his position today, with even more medals covering both sides of his chest and gold braids on each shoulder.

"You can drop the act, General. I know why I'm here and I have a pretty good idea what you're going to do to me. I can't stop you. But I want to see Trevor Moana. Right now."

His dark brown eyes narrow and he leans close enough for me to smell his stale breath. "Watch your tone, *puta*. You are a resident of La Cripta now, and you will learn that here, I control everything." He snaps his gaze to the guard behind me. "Search her. Thoroughly. Then put her in a cell on Sublevel One."

As the guards practically lift me off my feet and carry me into the elevator, the general calls after us, "I hope you enjoy your time with us, Señorita Monroe."

CHAPTER TWENTY-FOUR

Dani

Cold air hits my bare shoulders as I remove my shirt and place it on the table in front of me. The two soldiers—their name tags read Alvarado and Gurrero—removed my cuffs as soon as we walked through the door and ordered me to strip.

I don't have a choice. The room is small with only a single table in the center. A third soldier guards the room from the outside, so even if I could take both of these guys down, I wouldn't get anywhere.

Aikido taught me not only how to fight, but when not to. This is one of those times.

"Quitas el sostén y las bragas," Alvarado says when I lay my pants on the table next to the shirt.

Swallowing hard, I unclasp my bra, take off my panties, and cross my arms in front of me, trying to hide as much of myself as I can from these two men leering at me like I'm some prize they won.

But they don't touch me. My clothes, on the other hand... Guerrero scans them all with a metal detector and Alvarado checks every seam and fold. When they finish, they advance on me. "Face the wall."

Ryker prepared me for this, but I still want to cry when they run their hands through my hair, under my breasts, and between my ass cheeks. At least they spare me the horror of sticking their fingers inside me.

"*Vestirse.*"

I can't get my hands on my bra and panties fast enough when Alvarado gives the order for me to get dressed again. Guerrero examines everything in my bag, then asks me for my phone's unlock code.

"I'll give it to the general after I see Trevor Moana."

Alvarado grabs a fistful of my hair and wrenches my head back. "You do not give the orders."

"Neither do you," I snap, and he shoves me against the wall hard enough the impact ignites sparks of pain from my shoulder all the way down my arm, and my knees buckle, sending me to the ground.

"It is useless to resist," he says as he towers over me. "Everyone breaks here."

Peering up at him, I force strength into my voice. "I'll stop resisting as soon as the general gives me what I want."

They move faster than I expect, and I'm bent over the table with my arms pinned at the small of my back. Panic floods me, and I scream, but all they do is cuff me—making the bracelets so tight, my fingers start to tingle—before they take me to Sublevel 1, march me down a short hallway, and then lock me in a cell.

"Turn and press your hands to the bars," Alvarado says, and when I do, he removes the cuffs. "You will wait here until the general is ready for you. Do not expect it to be soon."

As soon as they leave, I sink down onto the thin cot and choke back a sob.

I'm not hurt. They didn't do anything my doctor hasn't done.

Well, except for sliding a hand between my ass cheeks. My doctor has *never* done that.

I don't know how long the general's going to make me wait, but there's a camera right outside my cell, so all I can do is look scared. Not difficult. Having mortar fire exploding all around me was less terrifying than this. At least then, I had armed soldiers protecting me. Now...I'm alone.

Drawing my knees up, I wrap my arms around my shins and bow my head.

"Look beat," Ryker says as we're going over the plan. "Make him think he's getting to you."

I start to rock back and forth in tiny movements. After a few minutes, I get to my feet and curl my fingers around the bars. "General Ochoa! How long do you plan on keeping me down here? I'm an American. There's a record of me entering this country. When I don't show up for work in two days, the Washington Post will break the story I wrote before I left. Want to know what's in it? You. Your name. Your face. And copies of all of our text messages. You were careful. Didn't use a traceable number. But I know it's you. And so will the rest of the world."

I barely have time to curl up on the cot again before the soldiers are back. But this time, there are four of them. I'm surrounded as they bring me down another level. According to the blueprints, this is the command center. We pass a room with dozens of monitors lining the wall, each showing a group of cells. I try to stop and catch a glimpse of Trevor, but one of the soldiers behind me yells at me to keep moving, and the other shoves me forward.

A break room of sorts is next, and then it's the general's office. He sits behind his desk, hands folded one on top of the other, that insincere smile along with his shiny medals making him look like a demented clown.

"Leave us," he says to the soldiers as he rises and rounds his desk to stand in front of me. The moment the door shuts, he backhands me, and I stumble, dizzy, my right cheek exploding in hot pain. "That is for taunting me."

I don't fight the tears that well in my eyes, nor the tremble in my voice. "Please. I just want to know Trevor's okay. You said—"

Another blow to my other cheek, and this time, I go down. The room is spinning now, and stars dot my vision. I struggle to get to my feet, falling over twice before I let my shoulders slump and stay down. The general, apparently bored by my pathetic struggles, turns and walks over to a side board where he pours a tall glass of water, and that gives me the opportunity I need.

The piece of rubber in the sole of my shoe doesn't look or feel any different from the rest, but Ryker made me practice a hundred times with my eyes closed, so I know exactly where I need to wedge my fingernail to pry it loose and palm the comms unit.

"I'm...s-sorry," I manage as I cup my cheek, shoving the little device into my left ear at the same time. Now, I have to hope he won't hit me again. "I just...he wouldn't have even come here if it weren't for me. I have to tell him how sorry I am."

"You will have the opportunity. After you prove yourself useful," the general says as he drains the glass and pours another, then holds it up to the light. "This is the freshest, purest water in Venezuela. In my office, and in my private quarters, there are only the finest things. Out there," he waves his hand towards the door, "it is very different."

In my ear, a tiny hiss of static is followed by Ry's voice. "If he touches you, he'll die screaming."

As pleasant as I find that mental image at the moment, there's nothing I won't do to get to Trevor. "Wh-what do I need to do to stay...here?"

"Cooperate. Luis Rojas has given up many secrets during

his time here. But not all. There are pockets of the Democrática Resistencia that still hide from us. Rojas knows how to find them, but he will not tell me, no matter how many times I send him to Sublevel Five. With his daughter in danger, however, the daughter he risked everything to smuggle out of this country, I believe he would give me the information I need."

"You want to hurt me to get him to talk." I scoot away as the general approaches, but before I've managed to move more than a foot, my back hits a chair.

"Not seriously, you understand." He holds out his hand, then nods at me to take it. I don't have much choice, so I let him pull me to my feet, then steady me as I wobble, still a little dizzy. "You would heal." He reaches out to skim my cheekbone.

What the hell is he doing?

"You are a beautiful woman, señorita." I hold my breath as he drags a finger from my neck to the first button on my shirt, then flicks it open and traces a line just above the cup of my bra. "A small amount of pain is worth your freedom, no?"

"And after? After he tells you what you need to know?" I don't have to fake the tremble in my voice now. Having him this close to me makes me want to vomit, and I'm scared I'll never see Trevor again, even with Ryker in my ear.

"Well, there is another matter. The CIA spy you say is so important to you? I need information from him as well. The names of all the other CIA assets in Venezuela. He will not break so easily. Unless you were to beg him."

Austin growls, "He'd die before he'd give up a single goddamned name," and Ryker tells him to shut up. If I could respond to them, I'd tell Austin the same thing. This isn't helping. I should have waited to put the earwig in, except now, they can hear—and record—everything the general's saying. It was always part of our plan. One of the contingencies Ryker built in.

"If I can get the names...get him to...to talk. Then what?"

"Then you will all be free to go. You, Rojas, and even the CIA spy. I will have no use for him after that." The general leads me over to the sideboard where he pours a second glass of water and hands it to me. "I am a reasonable man, Señorita Monroe. Or...Daniella. May I call you Daniella?"

"Y-yes. Daniella is fine." It's not. The only person I ever want to call me Daniella ever again is Trevor. While we're in bed. Safe. Away from this monster and everything he's built here. "I just want to see Luis—my father—and Trevor. Please. I'll help you. Hurt me if you need to. Just let me live." My words come faster and faster now. "I'll even send an email to my editor at the Post and tell him not to publish the story. I'll tell him anything you want me to." I set the water down and reach for the general's uniform jacket, holding on tight. "Please. General Ochoa, I'm a reporter. Getting people to talk? To believe me? It's what I do."

The general's lips curve into a smile, and this time, I think it's actually genuine. He believes he's broken me. Hell, I think I'd believe it if I were watching. Austin always said I could have been an actress.

"Then let us begin, Daniella." He stares down at my hands, still clutching his jacket, and I let go, sliding one of his medals free from his lapel and hiding it inside my clenched fist. If he notices, this could all go sideways in a hurry. But if not, it's one more weapon. And I have a feeling I'm going to need it.

General Ochoa pours a generous shot of rum into a rocks glass and offers it to me. "To strengthen you for what is coming. There will be pain, Daniella. That cannot be avoided."

"What the hell?" Ryker says in my ear. "Alpha Team, prepare to infil on my mark. We're not waiting for shift change."

"I'm fine," I say and hope Ryker understands I'm talking to him as much—if not more—than the general. "I can handle pain. It's nothing Lois Lane wouldn't do for Superman."

The general gives me a look that might be respect while Ryker swears. But he also tells the team to stand down.

"Very well." Pressing a button on his desk, Ochoa calls for the guards, and they march in, then clasp their hands behind their backs, awaiting his next order. Alvarado and Guerrero are in front, and my stomach does a somersault as I flash back to the moment I thought they were going to assault me before I squeeze my eyes shut and force myself to return to the present.

"Take her to Sublevel Three."

ALVARADO AND GUERRERO don't let go of my arms until they force me down into a chair inside a small room. Another chair sits facing me, empty, and they tie my wrists and ankles down, then step aside.

I managed to slip the general's pin into my pocket when I was in his office, but in this position, there's no way I can reach it.

Long minutes pass, and my insides are doing jumping jacks as my nerves ratchet higher and higher. When the door behind me opens, my entire body jerks.

"*Dios mio.*"

I crane my neck to see Luis being dragged into the room by two of the general's men with Ochoa following closely. He's no longer clean-shaven, or even clean. His face has aged a decade in the few days since the interview.

When he's tied to the chair facing me, I hold his gaze, hoping with everything in me that he won't give the general what he wants.

"Luis. *Lo siento,*" I whisper. *I'm sorry.*

He shakes his head, his eyes glistening. "General Ochoa, what is the meaning of this? She is innocent of any crime."

"She is not. She came here under false pretenses. She lied,

and she will pay for those lies unless you tell me where the Democrática Resistencia is keeping their money."

"I cannot. *Por favor.* I have been here for too long. There were plans in place if one of us were to be captured." Luis's desperation climbs with every word, and he struggles weakly, panting from the effort.

"That is unfortunate," Ochoa says. He slides a folding knife from his pocket and flicks it open. My stomach lurches, and I shake my head, unable to stop myself from whimpering.

It does no good as he lunges for me, grabs my hair, and forces my head back. The slice to my cheek is so fast that, at first, I don't even feel it. But a heartbeat later, my scream echoes off the walls and my thoughts fuzz. Something warm drips down my jaw, and fiery pain consumes the entire right side of my face.

The taste of blood makes me retch, which only makes the pain worse.

"Tell me!" General Ochoa shouts. "Where can I find the last of the dissidents? Who leads them? You will talk or she will suffer so much more."

"Please do not harm her!" Luis's cry rouses me from the haze of pain, and I force my head up, blinking hard to make sense of the shifting shapes before me. Darkness threatens to obscure everything, but after I manage a deep breath, the general's satisfied grin is the first thing I see.

Another flash of the knife and more flames lick along my collarbone. Shit. How much blood can I lose before I pass out?

"Do you wish to see her die?"

"No!"

"Then tell me what I need to know."

Yes. *Si.* I will," he says. "Anything. Do something for her, *por favor.* There is too much blood."

Ochoa's eyes take on an odd glean up as he pulls out a

lighter and runs the knife through the flame. My entire body starts to shake. No. He can't. He wouldn't.

"General Ochoa," I whimper. "I was wrong...about that drink."

He ignores me and presses the red hot blade to the wound on my cheek. The world goes quiet and dark, only muffled shouts reaching my consciousness as I drown in an ocean of agony.

"Stop. She cannot take any more!" Luis's voice sounds like it's coming through a long tunnel. One I have to fight my way through.

"S'okay," I mumble and blink back my tears. His horrified expression shifts in and out of focus.

Think. You need to focus. Tell him something. Anything.

"Catherine would want you to be free." I hold Luis's gaze. My birth mother never went by Catherine. It's the only thing I can think to say that might stop him from giving up everything he knows, because the truth is written all over his face.

Seeing me in pain broke him.

The soldiers untie him and drag him towards the door, but as he passes me, he reaches for my hand. His fingers slip quickly from mine—bound to the chair, I can't move to hold onto him, but he whispers, "Catherine would have loved you."

I hope to God that means he got my message, and when it's just the general, me, and Alvarado left in the room, I swallow hard and look up at Ochoa. "I did my part." Every word hurts as the very act of speaking tugs at the newly cauterized wound, but it has to be getting close to shift change, and I still haven't seen Trevor.

"*Si*. You did. If Rojas tells me what I want to know, he will be released."

"Let me see Trevor." When his eyes harden, I quickly add, "Please. He'll listen to me. Just...let me hold him. I can't do this from across a room. Not with him. After that, there's nothing else you can possibly want from us. Trevor hasn't been in the CIA for years, and I promise we'll never return to Venezuela again."

He inclines his head. "And the news article?"

"I'll call my editor. After I see Trevor. Bring me a phone, and I'll say whatever you want me to say. How much longer do I have to wait?"

"Not long at all." Ochoa nods to Alvarado, and they both leave, slamming the door on their way out.

Lowering my head so my hair hopefully hides my lips from the cameras at opposing corners of the room, I whisper, "What time is it at the Daily Planet?"

"Sixteen-forty-four," Ryker hisses in my ear. "One to ten, how bad off are you?"

I can't tell him. Not and be honest about it. My entire body hurts, and the cut on my collarbone is still oozing blood. At least that one wasn't as deep. So I lie. "Three."

"Roger that. Be ready."

If I could risk a reaction, I'd laugh. I was ready to get out of here exactly point-oh-one seconds after I walked through the door.

"I am."

CHAPTER TWENTY-FIVE

Trevor

THE SOLDIERS TOOK Luis maybe thirty minutes ago. I don't know where. I just know they haven't brought him back. Another patrol comes through, and heavy, booted feet stop outside my cell.

I squint up at the two meanest of Ochoa's soldiers—the ones who go off shift just before we're fed—as they unlock my cell and drag me out by my arm. Sparks of pain race down my fingers as the cuffs dig into my wrists.

That's good. It means my hands haven't lost all sensation in the cold.

"Where are you taking me?" I ask. The words are slow and unwieldy. It has to be close to mealtime again. The constant frigid air blowing over my skin means there's no fucking way a single cup of water can keep me from dangerously severe dehydration.

They don't answer.

Dani. I don't know how I can be so certain, but I am. She's here. And if she's here, I hope to God she's not alone.

Thoughts of rescue and escape help me focus, and though I only open my eyes to slits, I take in everything around me. The code one of the men enters on the electronic keypad next to the elevator: six-seven-two-three-nine. Where on their belt they clip the cell door keys. Each of the cameras we pass, including the one inside the elevator.

"Your eyes, ears, and brain are the three best weapons you have." My instructor at Langley used to repeat that bit of wisdom every fucking day. After the first week of training, we all joined in every time he said it. And he was right.

"You're taking me out for dinner, aren't you? Or to the spa. You shouldn't have." Joking with these assholes isn't going to end well for me, but their reactions are valuable intel.

Two swift punches to my gut follow in rapid succession, but I'm prepared, and while they hurt, they don't do any real damage. As the guards let me fall to the floor, I force out a hoarse chuckle. "A massage then. Great."

The guard on the left tenses like he's going to hit me again, but the other one stops him. "Not yet."

They don't want me to be a complete mess. Either Dani's here or she's demanding to see proof of life. Either way, it still means I'll have some sort of contact with her.

The guards stop just outside a closed door and remove the belly chain. "Stand up," one of them barks.

I try, but my legs won't hold me. "Fat chance of that. Should have gotten me that massage first."

General Ochoa emerges from the elevator with a look of pure excitement on his face. "You are a fortunate man, Señor Moana. To have someone who cares for you as much as Daniella? It is a wonderful thing."

I want to punch him in his smug face for calling her by her first name. But I can't. "What did you do to her?"

"Nothing she did not volunteer for. I give you my word."

Fear snakes cold tendrils around my heart. If he's hurt her...I won't be able to live with myself.

"She's the best of all of us, you know that?"

Austin's words from so long ago haunt me. She is. She always has been.

The general rests his hand on the door knob. "You have five minutes with her. After that, you will give me the information I require, or I will be forced to have her moved to Sublevel Five as well."

"You even *show* her Sublevel Five, asshole—"

"Watch your tone, *pendejo*," he snarls. "You have no power here, and unless you want Daniella to become a permanent resident of La Cripta, you will not speak to me that way again."

Ochoa punches in the code for the door, and the two guards shove me inside.

"Trevor! Oh, God."

I'm going to kill Ochoa. Painfully. Her face... Blood stains her cheek, all the way down to her jaw, and a thick line of burned and blistered skin follows the contour of her cheekbone. Another long cut along her collarbone is still bleeding. Fuck. She has to be in agony, and it's all my fault. Her just *being* here is my fault. I can't find my voice as she nudges my arms up so she can duck under them and rest her uninjured cheek against my neck.

"You're so cold, TJ. Just...hold on to me."

I do. For too long. But I might never get this chance again. As soon as Ochoa pulls me out of here, I'm going to kill him for what he did to her. I don't know how; I'm too weak to stand, but I'll find a way.

"Dani. What—what did he do to you?"

"It doesn't matter. You're all that matters," she says as she holds me tightly. "I'm sorry. I'm so sorry."

"For what?" Having her pressed against me makes everything else in the world fade away, if only for a few minutes, and I can't think of a single damn thing she should be sorry for.

"The article. It wasn't me. My editor published it. I left notes at the end of the article that said it couldn't go out, that it wasn't done, that lives depended on this staying quiet until I gave the word, but he did it anyway." Her tears soak into the dirty red prison shirt, and she hisses in pain. I don't give a fuck about the article. Or about anything but getting her out of here alive.

"Look at me, baby. Please."

Dani wriggles out from under my arms, and when I lock on to her haunted gaze, I hate myself for everything I've done. Pushing her away all those years ago. Not trusting her with my past—and Gil's—not protecting her from that bastard general, but most of all, for thinking, even for a minute, that she might have put her career ahead of my safety.

"You're not the one who should be sorry. I am. But we don't have much time. Ochoa said five minutes. If I don't tell him what he wants to know, he's—"

Her lips brush mine. Gently at first, then with pure, raw desperation. "Ten minutes," she whispers against my ear, her breath warm on my chilled skin. A low tone buzzes from some-where close, and I don't understand what it is until she corrects herself. "Seven."

She's on comms.

"You have to tell the general what he wants to know," Dani says, then winces and cups her cheek. "Dammit. That wasn't..." Her eyes flutter, and she collapses against me.

"Dani, breathe."

The door opens, and Ochoa's harsh voice makes us both jump. "Your time is up, Señor Moana." The general snaps his fingers, and two of his men appear behind Dani. "Take her back to her cell."

"Wait!" Dani's fingers curl around mine, and I tense when I feel her press something hard against my palm. Her gaze is almost...triumphant. "Tell him everything, Trev. Please. Then, we can get out of here."

She keeps repeating those words until the door slams shut, and the other two men who entered with the general pick me up and deposit me into a chair.

I still have whatever she gave me hidden, and as I look the general up and down, I realize what it is. One of his complement of medals. It's not much of a weapon, but it's the only thing I have, and it's better than nothing.

Ochoa drops a small notebook and pen in my lap. "What will it be, Señor Moana? Freedom? A long life with the beautiful Daniella outside of Venezuela? Or a very short one where you will both be in constant agony?"

Seven minutes. Less now. If I can stall long enough, we'll have a chance. "You're the worst kind of asshole, Ochoa. One who thinks he's better than everyone else. I'm only doing this for Dani. Because you hurt her, and I won't *ever* let that happen again."

With my wrists still cuffed and the medal hidden in my left hand, it's awkward as hell to write, but I start making up names and randomly picking cities and neighborhoods these fictional assets live in. I stop after the fifth name, pretending to be too tired to continue. "I could...finish this...a lot easier...if you gave me some food...shithead."

One of the soldiers knocks me off the chair, but before he can haul me back up again, the lights flicker and then go off completely.

Dani

Locked in a cell on the basement's top level, I grab the rough blanket off the bed and press it to the cut on my collarbone.

The pain makes me hiss, but it's nothing compared to the throbbing in my cheek.

It has to be shift change by now. Ry, Austin, and Graham should be inside.

"Lois. What's your location?" Ry asks.

I turn away from the cameras. "Sublevel One. Third cell on the right. Superman's on Sublevel Three. Door facing the elevator. Or was."

"Hold tight."

Only seconds later, something shakes the floor under my feet. Holy shit. All of a sudden, carrying that tin of thinking putty filled with C4 in my bag, only *inches from my heart*, seems like a very stupid idea. The lights flicker, and then I'm plunged into darkness.

The elevator doors inch open, a faint glow spilling from the interior. I squint as three men fan out in formation. Graham— he's all wiry muscles, as opposed to Austin's bulk and Ry's... mountain-like silhouette—heads straight for me. Less than a minute later, he has the cell door open. "Want to get out of here, Lois?"

"Hell, yes."

He holds out his hand, and I take it, letting him pull me forward until the men surround me.

"Put these on." Graham helps me with a pair of night-vision goggles, and I cry out as the rubber eye cup hits the fresh burn on my cheek. "Shit. Sorry."

"One to ten, Lois. How bad is the pain? Honesty this time," Ry says.

"Six."

He makes a low, frustrated sound. "Jimmy, get her out of here."

"No. Trevor's in bad shape. I'm not leaving him." I hold out my hand, staring at Graham through the goggles that make the world glow green. "Hand it over, Jimmy."

He looks to Ry, then pulls a Beretta from his vest. "Don't make me regret this."

I haven't fired a gun in ten years, but some things you never forget. Like the hours my dad—my real dad, the one who adopted me and never once looked back—spent teaching me how to shoot. "I won't."

Ryker sweeps his gaze over the other cells. In Spanish, he calls out, "We're putting an end to the Crypt tonight. In two hours, the Democrática Resistencia will liberate you all."

A chorus of cheers follows, and Ry nods. "Let's go get our boy back."

CHAPTER TWENTY-SIX

Trevor

"Find out what is going on," Ochoa spits out. A beam of light pierces the darkness, and one of the guards snatches the pen away from me before the three of them leave the room. The door locks, leaving nothing but pitch black around me. A moment later, a loud alarm starts blaring at regular intervals.

I trained for this. Too many years ago, but some things you never forget. My fingers are still stiff after so long in the freezing cold, but I pry the pin open and start to work on my handcuffs. Twice, I drop the medal, and to retrieve it, I have to feel around blindly until the sharp point digs into my palm.

But after the longest minutes of my life, the cuffs clatter to the ground. Now to get out of this room and find Dani.

My legs cramp constantly as I inch towards the door, but I force my body to ignore the pain. I'd crawl through fire for Dani, and now that I know we're not alone, I can endure anything if it means we have a chance to be together again.

On my knees, I fumble for the lock and get to work. With my hands free, I'm faster, and the door opens almost silently.

The two times I've been to this level, I've never seen anyone else, but that doesn't mean it's empty.

Staccato bursts of low, almost muffled sounds echo from above me. Gunfire. I have to find Dani and get the fuck out of here before there's more blood on my conscience. My family's blood. I don't know who's here with her, but it doesn't matter if it's West, Graham, Ford, or Ryker. Or anyone else from Hidden Agenda or Second Sight. They're all family.

Using the wall for support, I close my eyes and clench my jaw, then push myself up. My quads and hamstrings feel like they're tearing into a thousand pieces, and my eyes water, but I'm standing for the first time since they locked me in that frigid cell.

"You can do this. One foot in front of the other."

Three times, I fall. But I get back up. I have to find Dani. The guards and Ochoa aren't anywhere around, so there's a stairwell somewhere. In the pitch darkness, I have to rely on my other senses, and I feel along the wall, finding a window, another locked door right next to it, and then a second window. In another six steps, I'm at the end of the hall, and then a door next to me bursts open, sending my heartbeat skyrocketing.

"About damn time." Ryker. His voice shouldn't shock me. This is what he does. But we've barely talked since all the shit went down with Ripper and Cara. He only said half a dozen words to me at the wedding. I never expected *him* to lead the rescue team.

Yet, he's the one who catches me when my legs give out, and if I thought he'd let me, I'd hug him. I'm so damn overwhelmed that he'd risk his team breaking into the most notorious prison in the Southern Hemisphere, I don't know what to say.

"Relax, superman. We'll do the work from here." He claps his hand on my shoulder and holds on for the briefest of moments before passing me to another set of strong arms.

"Superman?"

"Just go with it," Austin says as he shifts me so he can still hold a gun. "We were running out of characters."

Somewhere close, I can sense Dani, and I look around blindly, needing to know she's okay.

"Can it. Gotta find Rojas, then we can get the fuck out of here," Ry says. "Gear him up and let's go."

"Put these on." This voice belongs to Graham, I think, who hands me a pair of NVGs, then shoves a comms unit into my right ear. As soon as I get the goggles situated, my surroundings come into focus, and I can see Dani between Austin and Graham.

"Eyes and ears, ready to go," I say.

"About to have company," Ronan says over the line, and if I wasn't certain we were going to find trouble at any minute, I'd have some words for him. Like how much more training he needs before coming on a mission like this. "A dozen hostiles breaching the exterior doors."

"This is gonna get messy," Ry mutters.

He's about to say something else when emergency lights start flashing, the sudden brightness burning our eyes through the night vision. Almost as one, we tear off the NVGs. A pained whimper escapes Dani's lips, and she grabs onto my arm. We're all blind, and we're sitting ducks.

"Move!" Ry orders. "Get Superman and Lois back up to the second level. Do *not* go any higher. Not with all the hostiles headed right for us. Base, what can you do about those goddamn lights?"

"Working on it," Wren says, tension lacing her tone.

The elevator starts to whirr, and in front of me, I can feel Ryker tense. "Go. Now!" he says and slaps Austin on the back as he and Graham raise their rifles and advance on the elevator.

The door to the stairwell closes behind us to a burst of gunfire, and we double-time it up the stairs. My legs are still screaming in agony, but Austin supports much of my weight, and each step is easier than the last. By the time we reach the second level, I think I might be able to stand on my own.

Austin passes me off to Dani, then cracks the door. Her arm tightens around my waist, and fuck, it's the best feeling in the world to have her next to me again. "I can manage, baby," I whisper in her ear. "As long as you're safe, I can do anything."

"Don't be an idiot," she hisses back.

"Clear," Austin says. "Let's go. We're headed for the security room. If base can't cut the power again, at least we'll be able to see what's coming for us. Plus, that door should be reinforced according to the blueprints."

We don't make it three steps before a barrage of gunfire erupts from the other end of the floor. I pull Dani against the wall while Austin starts to bob and weave, returning fire as he heads for the cadre of soldiers fifty feet away. "Go!" he shouts.

My quads strain as we rush forward, and those damn flashing lights make it almost impossible to get my bearings with any certainty. Dani pushes through a door and freezes as the overhead lights flicker to light and flood the room in sudden brightness.

"Drop the gun, Daniella," Ochoa says. His pistol is aimed directly at Dani's head.

She doesn't move, and I squeeze her shoulders before letting her go. We need to keep Ochoa occupied until someone hears we're in trouble or I can find a way to disarm him. "It's okay. Just set it down gently."

Dani inches in front of me, putting herself between me and Ochoa. "It's too late, General. I was lying when I told you the news article about you was coming out in two days. Part One went out two hours ago. And there's a hell of a lot more in it than just a few incriminating text messages."

"Gun. Now," he says, but there's fear in his eyes. Behind him, on the monitors, I can see Ryker and Graham moving through Sublevel Four, firing the occasional shot and dropping soldier after soldier who stands in their way. And then, one who holds up his hands in surrender and gestures something I can't understand.

Dani hasn't moved. Her right arm is down by her side, the barrel of the gun pointed towards the floor. She's not a threat. Not when the general is ready to fire. But she's not giving in either.

"Aren't you interested in what else I found?" she asks sweetly. "Because you might want to consider running far away from here. Presidente Farías won't be too happy with you when he learns you've been siphoning off a portion of the money *he's* stealing from the Venezuelan people."

"*Puta,*" Ochoa growls. Striding forward, he grabs Dani's wrist and wrenches it hard. She cries out in pain and drops her weapon while he jabs the barrel of his pistol against her side.

On one of the monitors, Austin heads straight for us, and the look in his eyes? That's the most controlled man I've ever met about to blow his stack and burn down the world.

"Call me a bitch one more time," Dani manages as the general pulls her away from me, "and you'll be sorry."

"I do not think so, *puta*. You will regret ever coming here. So will your CIA spy when he has to watch me have my way with you."

"Ready to breech," Austin says on comms. "Distraction coming in five, four, three, two, one." Multiple shots right outside the door pull Ochoa's gaze away from Dani, and she grabs the barrel of the gun with one hand and the general's wrist with the other, twisting sharply. He's caught off guard, and I surge forward, dropping my shoulder and catching him under his right arm. The three of us go down in a heap as Austin kicks the door in.

"I can't get a shot!" He's pissed as hell, but this bastard's mine. Dani wrestles the gun away from him, but Ochoa uses his free hand to punch her in the face, and she yelps, losing her hold on the weapon.

"Get Dani," I grunt as I ram my fist into the general's back, landing a hard strike in the vicinity of his right kidney. That gives me enough time to snatch the gun from the floor.

Austin grabs Dani around the waist and pulls her off of Ochoa, and as she sputters a protest, I hold the bastard's gaze, the gun pressed to his heart. "You should have known, asswipe. I don't break promises," I say, then squeeze the trigger.

***

Dani

Half a dozen armed resistance fighters help liberate the facility, and within an hour of Trevor killing Ochoa, The Crypt is nothing but a burned out shell. Ry, Graham, and Ronan went back through the lower floors after everyone still living had been cleared out and set explosives on every level.

"Blowing it now," Ry says from his position just outside of the open doors of the van. Trevor leans against me, and though he looks a lot better after two bottles of water and a protein bar, there's a haunted, almost vacant look in his eyes that breaks my heart.

The ground under us shakes, and even from half a mile away, we can hear The Crypt's windows shatter.

Trevor jerks, and I reach over and cup his cheek. "Look at me, TJ." As soon as he does, I regret asking. With the bright red wound now bisecting my cheek and blood staining my face and chest, every time he sees me, he blames himself even more.

I don't know how we can get past this. Or if we ever will. But dammit, I have to try to get through to him. "Listen to me. I am never going to give up on you. I lost you once because I was too scared to get in your face and tell you how I felt. I'm not now."

He starts to protest, but Austin clears his throat as he ducks his head inside the van. "Dani, Luis is here."

Letting Trevor go feels wrong, but Luis had to watch Ochoa torture me, and he's the reason for everything that's happened since I walked into Trevor's office two weeks ago. The good and the bad. "I'll be right back," I whisper as I brush my lips to Trevor's cheek.

Luis leans heavily on Franco and another man—one of the resistance fighters—and his eyes light up as I step out of the van.

"Mi hija—"

The term—*my daughter*—sends panic flooding me. "Don't. Please." Behind me, Trevor gets to his feet, and I glance back at him. He's in full protective mode, but I shake my head, and he sinks back down onto the bench seat, but keeps his eyes glued on me.

"I'm sorry," I say when I turn back to Luis. "That came out wrong." A deep breath shudders through me, and I try again. "Kate died when I was less than a year old. When I was eight, I was adopted by two amazing people. Steve and Betsy are my parents in every way that counts." Looking to Austin, I hold out my hand, and he joins me. "And this is their son, my brother, Austin."

Luis's eyes water, and he presses his lips together when they start to wobble.

"This...me coming here? It was never about replacing my dad. It was about finding the man who saved Kate from a dangerous, terrible situation, and being able to look him in the eyes and thank him."

A single tear spills onto his cheek. "I put you in great danger," he says. "I understand if you cannot forgive me."

"No!" I rush forward and take Luis's hand. "There's nothing to forgive. You have to see that." With a quick peek back at Trevor, I hope he understands my words are meant as much for him as Luis. "You are a good man. A fighter. A leader. Once I learned that, I had to do something. I thought writing an article for the Post would be enough. That if I did my job and prayed for a miracle, that I'd be able to help you—and the Venezuelan people. And learn a little about where I came from."

"You did that," he says.

"No." Shaking my head makes my cheek throb, but I hide my wince as I release Luis's hand and gesture to the men around me. "We did that. All of us. Along with half a dozen people back in the United States. And you."

"I did nothing but cause you pain. You were injured because of me. You could have been killed. Because of me. I abandoned you so many years ago, and now—"

I stop him. "Luis, you gave me so much more than you'll ever know. But, I can't stay here, and you can't leave. The people here need you. Once we release all the records we found of Farías and Ochoa's crimes, this country is going to need leaders who care. Who are honest and good and will do what's best for its people. You're one of them."

Luis's shoulders straighten, and his chest puffs out slightly at my praise.

"I don't think I can ever come back to Venezuela again. But...maybe when things settle down a bit, you could call me. Or send me an email."

He nods, another tear staining his cheek. "I would like that. To know you."

I hug the man I may never call father, but who will forever be a part of my family, and then watch as his brother and the other resistance fighter help him back down the street.

Ryker appears without warning at my side and stares down at me. "Ready to get the fuck out of here?"

Looking back at Trevor, I realize just how much I need to get him alone so we can talk about...everything. "Hell yes."

CHAPTER TWENTY-SEVEN

Trevor

Nothing around me feels real.

Dani and Austin on either side of me. Ryker behind the wheel with Graham next to him. Ronan sitting behind me.

Am I still in the cell at The Crypt? Dying from dehydration, lack of sleep, and starvation? Did that bastard Ochoa finally kill me and this is some sort of afterlife?

The van hits a pothole, and every muscle in my body protests, jolting me enough that some sense of reality bleeds through the fog in my brain, and I pull Dani tighter against me.

"Trev?" Dani rests her head on my shoulder. "What is it?"

I don't have the words to tell her how I feel, and it hits me that I never even questioned where we were going. "What's—" I cough, my throat suddenly too tight, "What's the plan now?"

Ry glances up at the rearview mirror, locking his eyes on me for a brief moment. "Safehouse so you and Dani can clean up and rest. Gotta pack up all of our shit and scrub the space clean. Wheels up at 0800 tomorrow morning."

Rest. I'm so fucking tired, and the idea of sleeping somewhere warm, somewhere I'm not cuffed, somewhere I can stretch my legs...it's all I want. Rest and Dani.

I let my thoughts wander, but I keep seeing her face when Ochoa's men dragged me into that room. The bright, angry burn. The blood staining her cheek, her neck, her chest.

"We're here," Dani says as the van coasts to a stop. "Let's get you inside."

I let her lead me, her arm around my waist. Ry directs us into a small bedroom with two sleeping bags laid out next to one another. Graham follows with a duffel bag, and Ronan brings in two chairs.

"Sit," Graham says. "Without West here, I'm the closest thing you have to a field medic."

I look to Ry, and he scowls. "I sent West and Inara to a SEER refresher course in the Everglades the day before you were arrested. They're not due to report in until—" he checks his watch, "—an hour ago. Gotta check in with Wren." He pauses at the door. "Graham knows what he's doing."

The look on Graham's face is pure shock. "You all heard that, right? If I asked you to repeat it, you would?"

Dani chuckles, then winces and cups her cheek. "Dammit. I'll repeat anything as long as you don't make me laugh again."

Graham's gaze pings between the two of us. "Trevor, take off your shirt."

"No. Dani first."

"Trev—" she protests.

I can't watch her in pain another minute longer. "Dani, please."

Whatever she hears in my voice gets through to her, and she tucks a lock of hair behind her ear, giving Graham a clear view of the cauterized wound. He swabs it with disinfectant, and Dani hisses and sways in the chair until I stabilize her with my arm around her waist

"Breathe, baby."

"Uh huh." Every second Graham works feels like an hour, but eventually, he cleans all the blood from her face and treats the burn with a thin layer of gel.

The slice across her collarbone is next, but it isn't deep, thank God. "This'll be fine in a few days," he says as he affixes the last of five butterfly bandages to her skin. "I'd be surprised if the hits you took to your face don't hurt more."

"They do," she says, and I stare at her. All I saw was the scar she'll have for the rest of her life, but now that I force myself to look closer, I hate myself even more. Both of her cheeks are shades of purple, and her left eye is swollen slightly.

"Fuck, Dani. What happened before—?"

"Later, Trev. Please. Let Graham take a look at you." Her gaze holds enough pain to last a lifetime. We're going to have a long talk when we're alone because I have to know everything that bastard did to her.

Other than the severe chafing around my wrists from the cuffs, bruises up and down my torso, and the lingering weakness and muscle cramps, none of my injuries are serious, and Graham packs up his kit, leaving us with an extra tube of burn gel and several packets of over the counter painkillers.

"Bathroom's there," he says, pointing to a door across the hall. "Dani, try to keep hot water off your cheek, but otherwise, you should both be fine to shower. Go clean up if you want. We'll get some MREs ready."

I stand when Graham does and reach for his arm. "Why did you come?"

To his credit, the kid—hell, he's only a couple of years younger than I am—the man doesn't ask me to elaborate. Just shrugs. "You're one of us. Why wouldn't I?"

DANI LEADS me into the bathroom and turns on the hot water.

The mirror's cracked down the center, and the tub/shower combination has seen better days. But for a safehouse on the outskirts of Caracas, this is pure luxury, and something I wasn't sure I'd ever see again. Just like the woman in front of me who unbuttons her blouse and throws it into the trash.

Her black slacks are next, followed by her bra and underwear. "I don't ever want to see those clothes again," she says. "Or these." Her fingers wrap around the waistband of the thin, dark red pants.

They land in the garbage along with the rough, prison-issue white briefs. "Oh, Trev..." Dani skims her hands over my ribs, circling me and cataloging every bruise, every scrape and cut. "Come on. You're still freezing."

Until she said the words, I hadn't noticed. But once I'm under the spray, I realize just how bad off I am. By the lack of steam in the room, the water's not much above warm, but my hands and feet feel like they're on fire, and I grit my teeth. Dani's worried enough about me already, and I don't know how to tell her about the past...however long it's been.

The scent of soap gradually replaces the stench clinging to me, and I close my eyes and focus on the sensation of Dani's hands on my skin.

"Hey, tough guy. You're looking a little unsteady there. Put your arms around me," she says softly, and when I do, she washes my hair. "You don't have to tell me what happened unless you want to. But you do have to forgive yourself."

I open my eyes to find her watching me, and I can't hold it in any longer. "You almost died, Dani." As soon as I say the words, I lose control, sobbing as I bury my face against her neck. "You never should have come for me."

"I will *always* come for you," she says as her lips brush my ear. "Always. Because that's what you do for the person you *love*, Trevor. You show up. You fight. You don't give up." She's crying now too. I can feel her shoulders shake, feel the shuddering breaths as she struggles to regain control. "I love you."

Her admission shakes me to my core, but she doesn't stop. She repeats it over and over again.

"I love you. I love you. I love you. You're it for me, Trevor, and you always have been."

My legs give out, and Dani sinks down to the floor with me, the water running over us as we hold on to one another. I want to say the words back to her, but I don't know how.

———

She has to help me dress, and I lean on her as we head for the main room with the rest of the team.

"For fuck's sake, sit your ass down, Trevor," Ryker says. "You look like shit."

"Yeah, I'm going to give The Crypt a terrible Yelp review. Accommodations left a lot to be desired."

Dani isn't having any of my gallows humor, and frowns at me as she accepts a cup of coffee from Graham.

"Sorry, Danisaur."

Ryker snorts. "Danisaur? That's fucking perfect for her." When Dani turns her icy stare on him, he arches a brow. "You're the one who convinced Dax and Ford to send you on this mission. You're a damn fierce woman, Dani." Ry offers her his hand and, after a minute, Dani shakes it.

Ronan passes me an MRE, and the scent of brisket and cheesy potatoes makes my stomach growl. No one says much as we eat, and when I finish my first meal, Ronan's right there with a second for me.

The coffee's every bit as good as it was on the mission to Afghanistan to liberate Ripper, even without West here, and after an hour, the exhaustion has caught up with me. Otherwise, I feel almost human. Though the distance between me and Dani is growing by the minute. She picked at her food. Even gave me her dessert of grainy cappuccino pudding.

I want to take her back into the bedroom, shut the door, and demand she talk to me, but before I can get up, a ringing sounds from one of the four laptops set up on the coffee table across the room.

Ryker taps a few keys, and the screen flickers to life, showing Dax and Ford in Dax's office.

"He's there," Ford tells Dax. "Looks like shit, but he's alive."

"Thank fuck," Dax mutters. "Trevor, when you get back, we're goin' to have a little talk about why you never told us you grew up best friends with the head of JSOC."

I gape at the screen. "I was arrested, extradited to Venezuela, and locked up in The Crypt. You had to finance a rescue mission, find people to risk their lives for me, and *that's* what you have a problem with?"

Dax pulls off his glasses and pinches the bridge of his nose. This ought to be good. He's pissed at me, and I'd rather he just spit it out.

"Yeah. That's what I have a problem with. We're family, Trev. I don't give a flying fuck what shit you got yourself into. Whatever it is, we'll fix it. For you and Dani. That's what we do. That's what *family* does. And I didn't have to find people—"

"Dax, I got this," Ry says. He turns to me, and flecks of gold flare in his multicolored eyes. "Listen up, Moana. Not likely you'll ever hear me say this again."

Ryker McCabe commands attention simply by existing. Looming in front of me with his hands on his hips, he's scary as fuck. I push up with a groan so I can look him in the eyes.

"When we found out about Ripper, you didn't hesitate. Didn't think twice about going with us, risking your life to get our brother out of that shithole. Back in September when those two bastards were after him, you not only called in Pritchard, but you rounded up every single member of this family to be there to support him. I'll never forget that."

Graham snorts. "You never forget anything, Ry."

Ryker gives the kid the side-eye and continues, "You're family, Trevor. Whether you want to be or not. You and Dani. You're stuck with us now. Dax didn't have to find anyone to go on this mission. All he had to say was 'Trev's in trouble.' If West and Inara hadn't been unreachable, nothing would have kept them off that plane, and they're both fucking pissed they couldn't be here to help. Ford only stayed in Boston to work his contacts and smooth things over for your return. Family shows up. No matter what. Are we clear?"

He studies me with narrowed eyes, waiting for an answer. For the words. They're there—on the tip of my tongue. But saying them? That's hard. *Hope* is hard. And that's what he's offering.

I clear my throat and manage a nod. "Crystal."

Dani

I unzip the sleeping bags so we can both stretch out on one and use the other as a blanket. Trevor winces as he sinks down beside me. Every time he looks at me, it's like all he sees is the new scar on my cheek. I haven't even tried to see it, but I spread some of the burn gel over it a few minutes ago, and it's...not small.

Seconds after he sprawls out, he's asleep, and though my heart aches and I want nothing more than to wake him up and ask him to talk to me, I know he's exhausted. The first-hand reports from survivors of The Crypt were so horrible.

Extreme sleep deprivation, constant blinding lights, frigid cold, barely enough food and water to survive. Ryker pulled me aside before we got into the van and told me he'd seen the cell Ochoa had kept Trevor in. So small, he'd have been unable to straighten his legs. No wonder he couldn't walk when the general brought him to me.

I don't touch him when I lie down, but I stay close. I need him. Need to know he's here with me. Even if only a piece of him.

"I love you, Trevor. I always will."

STRONG HANDS REACH for me in the darkness, and I mold my body to Trevor's. He's shaking, and as I wrap my arms around him, hot tears hit my shoulder. "Dani," he whispers, his voice hoarse. "You're really here?"

"Yes, *mi amor*. I'm really here." I don't know why I choose that particular phrase. I know Spanish like I know my own name, but I haven't spoken it outside of Venezuela since Gil died. Still, it seems right in this moment. "You're safe."

"Why did you come for me?" His tone holds so much pain, I want to cry. "I'm not worth—"

"Stop that. Right now." In the darkness, I frame his face with my hands and press my lips to his. I don't pull away until his fingers comb through my hair and land on the back of my neck. "You are everything to me," I whisper as I take his other hand and guide his fingers under my shirt to my tattoo. "You're my true north, Trevor. My home. The only place I ever want to be."

Trevor struggles to hold it all in, his entire body rigid.

"I know, Trev. I know." It's all I can offer him. "What was down on Sublevel Five. Wren found reports from two prisoners who'd spent time there. We saw the blueprints. The cells. The forced air system. I can put it all together, *mi amor*. You don't have to tell me. Just let me love you."

His quiet sobs break me, and I cry with him.

"I love you, Daniella," he whispers.

Something deep inside me settles, and when Trevor kisses me, I know he'll be okay. We'll be okay. Eventually. It'll take time, but we have each other.

CHAPTER TWENTY-EIGHT

Trevor

HOME. The plane touched down at Logan half an hour ago. Ronan said his goodbyes before we hit Customs since he still maintains his Irish citizenship. He's taking the T home, but Ford leans against a pillar just past the sliding doors, with Dax standing stiffly next to him. "Need a lift?" Ford asks as he pulls me in for a quick hug.

"Careful," I say when he moves to embrace Dani. "She's—"

"Fine." Dani glares at me for a split second before rising up on her toes to wrap an arm around Ford.

She's not. Though she tried to keep her voice down this morning, I overheard her telling Graham that her face hurt every time she moved. The bruises are so much worse today, and that damn burn on her cheek is going to pain her every day for weeks. Graham cleaned and treated it before we left, and when she came back to the little room we'd slept in, tears still shimmered in her eyes.

"Dax."

He doesn't like to be touched, so I'm not expecting him to

move, but he claps his hand on my shoulder and leans in. "You need to talk about what you went through, you call me. Understood? I made the mistake of keeping all my shit locked up tight for years. Don't do that to yourself or to Dani."

"Understood," I manage, though I don't know how. The lump in my throat feels like it's the size of a baseball.

"You ready to go home?" Ford says with a nod at the terminal's sliding doors.

Dani answers for both of us. "Yes. Very."

We don't have anything close to seasonally appropriate clothing, and I start to shiver violently as we head to Ford's SUV. Dani has her arm around my waist, but the memories still threaten. My wrists ache under the light bandages, and I swear I can't feel my toes anymore, even though the walk takes all of five minutes.

But once we're in the car, Ford blasts the heater, and with Dani pressed to my side, and the radio playing 80s rock, I pull myself out of my own head. "We have to talk about your terrible taste in music one of these days, man. Depeche Mode? Really?"

Ford laughs as he pulls out of the parking garage. "Good to have you back, Trev. But the music stays. My car, my tunes."

From the passenger seat, Dax mutters, "This is why I walk everywhere—or pay a car service."

It feels right to joke around with them. Even if it's a little forced. I run a hand through my hair and stare out the window as the wintery landscape speeds by. Three days. That's all it was. Three days. Most of my CIA training sessions on capture, evasion, and torture resistance were longer than that. I shouldn't be this off balance. I should be able to ground myself here, with Dani.

What if I can't?

She rests her head on my shoulder, her eyes closed. We're both still exhausted, even though Dax arranged for first class tickets from Panama City to Boston. Neither of us slept. Instead, we watched old movies on the in-flight entertainment system, curled up in the plush leather seats, hand in hand.

In the glow from the street lights, a fresh snow starts to fall as Ford pulls over in front of my apartment.

Dax turns in his seat and holds out his hand. "Keys, and Dani? A letter came for you this morning."

"To Second Sight?" she asks, accepting the envelope and running her fingers over the embossing from the Washington Post. "I guess Lincoln figured I'd still be in Boston. It's probably the bill for getting me out of jail."

"Why would they charge you for that?" My knuckles pop as I clench my hands, and I'd like to have a few words with her editor. Or a few minutes with no one watching.

"Because I quit."

"You...quit? Why?"

She tips her head up to meet my gaze. "Lincoln ignored my instructions, published an unfinished article without even contacting me, and nearly got you killed. You don't seriously think I'd ever consider going back there again, do you?" Her eyes shine, and she shoves the envelope into her small messenger bag. "They're lucky I'm leaving their part in this whole mess out of the exposé on Ochoa and the Farías government. The Post doesn't get any of this. The Boston Globe published a teaser article yesterday, and the full story will go out in a couple of days. All thanks to a contact your friend Clive got me."

"But this is your...you're a reporter. It's who you are."

She huffs and arches a brow at me. "I *am* a reporter. A damn good one. So good, I got an offer for a cushy job at the Globe *while* in Venezuela helping to rescue the man I love. The Post can suck it."

Dax chuckles. "Dani, welcome home. If Trev doesn't do a

good enough job of showin' you around Boston, you come to me."

"Um, Dax?" Ford says. "I hate to break it to you, man, but you're blind."

Dani's laugh is followed by a short hiss as she cups her cheek, then winces. "No more joking around. It hurts too much." But her lips are curved in a gentle smile.

"When you two are ready," Dax says, "we'll get everyone together. Everyone we can, anyway. Ripper...we don't ask him to leave Seattle. Ever. But you need to meet the rest of the family."

"Ry made me promise we'd come visit after things settle down," she replies. "I'll meet him soon."

As Dani eases herself from the SUV and holds out her hand for mine, I stare at the two men who gave me a job when I was so fucked up over Gil, I didn't know up from down. Who trusted me with their lives time and time again. Who organized a rescue mission that should have been suicide, and did it without a second thought.

"Thank you." I can't manage anything more than those two words, but I don't need to. Not tonight.

Ford jerks his head towards Dani. "Take her upstairs, Trev. And make sure you tell her she's home. Because this is where you both belong. Boston. Second Sight. Here."

Dax clears his throat and adds, "You're a part of this fucked up family. Both of you. And I'm sorry, but that's never goin' to change. Now go. We'll talk in a few days."

Dani slides her arm around my waist as I join her on the sidewalk, and we head upstairs together.

Home. We're finally home.

"FORD and I are going to have words," I say as I lock the door behind us. The bed's made, there are takeout menus and

Second Sight's corporate AMEX card on the kitchen counter, and a six-pack of beer in the fridge.

"Why? Because he made it so we didn't have to leave your apartment for a couple of days?" Dani asks as she sets her messenger bag on the chair. "You need to rest. I know Graham gave you a clean bill of health, but..."

When she puts it like that, I realize how ridiculous my frustration is. "You're right."

"Care to repeat that?" Sidling up to me, she drapes her arms around my neck. "I'm...what?"

I dip my head to kiss the smile off her face, and she leans into me. Her nipples harden under her t-shirt, and fuck. I need her.

"I'm still waiting," she says breathlessly when I pull back.

I scoop her up in my arms and carry her into the bedroom. "You're right. About a lot of things."

JERKING awake from yet another nightmare—dying chained and alone, in that tiny cell on the lowest level of The Crypt, unable to move or even speak—I reach for Dani. But I find only mussed sheets, no longer warm. Her scent fills the bedroom— along with that of the two of us together—and I force myself not to panic. A faint glow of light comes from the living room, along with quiet tapping.

My sore, tired muscles protest as I get up and pull on a pair of pajama pants and a t-shirt. "What are you doing up?" I ask when I find her at the kitchen table, her tablet in front of her and notes scattered over the polished wood.

She gives me a soft smile as I take a seat next to her. "I couldn't sleep. Figured I might as well get a jump on the Globe article. I promised to have it to them in two days, but they'll publish it as soon as I'm done. Did I wake you?"

"No." I don't mean the word to be so rough, and I shake my head. "Just a nightmare." Searching for anything to change the subject, I catch sight of the gray envelope from the Washington Post. The letter inside peeks from under her notes, and I pull it out and start to read.

Dear Ms. Monroe,

The Post would like to apologize to you for the unprofessional and unethical behavior displayed by one Lincoln Joynes, former editor of the Politics division. Actions such as that are not tolerated at the Post, and Mr. Joynes has been let go.

For the past five years, you have displayed exemplary dedication, perseverance, and courage, risking your safety countless times in pursuit of the truth. Losing you would be a blow to this organization, and as such, I am prepared to offer you a twenty-five percent raise and a promotion to Senior Political Correspondent. The position comes with a corner office, your pick of staff reporters to assist you, and a generous travel budget.

I hope to hear from you soon.

Respectfully,

JB

"Holy shit, Dani. You're taking this, right?" She stares at me like I've lost my mind, and I smooth the paper out on the table. "It's signed by the guy who owns the Post—and half the world."

"If I took that job," she says, her voice suddenly full of emotion, "I'd have to stay in DC. But more importantly, every morning, I'd walk through the doors of the place that almost killed you. How could you even think I'd be okay with doing that?"

"Baby, you told me you wanted to be a reporter the first time I met you. You weren't even ten. When you got the job at the Post, Austin said he'd never seen you so happy. That was your dream job."

"Dreams change." She takes the offer letter, folds it up, and tears it in half. "I'm still a reporter, TJ. The Globe assured me I could cover the types of stories I love. The ones that matter. That make a difference. So, they pay a little less. Or…a lot less given that offer. I don't care. Because this is where I belong." Dani places her palm over my heart. "You are where I belong."

Sliding my fingers into her hair, I pull her closer and slant my lips over hers. I still can't believe this intelligent, fierce, beautiful woman came for me, let alone that she wants to stay.

I do know that arguing with her is pointless. My Danisaur doesn't let anyone tell her what to do, and as I draw back, I whisper, "Come back to bed. I want to show you just how much I love you."

"Promise?" she asks when I help her to her feet.

That word holds special meaning for everyone at Second Sight. It was one of the first things Dax and Ford schooled me on. Promises are never broken. Three days ago, I didn't think I could ever say them to her, give her my heart and vow we'd have forever. But now…I can.

"I promise."

CHAPTER TWENTY-NINE

Dani

IT FEELS surreal to be back in DC. The last time I was here feels like it was a lifetime ago. The elevators ding, and I step into the familiar chaos of the job I loved for years. Now, the only emotions I can call up are anger and sadness.

I don't regret quitting. Not for a moment. There's no way I could come back here day after day. But I mourn the loss of the trust I had in my Post friends and colleagues. I started asking questions the day after we got back to Boston, and Lincoln wasn't the only one who agreed the story should go out.

Five other people helped make the decision that almost ended Trevor's life.

Sarita runs up to me, her arms open for an embrace, but I hold up my hand to stop her. "You don't want to do that."

Her eyes widen as she takes in my scar, the fading bruises along my cheek and jaw, and the thin, red line across my collarbone. I purposely chose a blouse that didn't hide it when I got dressed this morning. A little childish, but I don't care.

"Dani, I am so sorry," she says, her gaze riveted to my cheek.

The burn is healing well—according to the doctor I saw yesterday—but I'll have a scar half the width of my pinky finger and just as long for the rest of my life. "I didn't know—"

"So, you didn't bother to read my notes. Or call me. My phone was on. I was back in the States. Wouldn't have been hard."

Pushing past her with a small box under my arm, I head for my desk as she hurries after me. "You have to understand," she says. "It was late and we were about to go to press without a front page story."

"Oh, I understand." I set the box down with more force than necessary and whirl on her. "Now it's your turn. Because of what you did, a good man was arrested, put on a plane in full restraints, beaten multiple times, and locked in a cell so small, he couldn't sit up or straighten his legs. Oh, and the whole cell block was kept at near-freezing temperatures. He was deprived of food and water and not allowed to sleep for almost three days. And the only reason he's not still down there, the only reason he didn't *die* down there, is that he has enough friends and family with connections—including me—to coordinate a rescue mission, risk their lives, and get him out."

Sarita says nothing. Good.

"Understand this. I have no faith in this paper at the moment, and I likely never will. *You* could have killed all of us. For a story. I don't want to see your face ever again. I'm going to pack up my desk and get the hell out of here."

She nods, and when she heads back to her office, I scan the room to find a dozen people staring at me. The ones I want to keep in touch with already have a way to contact me. The rest... they'll fade in my memories, replaced by new coworkers I'll meet in a few days.

It only takes me ten minutes to dump my few personal items into the small box. My nameplate, a laminated copy of my first byline, two lipsticks, a tube of hand cream, and an emergency roll of deodorant. The final item? The picture of me, Austin, and Trevor outside my parents' home.

I used to think the photo showed three happy people. Now I know the truth. Austin was happy. Trevor and I...we were in love. We just hadn't admitted it. I can see it in how our heads gently angle towards one another. The look in our eyes. The closeness of our hands.

He broke my heart two months after that photo was taken. But with everything we just survived, my memories of that night don't hurt so much anymore. What we have now is so much stronger than anything we could have had then.

We fought for our love and we survived. I set the picture in the box and stand up, taking one last look around. I'll miss it here. But now, it's time for me to go home.

Trevor

Her key rasping in the lock dissipates some of the tension keeping my shoulders locked tight. I'm out of my chair and at the door before she can do more than turn the knob.

I don't know why today was so hard. It's been ten days since we landed back in Boston and started carving out a life together. Just yesterday, we finished moving into this two-bedroom unit across the hall from my old place.

"Welcome home," I say, my voice rough and strained. Easing the suitcase handle from her grip, I roll it into the bedroom where her half of the closet sits mostly empty.

"What's wrong?" Dani follows me, and when I turn around, I almost slam right into her. Taking the opportunity, I wind my arms around her waist, trapping her and easing the constant ache I've carried since she left for the airport this morning and refused to let me drive her.

"I need to do this on my own, Trev. All of it. I promise, next time I have to fly somewhere, you can drop me off. Or come with me. But this…I need to face them on my own."

Dani's hands frame my face. "Trevor…"

"Nothing's wrong, baby. Not anymore."

"Try again, tough guy. I'm not buying it." She flicks open the top button on my shirt and presses a kiss to my chest. "Your shoulders are like granite. And that's not a testament to your superior fitness."

Another button, another kiss, and I sink down onto the bed with her in my lap. "They've upped the salary on that job offer three times."

Her derisive snort wrinkles her nose, and fuck. She's the most beautiful woman in the world every day, but even more so in this moment. "Tomorrow, the movers are going to show up with all of my clothes, a coffee table, a desk for my home office, photo albums, and Mom and Dad's wedding china. Maybe *then*, you'll believe I'm really not going anywhere."

I lay her down, slipping my hand under her shirt to find her tattoo. My fingers trace the slightly raised skin, finding her true north. Mine too. "I believe this.

"It's a start," she whispers against my neck. "Make love to me, Trevor."

Her blouse slides up easily, and I kiss a line along the center of her stomach until I reach the bottom of her bra. "Gladly."

Undressing Dani is one of my favorite things to do. Every time, I find a new spot that gives her goosebumps. Today, it's the curve of her hip as I kiss my way to her mound. Her scent, her essence, surrounds me in our new bedroom with the dark purple comforter she picked out to go with my gray sheets.

My first taste has her moaning, and I pick up the pace, swirling my tongue through her folds. When I slip a finger inside of her, the moans turn into mewls and whimpers, and the only words I can understand are "more" and my name.

"I'll give you more, baby," I murmur against her clit as I add a second finger. She's so slick and tight, and I score my teeth gently over her tender nub, then pick up the pace with my tongue until her entire body stills, then combusts with the force of her release.

"Trevor!" she cries, and I drink her in.

Her skin chills as she comes down from her high, and I hold her against me, kissing the top of her head, her eyebrow, and back to her ear.

"You don't think we're done, do you?" Dani asks, her voice still husky with arousal. "I need you inside me."

"Oh, we're not done. Not by a long shot."

My hands are steady rolling the condom over my length, and she watches, her eyes hooded and a smile curving her lips as I nudge her entrance. She's always so tight, so perfect, and I take it slow as I fuse our lips together and let my tongue dance with hers.

This woman is my everything. She saved me. She healed me. But more than that, she loves me.

"Trevor, look at me," she demands when I start to thrust. I don't think anything could be more perfect than this moment, holding her close, feeling her body respond to mine in ways that I've only dreamed of before.

Until her gaze softens, and she whispers, "I'm home."

THANK you for reading Call Sign: Redemption. Trevor's story was one that I've wanted to tell since he first showed up in On His Six. He's a complicated man, and he'll definitely play a role in future installments of the Away From Keyboard series.

The last few Away From Keyboard books have included bonus scenes, but unfortunately, life intervened, and I wasn't able to polish up the bonus scenes in time to include them with this release. But I promise, there will be bonus scenes. I hope you'll sign up for my newsletter and join my reader group on Facebook. I'll release the bonus scenes there in February.

I want to explore a little more of Trevor's past. And of course, he and Dax have to have a few very serious conversations. These bonus scenes are not only for you; they're for me as well. I love giving these characters a voice. Their stories are inspiring, painful, and heartbreaking. But also so rewarding, hopeful, and wonderful too.

You can find my next release available for preorder now. It's the start of an Away From Keyboard spinoff series. Want to know who the hero is? I'll give you a hint. He's the head of JSOC. Or...is he now?

THE END

ACKNOWLEDGMENTS

Writing a book might seem like a solitary affair, but I assure you, it isn't. Many people helped Trevor's book to completion.

JW: You read my books when they're still half-finished ideas, rough and ugly. And then you read them again when they're done. That's a lot of reading. Perhaps even more importantly, you deal with all of my random insecurities and panic attacks when life gets in the way of...everything.

JF: We've had this discussion too many times to count. But even though, yes, I *can* write emotions, when you edit for me, you always seem to find that perfect place to add that perfect word or phrase at least a couple of times in every book.

Special thanks to AA, who asked me how much I loved her and then gave me Dani's nickname.

ABOUT THE AUTHOR

I've always made up stories. Sometimes I even acted them out. I probably shouldn't admit that my childhood best friend and I used to run around the backyard pretending to fly in our Invisible Jet and rescue Steve Trevor. Oops.

Now that I'm too old to spin around in circles with felt magic bracelets on my wrists, I put "pen to paper" instead. Figuratively, at least. Fingers to keyboard is more accurate.

Outside of my writing, I'm a professional editor, a software geek, a singer (in the shower only), and a runner. I love red wine, scotch (neat, please), and cider. Seattle is my home, and I share an old house with my husband and cats.

I'm on my fourth—fifth?—rewatching of the modern *Doctor Who*, and I think one particular quote from that show sums up my entire life.

"We're all stories, in the end. Make it a good one, eh?" — *The Eleventh Doctor, Doctor Who*

I hope your story is brilliant.

You can reach me all over the web...
patriciadeddy.com
patricia@patriciadeddy.com

ALSO BY PATRICIA D. EDDY

Away From Keyboard

Dive into a steamy mix of geekery and military prowess with the men
and women of Hidden Agenda and Second Sight.

Breaking His Code

In Her Sights

On His Six

Second Sight

By Lethal Force

Fighting For Valor

Finding Their Forevers (a holiday short story)

Call Sign: Redemption

Midnight Coven

These novellas will take you into the darker side of the paranormal
with vampires, witches, and more.

Forever Kept

Immortal Hunter

Wicked Omens

Elemental Shifter

Hot werewolves and strong, powerful elementals. What's not to love?

A Shift in the Water

A Shift in the Air

By the Fates

Check out the By the Fates series if you love dark and steamy tales of witches, devils, and an epic battle between good and evil.

By the Fates, Freed

Destined: A By the Fates Story

By the Fates, Fought

By the Fates, Fulfilled

In Blood

If you love hot Italian vampires and and a human who can hold her own against beings far stronger, then the In Blood series is for you.

Secrets in Blood

Revelations in Blood

Holidays and Heroes

Beauty isn't only skin deep and not all scars heal. Come swoon over sexy vets and the men and women who love them.

Mistletoe and Mochas

Love and Libations

Restrained

Do you like to be tied up? Or read about characters who do? Enjoy a fresh BDSM series that will leave you begging for more.

In His Silks

Christmas Silks

All Tied Up For New Year's

In His Collar

www.ingramcontent.com/pod-product-compliance
Lightning Source LLC
Chambersburg PA
CBHW070621170726
48291CB00003B/827